O9-BRZ-857

αβχδεφγηιϕκλμν

ΑΒΧΔΕΦΓΗΙϑΚ

ΩΞΨΖαβχδφγηιϕ

ψζΑΒΧΔΦΓΗΙϑΚ

ΘΩΞΨΖαβχδφγη

ωξψζΑΒΧΔΕΦΓ

ΤΥςΘΩΞΨΖαβχδ

τυϖθωξψζΑΒΧΔ

simon said

sarah r. shaber

simon said

A Thomas Dunne Book

St. Martin's Press

New York

A THOMAS DUNNE BOOK.
An imprint of St. Martin's Press

This book is fiction, and all the characters and incidents in it are entirely imaginary.

Design by Songhee Kim

Library of Congress Cataloging-in-Publication Data

Shaber, Sarah R.
Simon said / Sarah R. Shaber.—1st ed.
p. cm.
"A Thomas Dunne book."
ISBN 0-312-15207-8
I. Title.
PS3569.H226S55 1997
813'.54—dc20 96-34993
CIP

First Edition: April 1997

10 9 8 7 6 5 4 3 2

TO STEVE, KATIE, AND SAM;
MY BEST FRIENDS

My traveling companions are
ghosts and empty sockets;
I'm lookin' at ghosts and empties . . .

—Paul Simon

PROFESSOR SIMON SHAW HADN'T OPENED THE OLD-FASHIONED venetian blinds on his floor-to-ceiling office windows yet this morning. He needed his breakfast Coke to work its biochemical magic on his system before he could deal with the intensity of the North Carolina day streaming in.

He usually had a good view, too. He could even see the columns of Bloodworth House, the historic home that presided over the front corner of the small campus. This morning, if his blinds had been open, he could also have seen the police cruiser, its lights flashing, pull into the brick gates of the college, followed by a huge van marked INCIDENT INVESTIGATION UNIT, CITY OF RALEIGH and what was unmistakably a hearse. Within minutes, the porches of the college buildings that fronted the lawn were filled with gaping spectators, shading their eyes as they watched the police vehicles proceed paradelike around the traffic circle and pull into the parking lot of Bloodworth House.

But Simon was unaware of the scene outside when the departmental secretary, Judy Smith, knocked on his door a little later.

"Go away," Simon said.

"Can't," Judy answered from outside. She opened his door and walked in. She cracked her gum, put her hands on her hips, and studied him. "Try to pull yourself together," she said. "You're not going to make a very good impression." Judy was a small-town girl who wore cheap dark brown hose with white shoes and baby-doll dresses with lace collars. She had her long hair permed and dyed red (Autumn Mist) every three months and her nails done every week. She had come to Raleigh to make good money and find a new husband. She had left her ten-year-old son with her mother to simplify the process. She was almost thirty, and time was running out.

"I don't have to make an impression," Simon said. "I have tenure."

"There's a policeman here to see you," Judy said. "You're probably under arrest."

Sure enough, a real live cop followed Judy into the office. His hair, cut short at the back and sides, and his blue eyes set off the perfectly pressed dark blue of his uniform and the shine of his boots. Simon instantly felt guilty. He sat up straight and ran his hands quickly over his hair. He couldn't imagine why a policeman would come to see him.

"Good morning, Officer," Simon said. "Have I done something?"

The policeman was used to eliciting undefined guilt feelings from people. Unnerving the public was part of the fun of wearing a paramilitary uniform and carrying a sidearm and handcuffs.

"Not at all, Professor Shaw," he said. "I have a favor to ask, that's all."

So this is the prodigy, the policeman thought. What had the guy digging at the old house said? Dr. Simon Shaw was an A. B. Duke scholar, a Pulitzer Prize winner, and the youngest full professor in the history of the college. He didn't look it. The man was small behind the big desk. He had black hair, brown eyes, and hadn't shaved in a couple of days. He was wearing jeans, old Nike running shoes, and a rumpled black polo shirt with some kind of emblem on it. He had the same look in his eyes as the old homeless guy in the park the cop had rousted this morning, a look that happened when the bum realized that only half an inch of comfort was left in his bottle of Wild Irish Rose.

The office itself was a mess. Books were shoved into bookshelves every which way and were stacked deep on the floor. Papers, mail, and pink message slips littered the desk. The desk lamp was so covered with Post-It notes that it cast a canary glow. Obviously, the guy had not made much progress with his paperwork lately. Well, the cop had always heard there was a lot of slack in the academic life.

3

Underneath all the mess was some real good stuff, though. The cop was sure that the desk was an antique. It was the kind that two people could sit at facing each other. You could look into its dark mahogany surface and see your reflection two feet away. There was an Oriental carpet and two expensively framed bird prints on the wall. One picture showed every variety of hummingbird known to man hovering over a lone red trumpet vine. The other was of a giant pileated woodpecker perched on a branch. This could not be standard college-issue furniture. The guy must have brought it in himself.

"What kind of favor?" Simon asked.

The officer hesitated, obviously not sure how to word his response.

"Sir, this is not an official visit. I cannot compel you to come with me. But Sergeant Gates of the Raleigh Police Department requests that you come over to the Bloodworth House so he can ask you some questions. A Dr. David Morgan gave him your name."

Morgan was an archaeologist for the state of North Carolina, and one of Simon's closest friends. Morgan and his apprentices were excavating part of the grounds of Bloodworth House.

"What's going on?" Simon asked.

"They've dug up a woman's body, and the medical examiner says she died at least fifty years ago. Dr. Morgan told us you know the history of the house better than anyone. Sergeant Gates thought you might be able to add some information that would help us."

"Of course I'll come, Officer, but why is this so urgent?"

"There's a bullet hole in the back of her head."

ON THE WALK TO BLOODWORTH HOUSE, THE POLICEMAN FILLED him in, but Simon already knew the first part of the story. It had taken a long time to pinpoint the Colonial kitchen's location and to raise the funds to start excavating. Simon had attended the official predig conference at a local bar the previous Friday night.

Morgan had been sinking trenches at the site all week. Finding a corpse would have certainly startled him. There were no graves noted on any of the old maps of the property and no mention of a graveyard of any kind in the documents Simon had seen, and he was sure he had seen them all. And if there had ever been a murder associated with the history of the house, Simon would know about it.

"He found the corpse this morning," the policeman was saying. "And it looked recent to him. Recent, that is, compared with what he was used to. So he called the police. And we started the formal investigation procedure, called the medical examiner, had the incident van there, roped off the scene of the crime and everything. Then the ME tells us that the woman's been in the ground at least fifty years, and that she was shot in the head. It could be homicide, but we can hardly conduct a standard criminal investigation in this case. Dr. Morgan says you know everything about the house and who lived there for generations, so Sergeant Gates sent me to get you."

It was true: Simon did know the history of the place backward and forward. His monograph on the house and the Bloodworth family was sold at the gift shop and at bookstores and historic sites all over the state. He was on the house's board of directors and consulted regularly with David Morgan, who kept digging up bits of the property as funding became available.

Bloodworth House was located on the corner of the block that largely contained the college itself. Until it was given to Kenan College, it had been in the Bloodworth family since the late 1700s. In fact, Kenan was built on the original grounds and orchards of the house. The land had been donated to the college—leaving just the house for the family to live in—when the family lost interest in agriculture. Since one of the Bloodworths, Charles, had been a founder of the Chesapeake and Seaboard Railway and had figured in Simon's studies of industrialization in the South between the world wars, Simon had been the likely person to ask to write the history of the house. He was fascinated with the project. The house had been continuously lived in by the same family since the eighteenth century. Its furniture and other domestic paraphernalia had hardly been touched. The last resident was Adam Bloodworth, who had been a cousin of Charles's. Adam's heir, a nephew, had not wanted to pay the taxes on the house, so he had deeded it over to the college, who then leased it for ninety-nine years to the Historic Preservation Society to restore and maintain.

To get to Bloodworth House, Shaw and the policeman had to walk diagonally across the campus of Kenan College, where Simon Shaw had taught history for six years. The college had been founded as a women's institute in 1832 and barely survived Reconstruction, when cash for tuition and donations was scarce. Despite its troubled inception, Kenan College had grown and prospered into one of the finest small private colleges in the South. Bolstered by a number of large bequests, the college began to admit men in 1952 and offered a full curriculum, including a half a dozen master's-degree programs, by 1965. The campus itself was spectacularly beautiful; its historic buildings were set in landscaped grounds bounded by Hillsborough Street, St. Mary's Street, and the old Cameron Park neighborhood, where Simon lived.

As Simon and the policeman crossed the traffic circle in front of the college, they had to buck the opposite flow of a crowd dispersing. College employees and students who had gathered to view the scene were walking back to their offices and classes, having milked the event for as much time as they could. The last person Simon passed was Rufus Young, the public-relations officer for the college. He wasn't called that—he was vice president for community affairs—but his job was to keep the college's image positive. He looked as relieved as Simon had ever seen him. He mopped his face and the top of his bald head, then tucked his shirt into his belt.

"Thank you, God," he said, stopping next to Simon and clapping him on the back. "My secretary came running into my office, yelling about a dead woman. I thought a student had been murdered. Aged me twenty years right then. But it's just an old corpse—really old. I could throttle David Morgan. What business did he have calling the police before telling me about this? Thank goodness I had enough time to explain everything to the TV people before they slapped it on the noon news."

"He had to call the police," Simon said. "And it takes an expert to figure out the age of a corpse."

"He's an archaeologist, isn't he?"

"That's right—an archaeologist, not an anthropologist. He specializes in structures, not bones."

"Well, whatever." Young continued to pat Simon on the back. Simon was one of his favorite people. He generated good publicity for the college on a regular basis. "All I know is, I'm going to have a double bourbon with lunch." He walked off, then turned and called out to Simon. "Let me know if there's a human-interest angle to this. We could send out a press release."

The handsome 1826 Greek Revival addition of Bloodworth House faced the street, but all the action was taking place outside the back part, the original three-room house built in 1785. Yellow crime-scene tape surrounded an excavation between what was now the gift shop, which had been the old smokehouse, and a restored slave cabin. The kitchen garden, which was planted with authentic herbs and vegetables, fronted the excavation. The incident van was pulling out into the street, followed by a police car, leaving just the hearse and a patrol car behind. Standing in the middle of the excavation with Simon's friend David Morgan was a man Simon felt sure was a physician, as well as another person, who was the largest black man Simon thought he had ever seen. Morgan spotted Simon and called out to him with relief.

"I'm glad you were in your office, Simon," he said. "This is too much for me." He crossed over to Simon and ducked under the yellow tape. Simon's policeman escort did the opposite, joining the group near the pile of earth a few yards away.

"This is a cheap way to get off work," Simon said. "Couldn't you have just called in sick?"

"It has not been entertaining," Morgan said. "I had one student throw up, one burst into tears, the police are messing up my dig, and the PR guy from the college practically took my head off. I've had six cups of coffee and my heartburn is acting up." He patted his belly. "You don't have any Mylanta, do you?"

Said belly was hanging over Morgan's belt, not repulsively, but noticeably. Too much fast food and beer. But the belly was just one part of the total picture. Morgan dressed in stained pants, a flannel shirt, and work boots even at the office. His dark hair and gray beard were untrimmed and untended. Morgan's house was a mess, too. Simon had learned never to go into the kitchen if he didn't want to lose his appetite, and that the two chocolate Labs had first dibs on the sofa. He wondered if the excessive neatness required of a professional archaeologist explained Morgan's personal messiness. Hours of exact notation on graph paper, painstaking photography of sites from dozens of angles, and lengthy cataloging may have left him no energy for bringing order into his personal life. Morgan had never married. He was a misogynist, but whether by birth or training, Simon didn't know.

Simon dug around in his pockets and came up with an antacid tablet.

"It's probably too little, too late," Morgan said, popping it into his mouth.

"Are you sure this isn't a standard burial?" Simon said. "It wouldn't be extraordinary to find a grave on private property."

Morgan started shaking his head before Simon had even finished his sentence. "No way," he said. "There's no coffin, no marker, and besides, she was buried under the dirt floor of an unused outbuilding. Then there's the bullet hole."

"Oh, yeah." Simon said. "I forgot about the bullet hole."

Simon didn't usually forget anything. Morgan looked at his friend closely. The bags under Simon's eyes weren't quite as pronounced as they had been. Maybe he was getting some sleep.

The big black man Simon had noticed earlier joined them, and Morgan introduced him to Simon.

"This is Sergeant. Otis Gates of the Raleigh Police Department. He's the head of the major-crime task force."

"I'm glad you were willing to join us, Professor," Gates said. His huge hand completely enclosed Simon's and covered his wrist. Simon looked up to just about everybody, but he actually had to crane his neck to talk to Gates. The man was immense. His nose had been broken more than once. Simon instantly thought, ex-football player, then dismissed the thought as stereotypic. Considering his size, Gates should have been forbidding. But his look was softened by grizzled gray hair cut short and reading glasses that dangled from his neck by a beaded chain that had to have been made by a kid in crafts class.

Gates gestured toward the man Simon had decided was a doctor, who was kneeling over a trench in the middle of the site. He had a tool, maybe forceps, in his hand and was poking at something in the ground. Simon felt the acid in his stomach bubble slightly. He should have forced some real breakfast into himself. "That is Dr. Philip Boyette, the medical examiner," Gates said. Simon had guessed correctly.

"We've got a situation here, Professor," said Gates. "This corpse is too recent to be an artifact and too old to know exactly what to do with. It's probably homicide."

The medical examiner joined the group. "She was shot in the head, no question," he said. "Bullet entered at the back of the head—there's a classic bullet hole in the occipital lobe. I wouldn't be surprised if the bullet is still rattling around in her braincase."

Simon's stomach turned again, and he began to wish he had been anywhere but in his office this morning.

"What exactly can I do, Sergeant?"

"We're hoping you can give us some idea of what we're dealing with here," Gates replied.

"I told them if anyone could give the police any useful information about this woman, or connect her to the house in some way, you could," Morgan said.

Dear heaven, Simon thought, they want me to look at the body!

"She's pretty well preserved," the medical examiner said. "She's wrapped in a quilt, and the good drainage of the site kept the body very dry. I won't really be able to say how long she's been in the ground until I get the body in the lab. But from the color of the bones, I'd guess fifty years at least."

Simon couldn't believe that he was being asked to look at an old corpse on the grounds of an historic house he had written a book about, on the theory he could tell these three men something about the victim. The woman couldn't possibly be recognizable. She could have come from anywhere and been buried by anybody. Besides, he did not want to look at her. He began to feel a little warm.

The medical examiner cocked his head and gave Simon a look of the skeptical sort Simon had become all too familiar with recently. Without saying a word, the doctor's manner questioned whether or not Simon was up to what was being asked of him. Simon didn't like the way the doctor looked. The man had practically no lips and his mustache looked as if it had been penciled on. Although he was thin, his body was soft and amorphous. Simon could believe this man spent his life under fluorescent lights in a sterile room, poking at dead people.

Simon felt as though he was on the verge of failing some kind of a manhood test.

"Of course I'll take a look, if you think it would be helpful," Simon said.

They walked toward the excavation site. Simon's friend David Morgan was a proponent of the old-fashioned vertical method of archaeological excavation. That is, rather than remove the entire area of a site layer by layer, he believed in sinking trenches in careful patterns, leaving most of the site undisturbed. First, of course, he had used a metal detector and a magnetometer where he and Simon had deduced the old kitchen would be, and he had quickly revealed the stone foundations of the building.

Simon, Morgan, and Gates stepped over the pegs and string that marked off the site into grids. Simon could see that the first trench had been dug halfway across the site, until, he supposed, the body had been found. Picks and shovels lay scattered where they had been dropped. A sieve lay half in and half out of the trench.

"Watch it," David warned as he guided them around a large hole that was lined with stone. "That's an old cistern—Civil War era, maybe—and it's still holding water. We haven't got a secure cover on it yet."

As they approached the body, Simon remembered that David insisted on hand-digging his trenches, much to his students' chagrin. He wouldn't permit a Bobcat anywhere near his digs. Simon wondered who had been wielding the shovel when it struck the corpse.

Gates leaned down to remove a tarpaulin covering one end of the trench.

"You'd better take a deep breath," he said. "This is not pretty."

I'll bet, Simon thought. Uncharacteristically, David took his arm as Simon bent over the body.

Simon saw only the corpse's face for a few seconds before he looked away, but he would remember the minutest details for many days.

After all, the only dead people Simon had seen before were his parents laid out at a funeral home. Without the benefit of the embalmer's art, this creature in the ground in front of him could have auditioned for a part in a horror movie.

The body seemed to have been prepared for burial. It was shrouded neatly in a quilt of the wedding-ring pattern—he could just see the faded patches flowing in interlocking rings around her torso. Fingers that were mostly bone were crossed demurely over her chest. Most of the fleshy parts of the face, including the eyes, were gone, but some of the cartilage from her ears and nose still clung to the skull. Strands of short, curly black hair adhered to her head. He registered the miniature cameos in her ears and the larger matching one at her throat before he looked away.

"God," Simon said. He suppressed an intense urge to vomit. For a second, everything he could see was tinged with red and he was very hot. Morgan felt Simon quail and he tightened his grip on his arm. His friend's eyes looked out at him from deep inside dark sockets. Morgan mentally castigated himself.

"Take it easy," Morgan said. "You've had a shock—I should

never have suggested that you look at her. I forgot you weren't experienced at this."

Gates was concerned by Simon's reaction, too.

"I'm just sorry as hell," Gates said. "What a stupid thing for me to do."

"It's okay," Simon said. He took a deep breath and collected himself.

"No, it's not," Gates said. "Just because the three of us are used to looking at dead bodies of various descriptions doesn't mean we should go dragging a civilian into this situation. Can I get you anything?"

Something cold, Simon thought. "A Coke, please," Simon said. "There's a machine in the Preservation Society office at the back of the house."

With a gesture, Gates dispatched the policeman for the drink.

"No breakfast, huh?" Dr. Boyette said.

"Not much," Simon said. Not much sleep, either, he thought.

The policeman brought Simon his Coke and he drained it gratefully. Morgan was relieved to see that his color improved right away.

"It's going to be a lot of work to identify this woman after all this time," Gates said. "I was hoping you could give us a start. But she's not necessarily connected to the history of the house. She could have been brought here from somewhere else. She could be anyone."

"But she's not just anyone," Simon said.

The three men stared at him.

"What do you mean?" Gates said.

"I know who she is," Simon said.

"I TOLD YOU," MORGAN SAID TRIUMPHANTLY.

Gates looked at Simon incredulously. "Excuse me?" he said. "I didn't hear you say you could identify this body, did I?"

"Yes, I think I can," Simon said.

"Well, then, who is it?" said Gates.

"She's Anne Haworth Bloodworth," Simon answered. "She disappeared on April ninth, 1926. The whole state was mobilized to look for her—later even the Pinkerton Detective Agency got involved. She was never found."

"You can't possibly know the corpse is this Bloodworth woman," Boyette said.

"Believe me," David said. "If Simon says this is Anne Bloodworth, it's Anne Bloodworth. I've never known him to be wrong about something like this."

Gates shook his head in disbelief. "I have to say, son, that it doesn't seem reasonable to me that you could get a minute's look at a decomposed corpse and . . . well, we'll have to have more tangible evidence to go on."

Simon felt much better. He was on his own ground now. He pulled his arm away from Morgan. "Come with me," he said.

Boyette broke off from the group. "Not me," he said. "I've got to get this lady out of the ground and into the frig. Let me know, Sergeant, what your mouthpiece says about an autopsy."

The three men walked toward the house. Simon was on the

Bloodworth House's board of directors and had a set of keys. He let them into the original section of the house, the three rooms built in 1785. The rooms were narrow, dim, and the ceilings were low. Gates knocked his head on a doorjamb.

"They didn't grow them as big as you back then," Simon said. "The average person in the eighteenth century was around my size. But it was still crowded, with six or seven family members living in three rooms like this. Privacy is a twentieth-century invention."

He led them down a short, low hall, past a curving stair, and into a radically different atmosphere, the nineteenth-century addition. The Greek Revival drawing and dining rooms rose twelve feet in the air; the ceilings were covered with decorative moldings and the tall windows draped with yellow silk. Light poured in through the thick, rippled old glass.

"Still not a lot of rooms for a big family," Simon said, "but at least you don't feel you could suffocate in here."

He turned into the dining room. Except for repairs and some redecorating, the room had been left very much the same as when Adam Bloodworth had used it, and Simon's research showed he had altered very little in the house and its furniture. Neither had Charles Bloodworth, from whom Adam had inherited it, for that matter. The table was laid with dinnerware ordered from China and silver made in Boston. Some of it had the name Revere stamped on it. The buffet held a huge silver serving piece heaped with porcelain fruit and vegetables. A crystal chandelier was suspended over the table. It still held candles, but sconces positioned on the walls would have provided gaslight.

A display case holding a number of the Bloodworths' personal possessions stood against the wall. Charles's cigar humidor, pocket pistol, and fountain pen, together with Adam's silver cigarette case and mustache comb, were neatly labeled and locked inside.

"Look at this, Sergeant," Simon said, leading the men toward the fireplace. Over the mantel was the portrait of a young woman. Or rather, it was an enlarged photograph that had been touched with oils to simulate a color portrait. Simon suspected it was a high school graduation picture. The subject had a sweet face, framed by short, curly black hair and bangs—what they called "a bob" and "a fringe" back in the twenties. She was dressed in the unbecoming fashion of her time—a straight chemise with a dropped waist, which made everyone who was more than painfully thin look chunky. The dress was white and had a sailor collar, which contributed to Simon's conclusion that it was a graduation picture. The pose wasn't typical, though. She was sitting on a garden bench, leaning forward on her hands and smiling directly into the camera. Her gaze was eager and forceful. She looked as if she had a lot to look forward to.

"This is Anne Bloodworth," Simon said simply. "The portrait was done sometime after her eighteenth birthday. I believe it has hung here ever since."

Gates studied the picture carefully. "I agree there is some resemblance, if there can be a resemblance between a half-decayed corpse and a picture," Gates said. "But this is just a coincidence. I still say our body could be anybody."

"Look at the jewelry," Simon said.

The two miniature cameos in the young woman's ears and the larger one pinned to a ribbon at her throat seemed to jump out of the portrait.

"I'll be damned!" Gates exploded. Without another word, he turned and left the room. A few minutes later, David and Simon could see him out the back window, trotting toward the mortuary van.

"You're amazing," said David.

"No I'm not," Simon replied. "I just have a good memory. I studied this picture for a long time after I read about Anne Bloodworth's disappearance. Half of it's intuition, anyway—I just knew when I looked at the corpse that it was Anne."

"The police might need more proof than some earrings and your instincts," David said. "But I'm convinced."

Gates walked back into the room and up to the picture. He didn't look at either man, but he studied the picture for a full five minutes. He shook his head.

Then he turned and studied Simon just as intently. "A corpse from the right time period, the right hair color and build, and identical jewelry. And we know for a fact that a young woman disappeared. It's circumstantial, but convincing. However," and he sighed, "I don't think the medical examiner can officially ID her based on what we have here."

"What will you do now?" David asked.

"I don't know," Gates said. "The police attorney will have to tell me if this is a case or just a break in routine for us."

"It was hardly a routine event for Anne Bloodworth," Simon said quietly. He turned and offered Gates his hand. "I enjoyed meeting you."

"Listen," Gates said. "Are you going to be in your office tomorrow? I'd like to drop by and pick your brain some more."

"Sure," Simon replied. "Just don't ask me to look at any more corpses, okay?"

All three men laughed, and Simon left the room.

"That young man has a brain," Gates said.

"He has a photographic memory," David said. "He can remember anything he has ever read or jotted on a note card. But it's not just that. He's got instinct, or intuition, or whatever you want to call it."

The two of them could see Simon Shaw walking across the campus from the window in the dining room. "He'd make a good cop, then," Gates said.

THE MORNING'S EVENTS HAD SHAKEN SIMON. HE FELT HOT AND unsteady. He wanted to go home and pull himself together before his afternoon class. As he walked across the campus toward the nearby neighborhood where he lived, the sun seemed unnaturally bright and the colors of late spring were so strong they made his eyes hurt.

A migraine threatened him distantly, tapping at his temples and turning his stomach. He wished he had his car so he didn't have to walk the four blocks to his house.

Cameron Park was a very early suburb of Raleigh built in the 1920s. Now it was an island surrounded by Kenan College, a 1950s shopping district, and the downtown high school. Its streets, once paved with cobblestones, meandered around the hills and ravines of what had once been the Bloodworth estate. Most of the homes were of brick or clapboard, and retaining walls and chimneys were built of the stones that were upturned during construction.

If you knew where to look, signs of the age of the place were everywhere. The old trolley line had run down Hillsborough Street and ended where large stone pillars marked the entrance to the neighborhood. Most of the porches still had a square cut out of the door where a milk box could be slid in by the milkman. The old carriage house, where the residents had kept their horses and broughams, still stood, although converted into an arts center. It was a fashionable location for the type of person who enjoyed old-fashioned residential urban life and scorned the strip developments and congested traffic of the new suburbs. Simon found it similar in atmosphere to the neighborhood in Queens, New York, where his mother had been raised.

By the time Simon reached the 1920s southern bungalow that was his home, he knew that something other than the overall gruesomeness of the morning was bothering him. But he decided to worry about it later and concentrate instead on pulling himself together for his afternoon class.

Simon took two prescription headache pills, got a Coke out of his refrigerator, turned on the local oldies radio station on his stereo, and climbed into his only shower, which was on the first floor, next to the kitchen. His upstairs bathroom had an ancient footed tub, which was not conducive to the kind of repair his body and soul needed right now. He turned on the water, sat down, and chugged his Coke. His water heater was probably original to the house, which was built in 1926, so the hot water only lasted through three songs. When the water became lukewarm, he turned it off, but he stayed sitting on the floor of the shower to finish his Coke. Mercifully, this radical treatment stopped the development of his headache and quelled the insistent nausea in his stomach.

Simon went upstairs to dress. He paused in front of the mirror to check for bags under his eyes, and he decided that they were not too pronounced, despite lack of sleep and the morning's events. Simon was a small man, which had never bothered him except for the irritation he suffered when looking for clothes. But being a university professor allowed him to wear anything he wanted, and since his undergraduate days, he had lived in jeans, polo shirts or turtlenecks, sneakers, and any jacket he could find to fit. Occasionally, he wore a knit tie. Simon had played baseball in high school and college; he biked to work, and he had visited the local batting cage regularly until recently. He was still in reasonably good shape, with a well-developed chest and arms and slim legs and waist.

From his Jewish mother, Simon had inherited black—almost glossy—curly hair, which he kept short, brown eyes, and a Semitic nose. From his Irish father, whose family had lived in the mountains of North Carolina for generations, he got an engaging smile, a sense of humor, and his romantic nature. He was the only child of parents who had married late but were devoted. His father had been a classics professor at Appalachian State; his mother was a public-health nurse who had met his father while working at a rural mountain clinic. His parents died when he was in college, but his father's family in Boone and his Jewish relatives in New York City fought over his vacations, deluged him with care packages, and made him feel loved, even though he was on his own after the age of twenty.

In high school, Simon's academic prowess had isolated him somewhat. Only his starting position at second base on the varsity baseball team kept him from being considered a complete nerd. In college, though, as often happens, his intelligence became a social asset, and he found himself in the midst of a large circle of friends, both men and women. As an undergraduate, he attended Duke University in Durham, his parents' alma mater, from which he graduated summa cum laude in history. For graduate school, he defected to the University of North Carolina at Chapel Hill. Then he surprised everyone by accepting a teaching position at Kenan College. Simon wanted to teach undergraduates and live in North Carolina. Kenan and its environs became his home, and he had no intention of leaving, even when he developed his doctoral thesis into a best-selling book, *The South Between the World Wars,* won the Pulitzer Prize, and was catapulted to stardom two years ago.

Simon stayed on an even keel during the uproar that followed his receiving the Pulitzer. Kenan was ecstatic, issuing press releases wildly and giving him tenure several years before it was customary. He received telegrams and phone calls from people he could hardly place. His publisher flew him to New York, put him up in one of those fancy hotels where they give you a free bathrobe to use, sent him to the awards ceremony in a limousine, and threw him a huge party. He was even scheduled to appear on the *Today* show, but he was bumped when O. J. Simpson was indicted for murder. He didn't mind, though. He had a great time in the green room talking to Ray Charles, who got bumped, too, and took away a souvenir *Today* coffee mug with Charles's autograph on it.

After his brief exposure to fame, Simon returned happily to his life. Not so his wife, Tessa, who had loved the glamour and excitement of celebrity and who complained bitterly about the boredom of their everyday existence when life returned to normal. Simon, who had never been bored a day in his life, expected her to adjust in time.

Tessa adjusted by packing her things onto a carrier on the top of her Mustang and leaving for a job as a TV production assistant on a soap opera in New York City.

Simon was devastated. They had been together since graduate school—she taught high school just a few blocks away. He liked being married. He wanted a home and a family more than most men, probably to replace the one he had lost when his parents died. He seriously underestimated Tessa's restlessness, and he probably hastened her departure by suggesting that they have a baby.

Simon would never forget standing on the sidewalk begging her not to go, then watching her drive away from him.

In retrospect, Simon realized that she hadn't chosen their life—he had. His job had brought them to Raleigh. He had bought the house in the neighborhood where he wanted to live. He had taken his parents' things out of storage—the Steinway, the Oriental rugs, the countless books that filled two walls downstairs and the third bedroom upstairs—and furnished the house. Tess had never complained. She had seemed happy. Why had she thrown her lot in with his if it wasn't what she wanted? Charitably, Simon supposed she didn't know what she wanted until too late to avoid hurting him.

Simon walked downstairs and into the small kitchen and opened his refrigerator door. Three Cokes was not much sustenance for standing in front of a classroom all afternoon, but he was never hungry anymore. He knew he had to eat, so he took a container of cherry vanilla yogurt out of the refrigerator and sat at his kitchen table to force it down himself.

After she left, Tess had not responded to any of his attempts to contact her. When one of his cousins spotted her in Macy's, she simply said that she thought it was best that way. Best for her, maybe. When Simon realized how complete his loss was, he took an emotional nosedive. He was barely able to finish the semester's work. His troubled condition was so obvious that his friends worried about him aloud and everyone else talked about him behind his back. The chair of the history department, Walker Jones, came into his office one day shortly before the semester ended and gave him a kind but firm ultimatum: Get help or take a leave of absence.

First, Simon looked through the Yellow Pages under the listings for psychiatrists and psychotherapists. But he couldn't tell the good ones from the quacks. He hung out with a pretty balanced crowd, so no one he knew had any recommendations for him. In desperation, he went to his regular doctor.

"You have the common cold of mental illness," Dr. Wade Ferrell told him. "And you have company. About a third of all Americans, to be exact. You're depressed, and you have good reason to be. But unlike the common cold, we have a cure. You don't have to lie on a sofa for three years like Proust did until it goes away by itself. There's just one thing."

"What?" Simon had asked, wondering what could possibly be left about his private life that the man didn't already know.

"You haven't minimized your symptoms in any way?" Ferrell asked. "Have you thought at all about killing yourself?"

Simon was aghast, and it must have shown on his face.

"Good," the doctor said. "If you had said yes, I would have put you in my car, run by your house for your toothbrush, and taken you to a very safe place until the antidepressants kicked in. As it is, I think you can go home."

Ferrell wrote three prescriptions and tore them off his pad. " 'Better living through chemistry,' " he said, handing them to Simon. "But remember, these are not 'happy pills.' They're not going to change the fact that your wife left you. But you will be able to function."

Later, Simon stood outside his neighborhood pharmacy and inspected the little bottles of pills that would restore some part of his life to him. If Proust had had these, he wondered, would he have written *Remembrance of Things Past* when he got off that couch? But Simon decided to abandon existential musings for the time being and opt for feeling better. So he took his pills, and he did feel better—sort of.

As Simon inspected the last lump of cherry vanilla yogurt at the bottom of its container, he contemplated loss and thought about Anne Bloodworth. Did she have any notion that she was about to die and forfeit all the joys and sorrows of another fifty or so years of life? She had been shot in the back of the head, so the odds were that she had no inkling that she was going to die, and thus no opportunity to say good-bye, even to herself.

Simon walked out of the house and went over to his black Thunderbird. He had bought it when he was flush with royalties from the paperback edition of his book. Driving around town with the air conditioner on high and Paul Simon on the stereo was about the only activity that gave him any pleasure these days, so he figured the car was a worthwhile investment from a psychological standpoint. He got in the car, started the engine, shifted, slipped *Graceland* comfortably into its accustomed slot, and drove off toward campus, reveling in percussion all the way.

WHEN SIMON GOT back home from his class Thursday evening, he found a message from Sergeant Gates on his answering machine, asking if he could come to see him. So Simon arrived earlier than usual at the office the next morning. Judy Smith looked up at him in surprise when he walked into the departmental office to check his mail.

"What are you doing here?" she asked.

"I'm glad to see you, too," Simon replied.

"You know I didn't mean it that way. Besides, I was going to call you. Dr. Jones has called a departmental meeting for eleven o'clock."

"No kidding," Simon said. A departmental meeting during summer school was very unusual. For one thing, most of the faculty weren't in town. They vanished to the beach, mountains, abroad, or to a research site from early May, when the second semester ended, to the middle of August.

The faculty took turns teaching four courses, two in each summer session, every year. This year Simon was teaching *North Carolina History,* Alex Andrus was teaching *The Civil War,* Vera Thayer was teaching *European Imperialism and Colonialism,* and Marcus Clegg was offering his controversial *History of Science.*

"Got any idea what it's all about?" Simon asked.

"No," she replied. "But Dr. Walker and Alex were in crisis mode yesterday afternoon."

"What do you mean?" Simon asked.

"They spent two hours in Dr. Jones's office, and when they came out, both of them looked furious. Dr. Jones asked me to call all the faculty I could reach and tell them that there would be a departmental meeting this morning."

Simon was fascinated. What crisis could he have missed that would cause an emergency faculty meeting to be called when the rest of the faculty couldn't be on hand to enjoy the fracas? Of course, Alex Andrus could cause trouble about anything, anytime.

Simon walked on down the hall toward the lounge and the coffeepot, where he hoped to pick up some scuttlebutt about the meeting.

The history department was located in one of the original college buildings built in 1834. It was faced with hand-carved stone left over from the State Capitol's construction, and like the Capitol, it was early Greek Revival, complete with dome and pedimented portico. Every bit of the building was built by hand. There wasn't a right angle in the entire place, but the halls were wide and the windows were as tall as a man and could actually be opened during the spring and fall. The handcarved woodwork, wood banisters, and moldings were maintained meticulously by a fund specially set up for the purpose of preserving the four original campus buildings. Although the history faculty complained about the erratic heating and cooling and the unreliable plumbing, not to mention the mice, most would not have dreamed of forsaking the old building.

The lounge had once been the original library for the entire campus, and it was still lined with bookshelves that held faculty publications and part of the original collection. A few battered leather couches and a couple of tables filled the center of the room. A full pot of usually decent coffee sat on one table. During the academic year, one could find the entire history department in the lounge at this hour, but this morning, only Professor Vera Thayer was ensconced on one of the couches. She was drinking a steaming cup of coffee and reading the *Raleigh News and Observer.*

Vera looked up at him as he walked into the room.

"It's really good to see you," she said. "Where have you been all summer?"

Simon wished that everyone would stop noticing his comings

and goings. He really didn't enjoy explaining to the world that he had been having some difficulty getting out of bed in the morning because of a bout with clinical depression but that he was feeling much better, thank you.

Thayer suddenly seemed to realize the implications of her question.

"Oh, I forgot, *North Carolina History* doesn't meet until the afternoon, does it?" she said, covering for him.

"That's right," he said. Of course, he continued to himself, as he filled a cup of coffee to the brim and laced it with sugar, you're not teaching anything until second session, and you're here bright and early every day, loaded for bear. Professor Thayer was in her late fifties. She was always dressed meticulously in a suit, wore full makeup, and had her hair fixed twice a week. She was the type of middle-aged career woman who was so self-conscious about her success that she was constantly playing the part of the perfect academic. She was not brilliant, but she was tough and had written seven books, most of them now out of print. She was the first woman at Kenan to make full professor. She was not a popular teacher because she had no empathy with her students, but everyone who passed her courses knew the material backward and forward. Of course she knew that Simon's wife had left him, but she usually accepted no excuses for herself or anyone else, and it surprised him that she would excuse his "malingering." Simon, and everyone else on the faculty, except perhaps Walker Jones, tended to wilt under Thayer's scrutiny. Simon wondered if she would be chair of the department after Jones retired.

Simon picked up part of the paper and the two read in silence while the sun slowly rose higher in the sky and slanted into the room through the huge windows.

After a while, Simon became aware that Professor Thayer had let her paper fall into her lap and was studying him. He looked up at her, and she seized her opportunity to speak.

"I heard about all the excitement yesterday from Judy," she said. "I'm glad you could identify that woman," she went on. "It must have been an interesting experience."

"It was," Simon said. "Kind of gruesome, too. I thought about it half the night."

"I understand that the policeman in charge of the case is coming to see you this morning? What about?"

Simon shrugged. "I don't really know. He seems to think I might be able to help them more. Apparently, if she was murdered, there might be some kind of an official investigation, even though it happened a long time ago."

"It would be a mighty cold trail."

"But we historians investigate old, cold trails all the time," Simon said.

"True." She sat silently for a few minutes. It was clear that she had just been warming up to what she really wanted to talk to him about.

"There's going to be a faculty meeting at eleven."

"I know. Do you know what it's about?"

"I'm afraid it's going to be unpleasant for you," she said.

Simon felt his stomach constrict and his armpits grow damp.

"What on earth—"

"Simon," she said, "since you haven't been yourself this summer, which," she added quickly, "we all understand, under the circumstances, I'm afraid that there is an individual in the department who will use it against you."

Andrus, Simon thought. He wants my job. Always has.

Simon had been jumped over Andrus for tenure when his book won the Pulitzer. Andrus hated him for it. There were no more tenured positions available and wouldn't be unless someone left. Simon guessed that he was a candidate for that someone.

"Exactly what will be the context of this unpleasantness, Vera?" he asked.

"Bobby Hinton's senior thesis grade," she answered.

Simon had given Andrus's pet student a C on his senior thesis, and Andrus had been griping about it ever since.

"I'm not going to change that kid's grade, Vera, and that's all there is to it," Simon said.

"You know I agree with you," she replied. "But there is a formal process for appealing grades, and it starts at the departmental level, at this meeting this morning. Be prepared."

Now that he understood the issue, Simon wasn't concerned. The grade was final, and he was sure the department would back him up. He looked at his watch, then stood up.

"I've got to go."

As he walked out the door, Professor Thayer stopped him again.

"Simon," she said.

"Yes?"

"Just watch your back," she answered.

Simon worried about their conversation all the way down the hall to his office. The situation didn't seem to him to warrant Thayer's concern, and he wondered what he didn't know.

By the time he got back to his office, Sergeant Gates and the legal counsel for the police department were waiting for him. Gates looked older than Simon had thought at first—his short hair seemed grayer and Simon noticed deep lines cut into his forehead. Again Simon had an urge to step back a pace to get a look at the complete man. Judy, who knew everything about everybody in town, had told him that Gates went into police work after a very successful football career. The combination of the man's size and brains must have made him formidable.

Simon hadn't expected anyone other than Gates, and he quickly had to sweep a pile of papers and files off a chair before he could seat both his visitors. Gates introduced Simon to the young woman who was with him.

"This is Julia McGloughlan, the policeman's friend," Gates said. "She keeps us straight, legally speaking."

McGloughlan shook Simon's hand. His first thought was that she would be attractive if she wasn't wearing a gray suit with a burgundy-and-gray tie knotted under the collar of a stark white blouse. She had auburn hair and hazel eyes, and she looked particularly bad in gray. Nonetheless, Simon automatically checked her left hand. No rings. He caught himself mentally, surprised that he would care.

"I hope you don't mind my coming along, Dr. Shaw, but I'm very interested in this case," McGloughlan said.

"If it is a case," interrupted Gates.

"It's a case," she said. "A woman shot inside the city limits of Raleigh is definitely a case. The DA doesn't want to spend time and money on a case that is probably insoluble," McGloughlan continued. "He knows perfectly well that there is no statute of limitations on murder."

"We don't know that it's murder, although it seems likely," Gates said. "If it is, the murderer is dead by now, too. Isn't the point of solving a crime to bring the perpetrator to justice?"

"Maybe," she admitted. "But I don't know, it just bothers me. It seems wrong to ignore a crime just because it happened a long time ago."

"It bothers me, too," Simon said. "But historians are bothered by things that happened a long time ago. It's what we do for a living."

"That's sort of why we're here, Simon," said Gates. "We've pretty much decided to look into this, and the chief says it's okay as long as we don't spend too much time and money on it. We've got the authorization for an autopsy, but we have a favor to ask of you."

"Shoot," Simon said.

"We need a positive identification of the body. We think she's who you say she is mostly because of circumstance. The fact that we can authenticate her jewelry is important, but what we really need is a physical description of Anne Bloodworth to give the ME so that he can positively identify her and then give a death certificate that lists the cause of death as homicide."

"The sergeant has some good men on the police staff, but they're not historians," McGloughlan said. "We don't have any idea how to research this. The sergeant tells me that he thinks you might be willing to help us."

"What kind of information do you need?" Simon said.

"Stuff like her height, weight, age, any injury that might leave a skeletal record, maybe dental records," McGloughlan said.

Simon thought for a few minutes. He had run across newspaper articles about Anne Bloodworth's disappearance when he was researching his book, and he remembered the details fairly well. The police departments of the entire state had been alerted. Her father had hired the Pinkerton Detective Agency to search for her all over the country. Surely a detailed description of her must have been circulated by the authorities.

"I'll see what I can find out. If there is anything, it shouldn't take long to find it," Simon said. "I'll try to let you know something in a couple of days."

"Good," Gates said. "Let's see, today is Friday, and the autopsy is Monday. That should work out okay."

Gates and McGloughlan stood up to leave.

"Listen," Gates said. "I've got to get back to the office. Julia wants to see the site. Would you have time to take her over there?"

Simon checked his watch. He had almost an hour until his meeting. "Sure," he said.

"I'd appreciate it," Julia said. "But if you have something else to do, just say so."

"No problem at all," Simon said. If only she knew, Simon thought, just how little I have to do.

Together, the two walked across the Kenan campus, obsessing about the same things all North Carolinians obsessed about at this time of year: the weather and the pollen count.

Each year May brought rampant floral beauty and a massive accumulation of plant reproductive matter. Pollen and giant tree pods lay in clumps all over the ground. Little seeds with various wing configurations helicoptered out of the trees to the ground. Children couldn't go barefoot, for fear of stepping on the countless little round seed canisters with spikes that were thick on the ground.

The oak pollen was the worst. Huge clumps of oak flowers clogged up sewers and drains, gummed up windshields, and ruined car finishes. Everyone constantly prayed for rain to wash the stuff away and signal the coming of the month of June, that limited, blessed time that precedes the heat and humidity of July.

So Julia and Simon discussed the possibility of rain. Did all those black clouds and the oppressive atmosphere mean rain? If it rained, would all the pollen wash away, and would there be a final onslaught? Was ridding the neighborhood of pollen a worthy trade for canceling a Durham Bulls doubleheader and having to sandbag Crabtree Creek? Yes, they unanimously agreed as cascades of yellow dust drifted out of the trees around them.

After they had disposed of the weather as a topic, Julia wanted to talk about Anne Bloodworth's disappearance.

"Don't you think the FBI would have information on microfiche or something?" she asked.

Simon shook his head. "Probably not," he said. This happened in 1926. Most of the crimes we think of as federal crimes weren't designated as such by Congress until the 1930s, when the Depression caused a crime wave. For instance, kidnapping became a federal crime after the Lindbergh baby was abducted in 1932."

"So what did people do if they wanted to search for someone in another state?" Julia asked.

"If they had any money, they hired the Pinkerton Detective Agency. It had offices in every major city in the country. But the best place to begin researching anything is the newspapers. I'll start there tomorrow."

The crime-scene tape was gone from the site, and David Morgan was back at work excavating. He was watching the sky while supervising two students spreading plastic over the site.

"So you think it's going to rain?" Simon said by way of a greeting.

"I can't take the chance it won't," Morgan said. "This place will be pure mud if it's not protected. The trenches would fill up and we couldn't empty them for days."

Simon introduced Julia McGloughlan to him. David acknowledged her with a noncommittal nod. She could have been seventy and walking with a cane for all the attention he paid her. Most women were insulted by this—Tess certainly had been—but Julia seemed unconcerned. She was only interested in information.

"If you have the time, Dr. Morgan, please show me where you found the body," she said.

David obligingly walked her around the site, pointing out how and where the corpse was found.

"How could she have been buried here without anyone knowing it?" McGloughlan asked.

"The kitchen was abandoned before 1926," David said. "But you really need to ask Simon about the chronology of all this."

McGloughlan turned to Simon.

"This building had a dirt floor, a fireplace, and a wood-fueled stove. It was used for over a hundred years. A modern kitchen was added to the house right before the First World War," Simon said. "Then this building was used for storage until it burned to the ground in 1933."

"How can you be sure of that?" she asked.

"The draftsman's drawings for the kitchen addition are in the Preservation Society's library," Simon said, "and they're dated. Plus, a watercolor of the house done shortly afterward shows what the house looked like after various improvements, including the kitchen addition. There's a 1924 date on the back of the watercolor, which is hanging in the house, by the way. And we know the building burned in 1933, because it was reported in the newspaper in a story that included the information that it was being used for storage. All this is in the monograph I wrote."

David jumped into the ditch. "And look—Simon, I haven't had a chance to show you this yet—it verifies the written record." With his finger, he traced a line of black not far beneath the surface of the sides of the ditch. "This is a layer of carbon, which proves that the building did burn at about the time we believe it did." Simon and Julia climbed into the trench to inspect the evidence. Julia knelt in the dirt for a closer look.

"Look," Julia said, pointing to another layer of black about a foot farther down the trench. "Is that another fire?"

"In the early nineteenth century," David said, "but there's no written record of it."

"Detached kitchens burned all the time," Simon said. "That's why they were built away from the house to begin with."

Julia contemplated the wall of the trench while the two men climbed out of it. Simon turned and reached out a hand to help her, and she scrambled up, oblivious to the mud collecting on her shoes and stockings. David handed her a towel, and she wiped her hands carelessly, staring off in the general direction of the house.

"This all seems very suspicious to me," Julia said.

"I think so, too," said Simon.

"What are you two talking about?" David asked. "It's not suspicious, it's clear as a bell. The woman was killed and her body was hidden to conceal the crime. What could be clearer than that?"

"There's more to it. I think that we can make some other assumptions from what we know so far," Julia said. "First of all, we can assume that Anne Bloodworth was murdered that day in 1926 when she supposedly disappeared. She was shot in the back of the head, which is odd if she just surprised somebody on the property who was doing something they shouldn't have been doing. Did she even see the guy? If she was running away, why shoot her?"

"I want to know where everyone else was," Simon said. "Where were her father and the servants? Someone should have seen something. It's unlikely she was on the property alone."

"And the person who killed her knew the area pretty well, because he buried the body right here, in a building that had been abandoned except for storage," Julia added. "Hidden so well, in fact, that it wasn't found for seventy years."

"It would be far-fetched to think the building was burned down a few years after her disappearance to further hide the crime," Simon said.

"Far-fetched is an understatement," David said. "There's no evidence of that at all."

"But it certainly is a coincidence," Julia said. "And I think there is one solid conclusion we can draw from all this: Anne Bloodworth's murderer was someone who knew her, which isn't really surprising. That's true in most murders."

"I think he definitely knew her fairly well," Simon said.

"Hold it—that's going too far even for you," David said.

"The body was laid out for burial," Simon said. "Anne Bloodworth was shrouded in a quilt and her hands were crossed across her chest, just as if she'd been buried formally. Her jewelry hadn't been stolen. Would an ordinary criminal, a stranger, do something like that? Especially if he was in a hurry? Hell, where did he get the quilt? Did he go into the house?"

"It's a mystery, that's for sure," said Julia, "and one I would like to solve."

"No way," David said, "the trail's too cold."

"No trail's so cold that we can't at least try to make sense of it," Simon said. "Look at what we know already."

"And by next week, we should know a lot more," Julia said. "Simon's going to do his historical research thing, I'm going to search our files, and the ME, we hope, will be able to ID the corpse positively, and who knows what else he may find." Simon and Julia both looked at David expectantly, waiting for his contribution.

"I think you're both crazy," he said.

"Well, I've got to go back to the office and pretend to work on something a little more current," Julia said. "But what I'm really going to do is find out what happened to our own files from 1926, if we even had any." She declined Simon's offer to walk her to her car, then went off by herself toward the parking lot. Simon watched her walk away from him. She had a good figure.

"I would think you'd be cured of women," David said. It was the first reference David had made to Simon's troubles, and Simon chose to ignore it.

"What do you think of her?" he asked.

David shrugged. "She's okay. At least she doesn't mind getting a little dirty."

Simon liked just about everything about Julia McGloughlan except that awful gray suit.

As Simon walked back to his office and his meeting, he noticed that the sky was becoming very dark with promised rain. Some of the cars on Hillsborough Street already had their lights on. Hillsborough Street was a broad thoroughfare even back in the twenties, when Anne Bloodworth had disappeared. The first mass-produced automobiles mixed with horse-drawn vehicles of every description. The trolley, its bell constantly sounding, ran under a tangle of wiring between downtown Raleigh and State College, now North Carolina State University. Anne Bloodworth would probably never have ridden the trolley, even though it had passed right in front of her home. Her set had its own carriages or automobiles to drive to one of the houses on fashionable Blount Street for chicken salad and pickled oysters, or perhaps to the Nine O'Clock Cotillion in the ballroom on the second floor of the Olivia Raney Library. Had Anne heard of the Scopes trial? Did she care that women got the vote in 1920, although without the approval of North Carolina? What kind of young woman had she been? And who cared now, anyway?

Finally, whatever had been eating at Simon had worked its way into his consciousness. He realized that he cared. A lovely and intelligent woman had died violently long before her time. In the natural order of things, she should have lived, married, had children, enjoyed the good times and endured the bad, and died in bed. Someone took all that away from her. Simon wanted to know who and why.

5

EVERYONE ELSE HAD GATHERED IN THE LOUNGE BY THE TIME Simon arrived for the faculty meeting. Nonetheless, it was a sparse assembly, with just Walker Jones, Vera Thayer, Alex Andrus, Marcus Clegg, and himself.

Marcus Clegg held a joint appointment in the departments of psychology and history. His research in both fields was brilliant, original, and meticulous. Despite his accomplishments, Marcus probably wouldn't be welcome at a major university. He just didn't fit into any standard academic niche. Kenan College was happy to have him move between his lab, where he studied the neuroanatomy of rats in the context of behavior, and his crowded office in the history department, where he was finishing a book on the recantation of Galileo.

Marcus's views on psychology and psychotherapy were unfashionable, too. He was a social liberal only because he believed that either the carrot or the stick would solve any problem known to man, but that the carrot was more humane. Buying off the masses was just plain more acceptable to him than locking them up. He was especially critical of talk therapy, which he believed encouraged self-pity and helplessness. "I hate to hear people whine," he once told Simon. "I don't want to spend years listening to the same people try to figure out why they can't get on an elevator without having an anxiety attack. I want to get them on that elevator—as soon as possible. And never see them again."

Simon was glad that Marcus was in town. He was the only one

in the room with whom Simon had a personal relationship. Marcus was about ten years older than Simon, and he still cultivated a sixties' image. He wore Birkenstock sandals with socks practically all year, wire-rim glasses, and his brown hair curled over his collar. He professed to be a radical, but he had an essentially conservative nature. The man worked hard at his job, adored his wife of fifteen years, and was devoted to his four daughters. He spent most of his free time with his family at soccer games and Indian Princesses meetings and other such family events. Simon was jealous as hell of him.

As always, Walker Jones presided paternally at the head of the table. White-haired, dignified, and poised, he reminded Simon of Walter Cronkite. He had been department chair for twenty years and took it just as seriously today as he did his first week on the job. Vera Thayer sat rigidly next to him, poised like Athena determined to defend Troy from the Greeks. She wore her business suit like armor and her beehive hairdo like a helmet. All that was missing was a sword and a shield. Alex Andrus was pacing in front of the windows, carefully balancing a well-worn chip on his shoulder.

Andrus was on his second career and was sensitive about it. After being passed over for captain twice, the navy refused to renew his enlistment contract. He was a fanatic Civil War hobbyist, so he went to graduate school to get his doctorate. He worked hard and produced dozens of articles published in Civil War journals and magazines. Most of them were bibliographies and catalogs of artifacts. He was a popular teacher because he taught the Civil War anecdotally and adhered to the standard southern line that slavery had not been the cause of the Civil War. If Simon had not come to Kenan and won the Pulitzer Prize, Andrus would have been a sure bet for tenure.

Simon kept his mouth shut around Alex. He disliked the man, but he also despised his attitude toward southern history. Simon was a devoted southerner. He wouldn't live anywhere else in the world. But he hated the unquestioning idolatry of most of the South toward the Civil War experience. He believed that the decision to secede was indefensible from any standpoint, whether social, economic, or military. It was even more irresponsible to keep fighting when the odds against the South became clear. Many thousands of young Southerners died unnecessarily for "the cause" long after it was hopeless. In any other nation in the world, everyone from Jefferson Davis to General Lee would have been shot for treason after the surrender at Appomattox. Then what the outmoded economics of slavery didn't do to delay the development of the South, Reconstruction did. It was a hundred years before the South recovered. It gave Simon a headache to drive past the capitol on Robert E. Lee's birthday and see the Confederate battle flag flying.

But Simon was smart enough to say very little on the subject. He did once suggest mildly to Andrus while he was holding forth on states' rights that he really ought to read the Constitution. But he didn't want to get ridden out of North Carolina on a rail. Just because he thought the Yankees' victory was inevitable, he didn't want to have to go live with them.

Simon sat down next to Marcus. Everyone looked at him. Although Simon knew he was the focus of this meeting, he was relaxed. He was right and Andrus was wrong.

Walker Jones called the meeting to order.

"I really dislike holding a faculty meeting when we have so few of our people here," he began, "but I have come to feel that it is necessary to keep a certain situation from becoming out of control." He looked at Simon directly. "Vera tells me that she mentioned the purpose of this meeting to you earlier this morning."

"Yes," Simon answered. "Bobby Hinton's senior thesis grade is being appealed."

"That's correct," Jones said formally. "Let's summarize the situation briefly." He looked at his notes. "Mr. Hinton was a senior history major, one of our best students. Along with nine others, he was selected to participate in the senior honors seminar, which requires the writing of a long research paper over the course of the year. This paper is expected to be of graduate-school quality. Last year, the seminar was taught by Simon. In addition, every student has a faculty adviser who is a specialist in the period he or she has selected. As Mr. Hinton's topic was the Civil War, Alex Andrus was his adviser. At the end of the year, Hinton received a C from Simon. The other grades in the class were six *A*s and three *B*-pluses."

"It was absolutely ridiculous—" began Andrus.

"Hold on, Alex. I'm not done yet," Jones said. "Please tell us, Simon, your rationale for that grade."

"A senior thesis of the quality we expect must be written to graduate-school standards," Simon said. "We tell the kids that when they sign up for the course. Most of them live, eat, and breathe this paper for the course of the year. It gives them a huge edge in graduate school. They all know that. All the senior faculty take turns teaching the seminar, and we emphasize critical reading and thinking, and the use of primary sources. I repeatedly warned Hinton after reading his drafts that his primary research was unacceptable. In fact, it was practically nonexistent. He ignored me. He writes very well, and he did an excellent survey of the literature on his topic. But he didn't add an iota of original knowledge or thought to the subject. So he got a *C*. It would have been unfair to the other students to give him anything else."

"I hope you realize that he will lose his spot in graduate school because of this," Andrus said.

"That's completely irrelevant," Vera Thayer said.

"Hold on, please," Jones said. He turned to Andrus.

"Now, Alex, did you know of Simon's comments on Hinton's drafts?" he asked.

"Of course I did. And I referred him to a number of sources."

"And did he make any use of these?"

"Yes. But he said that they didn't add much to his discussion."

Jones turned to Simon. "Simon?"

"All the students are supposed to make sure there are sufficient sources for their topic before they formally select it and begin work. In fact, his bibliography referred to a number of primary sources. But there was no evidence at all in his paper that he actually used any," Simon said.

"Listen," Andrus said. "The boy was carrying a huge load. He was taking an extra course, and doing research for me at the same time."

"Then he shouldn't have signed up for the senior seminar," Vera said.

"I think," Simon said, "that Hinton expected that his writing facility would see him through. He expected a *B* just from participating in the seminar and completing a paper. But I gave *B*s to others whose papers were much more thoughtful. If I'd given him a *B*, I would have had to raise three others to *A*s, and they just weren't that quality."

"Listen, damn it," Andrus said. "I read his paper and I thought it was a *B* effort."

"But you weren't teaching the course," Marcus Clegg said quietly. "Simon was. He gave the grades, not you. We must support his decisions."

"Not if he's incompetent, we shouldn't."

A stunned silence fell over the table. Jesus God, thought Simon, so this is what this is all about. He felt dampness begin to collect under his armpits and around his groin.

Marcus exploded. "Of all the ignorant, insensitive things you have ever said and done, Alex, this is the worst. You—"

"Hold it!" Jones said. "Alex, you owe us an explanation. Right now."

"Ask Professor Shaw if he isn't taking medication for emotional problems," Andrus said.

"This is reprehensible," Marcus said.

"It's okay, Marcus," Simon said. Perspiration began to trickle down his back and sides, pooling in the crevices of his body. His head began to pound.

"It's true that I've been treated for clinical depression recently," Simon said. "You all know that my wife left me, and the last few months have been very difficult."

"If I thought Simon couldn't do his job, I would have suggested that he take a leave of absence," Jones said.

"Most normal people, Alex, of which I am sure you are not one, have some down times in their lives when they aren't as productive as others," Marcus Clegg said. "If Simon had broken his leg, we would give him time to heal from that. Emotional illness is no different."

Let's just hang out a sign, Simon thought. Let's get the cable access channel for an hour. Maybe CNN would pick it up and tell the world, right between the invasion of the week and the disease of the month.

"If I thought I wasn't fit to teach, I wouldn't teach," Simon said. "Bobby Hinton's paper is a C paper."

"I think we should all read it and see if we agree," Andrus said.

"Out of the question," Vera Thayer said. "We don't check behind senior faculty."

"Goddamn it!" Andrus shouted. "Let's just all stand behind our famous Pulitzer Prize winner! Never mind that he can hardly make it into the office in the morning. Never mind that my protégé's career is ruined!"

"You're excused, right now, Alex. Don't show your face in this building until you are prepared to apologize," Jones said.

"I'll appeal this to the dean. Don't think I won't!" Andrus said as he stalked out of the room.

"If you've ever needed a reason not to renew his contract, you've got it now," Marcus Clegg said to Jones. "The man has navel lint where his brain should be."

"I don't have cause to cancel his contract. You know that," Jones said.

"Can't we squelch the appeal somehow?" asked Thayer. "This could be embarrassing to the whole department."

Simon knew now why Thayer had defended him. She was a tough grader, and she didn't want this case to set a precedent.

Everyone avoided looking at Simon, who was fighting to subject his nervous system to manual control. His clothing was damp, his stomach hurt, and a migraine aura appeared in the left corner of his field of vision. To his surprise, his voice sounded fairly normal when he spoke.

"If you want my resignation, you have it," Simon said. Hell, he'd always really wanted to teach high school. Maybe junior college. Anything would be better than having his personal problems spread all over the campus.

"If you resign, I'll resign, too," said Clegg.

"Don't you dare!" snapped Jones. "I'm not accepting any resignations from anybody. I refuse to lose my faculty to some stupid, jealous departmental bickering. Is that understood? We'll deal with this." He didn't leave any time for a response before he went on.

"We can't stop him from appealing to the dean if he really wants to," Jones said. "But I'll talk to Alex and do my best to convince him that he'll look like a fool. If he insists, it would probably be best to get the whole thing out in the open and let the dean put an end to it."

"Make sure that you mention to Alex when you have this little conversation that he isn't tenure material under any circumstances," Clegg said.

"For a psychologist, you're not much of a diplomat," Jones said. The chairman left the room, followed by Thayer.

"Shit," Simon said.

"Life sucks sometimes," Clegg said. "When my brother died in Vietnam, I felt like I was living outside my skin for three years. And I'm a psychologist. I'm supposed to understand this mental stuff."

"I was actually feeling pretty good, until about an hour ago."

"Alex is an ass. If he goes any further with this, he'll just look like an ass to more people. Forget about him. Come on, let's go get some bad food for lunch."

"I'm not hungry, and I'd be terrible company."

"You call me anytime," Clegg said. "I'm a trained psychotherapist, you know. Electroshock is a hobby of mine."

"I wouldn't let you anywhere near my brain. God knows how you'd rewire it."

After Marcus left, Simon was alone in the lounge. He stood up and inspected his armpits. He felt soaked. He walked over to one of the huge windows and opened it, standing in the damp breeze so that he could cool off and be able to walk out of the department with dignity. Rain was falling in big, heavy drops, knocking aside leaves and twigs as it fell straight down from the sky.

Simon wondered if he shouldn't resign despite what Walker Jones had said. If Andrus appealed further, everyone on campus would know the details of his personal misfortune. But wouldn't that happen anyway if he resigned? Why did he have to lose everything? Surely this, and worse, had happened to other people. It would pass when something hotter got everyone's attention. He would just have to manage the embarrassment as best he could until then.

He spent the afternoon in his office grading papers so he could return them to his four o'clock class. Alex Andrus walked back into the department in time to teach at two, then walked back out again. He didn't speak to anyone, much less apologize.

Back home for dinner, Simon contemplated the contents of his refrigerator with revulsion. He knew he couldn't get rid of his headache, Coke and pills notwithstanding, unless he put something in his stomach. He decided that scrambled eggs and toast might be gentle enough, but beating the glutinous eggs almost made him throw up. Once they were cooked, he managed to eat them, buffered as they were by a lot of toast and peach jelly.

His doorbell rang. Standing there was the little boy from next door, dressed in regulation Little League from head to toe and wielding a catcher's mitt and the Louisville Slugger Simon had given him for Christmas. Oh no, Simon thought.

"I can't, Danny, not now," Simon said.

"Please, Simon, you haven't pitched for me in ages. Please."

"I know, but I just don't feel like it. I'm sorry. Some other time."

The boy was too polite to whine, but he continued to stand at the door, waiting for a break in Simon's resolve. Simon remembered how little the boy saw his father, and what his mother had said Simon's attention meant to him.

"Sometime soon, I promise," Simon said.

"Sure," the boy answered.

Simon watched the boy despondently walk down his steps and back to his house, dragging his bat behind him. Great, he thought. What a time he had been having. He had almost fainted at the sight of a corpse in front of the Raleigh police and his best friend, been accused of incompetence by a peer at an open faculty meeting, and disappointed a small boy. What a guy he was. And it was just seven o'clock in the evening.

What he really wanted to do was go to bed and to sleep, to obliterate his problems at least for a few hours. But if he went to sleep now, he would wake up at three o'clock in the morning with nothing to do but think about his life—which was to be avoided at all costs.

Then he remembered his promise to Julia McGloughlan. He was supposed to find information somewhere that the medical examiner could use to identify Anne Bloodworth's body positively.

He was saved from Friday night television.

Simon went upstairs to his library, where the index cards with notes for his book were stuffed into shoe boxes in the back of a closet. Unfortunately, the cards were no longer organized chronologically or by subject, but the way he had sorted them to write the book. He would have to go through them one by one to find what he was looking for. Simon sat cross-legged on the sofa and contemplated the four boxes. Charles Bloodworth had left few papers that could have been called personal. The documents Simon had read were mostly business correspondence and a daily diary that listed his appointments along with a few personal comments. However, the disappearance of a daughter was obviously a momentous event, and Simon remembered several references to it in Bloodworth's diary and at least two letters on the subject, one of which was to Pinkerton's main office in Chicago. The problem was, he hadn't taken any notes on these. If he didn't want to reread Bloodworth' papers completely, he had to go through the cards and correlate what events he had documented with what transpired concerning Anne Bloodworth's disappearance. When he had located what he needed, he would have some dates and document numbers he could take over to Chapel Hill and the Southern Historical Collection. That way, he could quickly locate the files he needed. His hope was that somewhere in Bloodworth's business diary or in a letter, he had described his daughter in some way that would be helpful to the medical examiner.

Simon had just used newspaper accounts to write the very brief section on her disappearance in the monograph on the house, and he had those references easily at hand. He could start rereading the newspaper files tomorrow.

Painstakingly, Simon went through every note card in every box. Three hours and a lot of CDs later, he had found several cards that he was sure would lead him in the right direction. He realized that he was starving, so he went downstairs and got a huge bowl of freezer-burned vanilla ice cream with some stringy, old chocolate sauce on it. It tasted wonderful. It was nearly eleven o'clock when Simon went to bed. He slept like a log for almost nine hours.

The next morning found Simon at the door of the Kenan library when it opened. It was crowded even on Saturday. Summer school was so compressed that students studied every free minute. A few faculty members were there, too, trying to stay one lecture ahead of their students.

41

Simon walked to the back of the library and unlocked the door to his carrel. He hadn't been here in weeks. Books, papers, and file folders were strewn everywhere over the cheap wooden desk and bookshelf, but everything was coated in a thin layer of dust. Simon looked warily through the stack of stuff on his desk. He had a momentary fear that somewhere in this mess was a pile of student papers he hadn't graded and that neither he nor his students had missed. Apparently not. There was, however, a caustic note from the librarian that announced she had removed some long overdue materials and returned them to the stacks, and that he really should be more considerate. Simon hardly remembered what he had been working on when Tess left. When he scanned the last few pages he had written, it seemed like someone else's work that had been accidentally left on his desk. This is one article that won't ever be finished, Simon thought. The hell with it. The world will hardly stop orbiting the sun. He dumped his briefcase on the chair, picked up a yellow pad and pen, locked the door behind him, and went to his favorite place, the microfiche reading room. Oddly, his heart was pounding.

He found the spool of microfiche labeled April–May 1926, unrolled it onto the spools on the reader, and flipped on the power. The process was so familiar and automatic that it had a tranquilizing effect on him. When he immersed himself in any kind of primary research, he tended to block out his own present and identify completely with his subjects. It was such an intense experience, he never discussed it with anyone, even other academics, because he worried that it was a little abnormal.

Anne Bloodworth's disappearance on April 9, 1926, had driven other stories about Byrd's expedition to the North Pole and the attempted assassination of Mussolini off the front page of the paper. In a tabloid style the *National Enquirer* would have been proud of, the paper dwelt on the mystery of Anne's disappearance, the bafflement of the police, the grief of her father, and the desperation of her fiancé. Apparently, Anne Bloodworth and her father, Charles, had been alone in their house—the live-in help had gone to a movie. Her second cousin and fiancé, Adam Bloodworth, was on a fishing trip. She went upstairs to bed to read; Charles worked in his study. Before Bloodworth went to bed, he knocked on his daughter's door to say good night. When there was no answer, he assumed she was asleep. The next morning, the maid taking her tea upstairs found that her room was empty and that her bed had not been slept in. All hell broke loose.

Motorcycle patrolman Peebles arrived at the Bloodworth home first. He described the scene as extremely confused—the wailing servants had the house in an uproar and "Captain Bloodworth" was prostrate. Dr. Zeb Caviness, who lived up the street, was plying him with sleeping salts to keep him coherent. Officer Peebles found, to his dismay, that Anne Bloodworth's room had been completely overturned by her father, who had been looking for some answer to the riddle of her disappearance. The back garden and orchard had been trampled by neighbors searching for her. This "well-meaning but unorganized search," said the reporter, "seems likely to have obscured important clues."

The entire Raleigh police force, on horseback and motorcycle, searched the city from top to bottom. The next day, Police Chief J. W. Bryan told readers that there was no trace of Miss Bloodworth anywhere in the city. They had even searched the saloons and whorehouses, he said, in case she had been abducted by white slavers. Telegrams had been sent to Charlotte, Charleston, and Richmond. She had not been seen at the train station, and she could have gotten no farther than Charlotte by motorcar. Bloodworth had hired the city's only detective, Robert L. Lumsden, of the Southern Detective Agency, to help search for her. The police of the time, Simon knew, were trained to keep law and order, not to detect.

By the end of three days, the story of Anne Bloodworth's disappearance had dropped to below the fold of the front page. Nothing had been heard from neighboring cities. Her fiancé denied rumors that she had run off with a lover—their engagement was a devoted one, he said, and a wedding date had been set. No ransom demands had been made. The local detective agency had contacted the Pinkerton National Detective Agency. The Pinkerton system of employing underworld informers and railroad spies held the last hope for finding her if she had been kidnapped or had run away.

For weeks, a full-page ad offering a five-thousand-dollar reward for information leading to her return ran in the newspaper. The picture that illustrated it was a line rendition of the same portrait that hung in the house. She was described as of medium height and weight, with black hair and brown eyes. She had a mole on her left cheek and was never without the cameo earrings and brooch she had inherited from her mother. Miss Bloodworth was an accomplished pianist, the ad said, had completed two years at Kenan Institute for Women, and intended to graduate. She was "unusually interested in intellectual matters for a woman," the article went on. There was nothing here that would help the medical examiner, but Simon photocopied the page anyway.

The last paragraph written about Anne Bloodworth's disappearance stated that her picture and description had been placed in all the major American newspapers, as well as in newspapers in London, Paris, and Rome. Her father vowed to search for her forever if necessary.

The glare of the microfilm screen and the persistent hum of the machine wore Simon out after about two hours. With relief, he turned it off, rubbing his eyes and stretching back in his chair. He reread the photocopy he had made of the advertisement offering a reward for the return of Anne Bloodworth. What did "unusually interested in intellectual matters for a woman" mean?

Simon's eyes hurt when he tried to focus on the clock on the opposite wall. It would take a few minutes for his far vision to return after reading blurred newsprint. Then he spotted Bobby Hinton through the open doors into the seniors' study room, and his body tensed.

Might as well get it over with, he thought. He got up and walked out of the reading room and over to Hinton. The boy was stripping his carrel.

"Bobby, I want you to know that I believe the grade I gave you was fair, but I'm sorry about graduate school." The thin, long-haired blond boy stopped stuffing pens and papers into his backpack. Simon had never felt that he knew him as well as he did other students in the seminar. He often seemed to be somewhere else mentally. Now Hinton just grinned at Simon.

"Don't worry, Doc, Professor Andrus is more upset about that grade than I am. I knew I was just sliding through. I mean, I thought a *B* was automatic, but it was a stupid assumption."

"What are you going to do? Apply to a master's program, maybe?"

The boy slung his backpack over his shoulder. It was a nice backpack—black tooled leather—definitely a cut above what most students bought at the student store.

"I'm not sure graduate school is what I want at all, now. I'm not going to go anywhere, for a few years anyway."

"What are you going to do?"

"My mother owns a real estate firm in Charlotte. I figure all I have to do is sell one house a month to make ends meet. And I can go to the beach and play golf all I want."

Damn Andrus, thought Simon as he watched Hinton walk away. The kid himself didn't care about the grade.

"I told you," Marcus Clegg said when Simon joined him for lunch at the student union. "It's not the grade at all; it's the chance to get at you that Andrus is after. You have to hang in there."

"It's going to embarrass me if this gets around campus, Marcus," Simon said.

Clegg leaned over his bowl of chili so Simon could hear him over the din of student conversation.

"Be realistic. The academic community isn't any more discreet than any other small, intense, people-oriented environment. Everyone knows everything there is to know about you right now."

Simon's stomach began to react. "Like what?" he said.

"Like your wife left you to go to the bright lights of New York City, and that you're upset as hell about it. You think this is a scandal? Have you watched daytime television recently?"

"It's mostly pride, I guess. I hate to screw up my life in public."

"You didn't screw up your life," Carver said. "Your wife screwed it up. Let her go. And on that word of patronizing and unrealistic advice, I have to leave. My mousies need their next injection."

"Someday somebody from PETA is going to overhear you and you're going to wish you hadn't spent your career torturing small animals."

"Some torture. My subjects get all the food and sex they can handle just for pushing the red button instead of the green one. Our lives should be so good."

A MESSAGE FROM Julia McGloughlan was on Simon's answering machine when he got home.

"Guess what," she said. "The police department here didn't even have a filing system until 1950! There are some filthy old boxes in the back of a storeroom that might have something on our case, the file gnomes tell me. I'm going to riffle through them this afternoon. Call me."

Simon carefully wrote down her number and silently rehearsed a message, if, as he expected, he got an answering machine, too. Simon loved answering machines. Communication without the distracting presence of the other person allowed one to tailor one's thoughts precisely. As the phone rang, he silently hoped that she didn't have a stupid message. He would have to scratch her name off his list if she did. She didn't.

When he got the beep, Simon did his best to sound like a grown-up Pulitzer Prize–winning history professor entitled to her respect and even admiration.

"This is Simon Shaw. I'm going over to Chapel Hill to the Southern Historical Collection this afternoon to look at Charles Bloodworth's papers. Want to meet for dinner and compare notes? If you do, meet me at the Chinese place across from Kenan at seven."

6

SIMON ALWAYS LISTENED TO JAMES TAYLOR WHILE DRIVING TO Chapel Hill. It just seemed appropriate. He had *New Moonshine* blaring on this trip, but he wasn't hearing it. He was so preoccupied with the Bloodworth murder puzzle that he arrived on the outskirts of town without any recollection of the passage of time or of the landmarks he must have passed on the way. Automatic pilot brought him straight to the library, where he found a place to park only because it was too pretty a Saturday afternoon for anyone other than the most desperate students to bury themselves in the windowless stacks. Simon had a sudden urge to defect himself, but instead, he found his way to the Southern Historical Collection and presented his requests to the student in charge. She looked at his request slips in horror.

"Do you know where this stuff is?" she asked. "I don't usually work here."

The girl was obviously in the middle of an intense cram session. She had bags under her eyes and her hair needed washing. Books and notes were piled at the desk where she had been working. She had probably planned to study during her entire shift.

"Exactly where," he said. "I've used these materials many times. Why don't you just let me go get them myself?"

"I'm not supposed to do that," she said. "The Southern Historical Collection stacks are closed. I'm supposed to find them and bring them to you." She didn't move, though, just looked at the slips of paper and then at the monster card catalog in the middle of the reading room.

"Look," Simon said. "Let me find them myself. I went to grad school here. I just need a few minutes. I'll use them right there in the stacks and put everything back. You don't need to do anything."

Still she hesitated.

"I'm a full professor at Kenan College," Simon said. "I'm not going to steal anything. I just want to look a few things up. I can do it and be gone before you could probably find the stuff. You can hold on to my driver's license as collateral."

"Okay," she said. She carefully looked around before unlocking the barred door that guarded the collection.

Simon walked down two flights of steps and turned left into a regiment of shelves piled with file boxes. He found the aisle he was looking for, then pulled two of the boxes off a shelf. They were labeled CHARLES BLOODWORTH PAPERS, CHESAPEAKE AND SEABOARD RAILWAY. Bloodworth's papers were a small part of the huge inventory of files that the railway had given to the collection when its original Victorian-style building had been torn down. The files covering the 1920s had been an important source for Simon's thesis and book.

He hauled the boxes over to the nearest table and began to look for Bloodworth's appointment book and correspondence for 1926. Bloodworth left no other written records than these, Simon knew, because Simon and the local historical society's curator had thoroughly searched the Bloodworth House for documents when it had been deeded to Kenan College. Adam Bloodworth had left no written records behind at all.

He found the appointment book first. Among the usual business entries, Bloodworth occasionally jotted a few personal notes to himself: "Have Robt. grease the Ford," or "Lunch at club with Anne today." On April thirteenth, four days after his daughter's disappearance, he wrote, "The search is futile. She is gone." On the fifteenth, after an appointment with private detective Robert Lumsden, he recorded: "Lumsden will communicate with Pinkerton. Adam is all I have left." Bloodworth wrote nothing else about his daughter for the rest of the year.

Simon found three letters in the file about the disappearance. One was from the Southern Detective Agency ("Legitimate detective work of every description handled in every part of the United States. Connections all over the world"). It promised to forward Bloodworth's physical description of his daughter to the Pinkerton Detective Agency in New York and to send a complete written report on progress in a week. A very businesslike letter from Bloodworth to an advertising agency, also in New York, arranged for the ad Simon had already seen in the *News and Observer* to be placed around the country and the world. The final letter was from Bloodworth to the detective agency, dated about three months after the disappearance, enclosing a check "in final settlement of my account."

The sparseness of the documents left Simon with more questions than he had had when he started. Where was the description of Anne sent to Pinkerton? What did it contain? Where was the detective agency's final report? How could a worldwide search for anybody in 1926 be concluded in just three months? Simon knew that nothing he had found so far would help the medical examiner positively identify the body.

"EVEN IF WE CAN IDENTIFY THE BODY, THE POLICE DEPARTMENT won't do anything officially," Julia McGloughlan said. "This case has a poor solvability factor."

The two were sitting at the local Chinese eatery decorated with tacky red chandeliers with tassels, paper place mats that told you whether you were a rabbit or a horse, and giant plastic Chinese letters stuck to the walls. It was the same stuff you saw in every other Chinese restaurant in town, and probably the world. Somewhere, Simon thought, there must be one huge warehouse that has a total monopoly on Chinese restaurant decorating supplies.

Julia was wearing a black denim skirt, a green sleeveless T-shirt, black canvas shoes, and gold hoop earrings. A vast improvement over the grey suit, Simon felt. He noted that she was eating her shrimp toast with gusto. Simon hated it when women didn't eat. Diets, if they were necessary at all, should be conducted in private, where they couldn't ruin dinner for anyone else.

"What, pray tell, is the solvability factor?" Simon asked.

"That's the degree to which we might actually have a chance to solve a case," she answered. "In modern police work, we don't spend time investigating cases that look hopeless. It's a waste of time and taxpayers' money. It sounds obvious, but it used to be that a detective was assigned to follow every case forever. So if your bicycle was stolen off your back porch in the middle of the night and no one saw anything, you could count on a detective following up. Not today. You'd be lucky to get a phone call back from the investigative division. It irritates people sometimes, because they like to think something is being done about a crime. But it's not efficient. Investigating this murder just won't make sense to our administrative people."

"So even if the body is positively identified and we think it's murder, there won't be an official investigation?"

"We'll be able to open a file. But we won't be able to use any of the department's resources to work on it. The chief's attitude is, the perp is dead. Everybody else involved is dead, too. What would be the point?"

"The point is, I want to know what happened."

"Me, too."

"What about Sergeant Gates?"

"He's probably the best investigator we've got. He'll follow the rules. But he's definitely interested, so we can probably count on his unofficial help."

Simon liked the sound of that "we."

After they finished their crispy duck and seafood delight, Julia pulled two single sheets of paper out of her handbag and gave them to Simon.

"This is it," she said. "I found these in a box of old papers in the back of the file-storage room, in an envelope full of stuff, with just the month and date written on the outside. It's the patrol officer's report."

"Peebles," Simon said.

"That's right. He couldn't spell."

Simon read the pages over closely several times. It was written on what looked like plain-ruled school paper, the kind with blue lines—in pencil no less. It was an account of the incident exactly as Simon had read it in the paper, with the addition of several indignant remarks about the mess in Anne Bloodworth's room and around the outside of the house. Peebles noted that during the time Bloodworth must have disappeared, the servants were away, her fiancé, Adam Bloodworth, was on a fishing trip, and her father was working in the study on the first floor. The next page was a paragraph, probably written later, which simply observed that no clues to Bloodworth's disappearance had been found and that an intensive search of the city had failed to find her or any evidence of what had happened to her.

"There's precious little there," Julia said. "You couldn't consider this any kind of official report. It's just the patrolman's notes to himself."

"Remember that police departments didn't do much investigating then. For that, you hired a detective agency, which Charles Bloodworth did." He told her what he had learned from the Bloodworth papers.

"It sounds as though he didn't have much hope of finding his daughter from the beginning," Julia said.

"I noticed that, too. And there are a lot of relevant documents missing. The final report from the detective agency, for one."

"Gone forever, I guess."

"Not necessarily. The agency Bloodworth used was the Southern Detective Agency. I looked it up in the Raleigh city directory for 1926. It was affiliated with all the right organizations—the Association of American Detective Agencies and the International Association for Identification, among others. They had the resources to search effectively for Anne Bloodworth, and should have kept good records."

"You think their files could still be around?"

"Maybe. And there should be a record somewhere at Pinkerton. The Pinkertons were sticklers for paperwork. I know the agency's archivist in New York. But I can't call him until Monday."

"I'll see if I can get the medical examiner to delay the autopsy for a few days."

"What happens if he does the autopsy and can't positively identify her?"

"She's a Jane Doe forever."

SIMON WAS HAVING A GOOD TIME. HE STARTED TO ORDER MORE wine for the two of them, then noticed the lines of hungry people waiting at the entrance to the restaurant. It was Saturday night, after all, and in just an hour or so the nine o'clock movies would start.

"Maybe we'd better go," Julia said. "Other people are waiting."

Simon was surprised by the disappointment he felt. This was interesting.

Julia had insisted on separate checks when they first ordered, and as they groped for money, she dropped her purse on the floor. As she leaned over to retrieve it, her skirt rode up slightly and her T-shirt stretched over her breasts. When she sat up, she pushed her auburn hair out of her face and disentangled it from her earrings with long fingers. Her nails were short and lacquered with a clear polish.

Every pilot light in Simon's body flicked on, and kept flaring, despite his efforts to tamp them down. He managed to hide his arousal while they paid the check and argued over the disposition of the tip. Walking behind her as they left the restaurant didn't help matters any.

They had come in separate cars, and Simon couldn't think of an excuse to spend more time with her. After all, they were just supposed to be talking about the Bloodworth case. It wasn't a date or anything, although he recalled having been a little nervous when he left his message on her answering machine.

Waiting for the light to change before turning onto his street, Simon rested his hot face on the cool steering wheel. Whether the flush was from desire, embarrassment, or just plain shock that he had been attracted to a woman other than his ex-wife, he didn't know and wasn't even going to try to figure out.

It was not soothing that "Layla" was playing on the radio the rest of the way home.

DAVID MORGAN WAS reluctantly scrubbing dried food off plates before loading his dishwasher when the phone rang. He washed dishes only on Saturday night, after his stock of plates and glasses was completely exhausted from the week's meals. Until then, they piled up on every available surface in his kitchen.

"This is Julia McGloughlan," said the voice on the phone.

Morgan remembered—the lady police lawyer who didn't mind getting dirty. What on earth did she want?

"I was just wondering if you had located anything else at the site," she said.

"Like what?"

"Oh, evidence that could be related to the corpse. You wouldn't throw anything you found away before we could get a look at it, would you?"

And he had thought briefly that this woman might have some intelligence.

"Lady, I'm an archaeologist. We don't throw anything away. Every site I supervise is thoroughly mapped and sieved. Not a button or a tooth will get by us. I will let you or Simon know if we find anything."

"Simon and I had dinner tonight. To talk about the case."

"This is a case?"

"As far as I'm concerned." She filled in Morgan on their conversation. He was interested in spite of himself.

"Look," he said. "I'll be very alert when we sieve. Okay?"

"About Simon."

What was this all about? His suds were collapsing.

"Yes?"

"Is he married or what? He's not wearing a ring."

"Divorced. Recently."

"Oh. Thank you."

They hung up simultaneously. Morgan went back to his dishes. Women are all alike, he thought. Poor Simon.

SGT. OTIS GATES and his teenage son were locked in mortal computer-game combat when his wife called him to the telephone. He reluctantly paused just as he was about to break out of the novice level of *Rebel Assault II* and went to the phone. At least it wasn't police business. He could tell that from the tone of his wife's voice.

"Yes?" Gates said.

It was Simon Shaw, the young professor who was consulting on the case of the corpse found buried on the grounds of the Bloodworth House. Gates conjured up Shaw's image and placed him: small, dark, brilliant.

"What can I do for you?" Gates asked.

"I've been talking to Julia McGloughlan," Simon said.

"Uh-oh." Gates laughed.

"What does that mean?" asked Simon.

"It means I have a feeling that the two of you intend to get intense about solving the mystery of our unidentified corpse," Gates said.

"She's not unidentified. It's just not proven yet. But that's not what I'm calling about. Can you tell me if Julia is dating anybody?"

"She's not right now, I don't think. She just broke off an engagement a few months ago. A banker, I think."

"Oh," Simon said.

"Don't worry, she's fully recovered and well out of it. He was a jerk. The whole department chipped in and bought her a bottle of champagne to celebrate after they broke up."

This was an interesting development, Gates thought as he hung up, but he felt sorry for Simon. He was just not Julia's type. She socialized with a coat-and-tie crowd, and he didn't see Simon fitting into their symphony and Sunday brunch existence.

WHAT SIMON REALLY WANTED TO DO ON SUNDAY WAS CALL THE Pinkerton Archivist in New York, contact the Raleigh Chamber of Commerce to find out if the Southern Detective Agency still existed, and talk to someone at the North Carolina Dental Society about the practice of dentistry in 1926. Of course, he couldn't do that, so he vented his frustrations by cleaning his house, which was filthy. He changed the Kitty Litter for his cat, Maybelline. Actually, she was Tessa's cat, but she had left Maybelline behind when she went to New York. Maybelline had always liked him best anyway.

After he cleaned both bathrooms and dusted and vacuumed, Simon tackled the laundry. He wasn't an expert, so he washed everything in cold water, just to make sure. He even washed the sheets that he had left in the hamper in the basement when he first changed the bed after Tessa left. He had slept on them until he couldn't detect her odor anymore, then left them in the hamper for months. Now he didn't even think about her as he dumped them into the washing machine.

Even after his chores were done, Simon was restless. So he went next door, detached Danny from his homework, and took him to the batting cage, where they practiced hitting high ones for almost two hours. Then they went to the Char Grill on Hillsborough Street and ate a surprising amount of cheeseburgers, fries, and chocolate shakes, considering their respective sizes. Simon then delivered Danny home. The boy was completely incapable of finishing his homework, but his mother didn't complain.

56

The next morning found Simon at his kitchen table, drinking coffee and watching the clock as it crawled toward 8:30. It was far too early to call anyone in New York, but the day had begun hours ago in North Carolina. Half the state had probably done two hours' worth of chores before going to work. He dialed the number of the Raleigh Chamber of Commerce.

The very kind young woman who answered the phone led Simon to a disappointing dead end. According to her records, the building that housed the Southern Detective Agency offices had burned in 1937, and the business had never been rebuilt. Good-bye files, thought Simon. Did Simon need a detective agency? she asked. If so, she had a list of reputable ones. He thanked her for her time and trouble and hung up.

Simon knew that dental records were the best means of identifying a corpse and had been for decades. He also knew that a young woman of Anne Bloodworth's class had undoubtedly had a dentist. He already had a list of the dentists practicing in 1926 in Raleigh, which he had gotten from the city directory. There were twenty in the city—seventeen white and three black. There was no way she would have gone to a black dentist, so he had seventeen names to research. Unfortunately, the public-affairs officer at the Dental Society told him not to waste his time. There were no records extant from that long ago. They would have been discarded whenever the patient, or the dentist, died. Period. End of discussion.

As soon as Simon hung up the phone, Julia called him. He told her about his negative results so far.

"It gets worse," she said. "Dr. High-and-Mighty Boyette won't delay the autopsy. He says it's not a priority case and that it doesn't matter to him or to the police department if she's identified or not. He says there's not enough of her left to do a real autopsy anyway, and they don't want a corpse in such an advanced stage of decay lying around the morgue any longer than it has to."

Simon could understand that.

"When is he going to do it?" Simon asked.

"After lunch. Probably about two o'clock. Do you think you can get in touch with your friend in New York?"

"My chances of getting any information in time are pretty slim," Simon said, "but I'll try."

57

Simon placed a call to his friend Mark Mitchell, the archivist of Pinkerton Investigations in New York City. Simon had a lot of respect for Mark. While the rest of their classmates derided Mark's decision to become a company historian instead of an academic, Simon thought that it showed infinite good sense. The job paid well and was never boring. Pinkerton's had been in the middle of just about everything interesting that had gone on in the country from 1850. Mark was besieged with requests for information from historians studying everything from the Wild West to Prohibition to railroad strikebreaking. And he didn't have to worry about getting tenure.

"You want this by when, Simon?" said Mark.

"By one o'clock," Simon said.

"You don't ask much," his friend answered.

"If we can't get this body identified properly, we'll never know who she was for sure or what happened to her."

"Who cares?"

"I care. I care a lot. I dream about it at night."

"I'm sorry, I just can't drop everything and go look for one letter right now. It's probably on microfiche, if it's still here at all. It's Monday morning. My assistant is sick, and I've got stuff on my desk up to the ceiling. I'm teaching a class at NYU and I'm going to have to grade papers during my lunch hour. I could maybe do it toward the end of the week."

"I'll buy you dinner the next time I'm in town."

"When will that be? When you win your second Pulitzer?"

Simon played his best and final card.

"Did you ever meet my uncle, Morris Simon?" asked Simon.

"I don't know. Maybe."

"He owns that deli on Pearl Street. You know, the one with the great potato salad. We've had lunch there."

"And?"

"How about lunch? My treat."

"I can't make it today."

"Anytime. Let's make it . . . a week's worth of lunches. I'll set it up with my uncle."

"This is really important to you."

"Yes."

"Okay. I'll do my best. Do you have a fax number?"

Simon gave him the fax number at the history department. Then he called his uncle's restaurant. He was out, according to Simon's cousin Leah, so Simon left his Visa number with her. Leah wasn't very happy spending her summer slinging hash. She wanted to be a meterologist, but her father forced her to work in the deli when she wasn't attending college in hopes that she would take over the business. "What it is," she told Simon, "he thinks the smell of pickles and corned beef and Hebrew National mustard is going to grow on me until I pine to spend the rest of my days slapping it all over pumpernickel. I keep telling him there's no gene for Jewish food preparation."

Simon drove to the Kenan campus to wait for Mark's fax. He felt sure it would come. It was a beautiful clear day, with a limpid yellow sun shining brightly in a Carolina blue sky. It was not yet as hot and humid as it would get later, so Simon turned off his air conditioning and let the wind blow around him. He waited for two cycles at the light so he could listen to all of "Late in the Evening," rolling into his parking space just as the song faded away.

Simon felt fine. He had slept well, he had eaten well, he liked a woman, he had driven in his car with the stereo blasting, and he was working on an interesting problem.

When he walked into his office, his luck changed. Alex Andrus was sitting there. Simon went behind his desk and sat down.

"What are you doing here?" Simon asked.

"Dr. Jones tells me I am to apologize," Andrus said.

"Don't feel compelled to be sincere."

"I won't. I'm here only because I have to be. I've been ordered to apologize for the scene I made at the faculty meeting. But I don't have to tell you that I still don't think you're doing your job. Anyone who hasn't won a Pulitzer Prize wouldn't get the consideration you have."

"Did it ever occur to you that maybe that's okay, Alex?"

"What do you mean?"

"Maybe I have gotten some leeway just because I am productive. Maybe I deserve it."

"You'll be happy to know that Hinton's appeal will not go forward," Alex said. "The boy won't cooperate. So there's really nothing else I can do. You've won."

"This isn't a race. When are you going to understand that? We're teachers. We have different specialties, different interests, different abilities. There's room for both of us here."

"I understand that you're doing some consulting for the police department."

"That's right."

"I'm glad you have the time. You must be carrying a pretty light load."

Andrus got up and left the room. Judy Smith poked her head around the corner of the door.

"Are you in one piece?" she asked.

"Barely."

"Would you like me to get you some coffee?"

"Is that politically correct?"

"I won't tell anyone if you won't—just this once."

"Yes, please."

Why on earth had he let Andrus make him so defensive? Probably because Simon felt the man had some right to a grudge. Andrus had been at Kenan for two years when Simon arrived. Simon won a Pulitzer and got tenure when Andrus didn't. Simon was carrying a light teaching load while he recuperated from emotional problems. It was all true. But exactly what was he supposed to do about it?

Judy came back into the room with his coffee.

"Here it is," she said. "Hot as hell and sweet as love."

"Thank you," Simon said.

"You should not let Alex Andrus talk to you that way," Judy said. "It makes me sick."

"I know," Simon said. "But I don't know how to deal with someone like him. I don't have the right weaponry."

"Sugar, you're not even fighting on the same battlefield. Just because you're polite and fair doesn't mean everyone is going to treat you the same way. You've got to learn to cover your tail."

"I suppose. But I think this business about the grade is finally over. It's not going to be appealed."

"There'll be something else."

Suddenly, Simon could not stand the sight of his chaotic office.

"Do you think you could help me in here for a while this morning?" Simon asked.

"Sure thing. Let me forward the phone to your extension."

Between the two of them, they quickly made progress in the tiny office. She filed while he threw away. Simon feared finding neglected responsibilities tucked into the stacks of papers, and he was not disappointed. He found an entire manuscript that had been sent to him by a publisher to be critiqued.

"Damnation," Simon said. "This is really inexcusable."

"Let me see," said Judy. "Oh, that's nothing."

"How's that?"

"I'll just write and say it got put on the wrong shelf in the mailroom or something, and that if he still wants you to read it, you'll do it right away."

"But that's not true. The truth is, I screwed up."

"Let's not worry about that today. Let's just get you out of trouble. You can be honest and forthright starting tomorrow."

Even worse, Simon found a request from a student for a job recommendation, and he knew he had never written it.

"I deserve to be tarred and feathered," he said. "Every word Alex has ever said about me is true."

"Relax," Judy said. "I wrote it."

"You wrote this letter for me?"

"Sure. I knew the girl as well as you did. I can sign your name good, too."

"I really owe you, don't I?"

"Don't worry, I'll collect someday."

By the end of the morning, Simon's office looked like a human being worked there. Not a perfect human being, but a functioning one. He was hugely relieved. In retrospect, to uncover only two big screwups was not too bad. It could have been worse.

"Let me take you to lunch," Simon said to Judy.

"Some other time," she said. "On Mondays, a bunch of us order in Cooper's barbecue and watch *The Young and the Restless."*

Simon remembered the fax. He followed Judy back to her office. The fax basket was empty.

"Is this thing on?" he asked.

"Absolutely," Judy said. "Scoot. I need to lock up."

Simon talked her into letting him stay in the office while she went to meet her friends. He drank a Coke and ate a package of Nabs and a Moon Pie while watching the machine. Nothing.

At quarter to one, just as Simon was losing hope, the machine began to hum. Paper slipped slowly out of it, curling into a tube and then dropping into the basket. It was a cover sheet with a Pinkerton logo. "Bingo," Mark wrote. "You're out a Reuben all the way and potato salad for a week. Call me and let me know what happens. Mark."

The machine gave birth to the next sheet of paper very, very slowly. Simon thought he would get a headache waiting for it. Finally, he had it in his hands, smoothing the curl out of it and trying to decipher Charles Bloodworth's handwriting, made more difficult by the facsimile reproduction.

Anne Bloodworth had been five foot five, with curly black hair in a bob and brown eyes. She had broken her lower left arm falling out of a tree when she was eight. She wore magnifying glasses to read or do needlework. She was wearing her mother's cameo earrings and brooch when she left—Bloodworth felt that she would not part with them under any circumstances. He thought she could easily make her own living if necessary, either as a governess or as a music teacher. Interesting observation for the wealthy father of a daughter in 1926, thought Simon. That was all, but Simon was excited. Surely the break in her arm would show on the skeleton.

To Simon's surprise, another piece of paper began to emerge from the fax machine. He wasn't really expecting anything else from Mark, so he assumed it was a different letter addressed to someone else. He picked it up, prepared to route it to one of the faculty mailboxes outside in the hall. Instead, he stood rooted to the floor, staring at the neat hand-drawn diagram of Anne Bloodworth's dental chart. It was drawn on a dentist's letterhead, dated April 13, 1926, and signed "Louis J. Pegram, D.D.S."

At quarter to two, Simon's Thunderbird screeched out of the entrance to Kenan College on its way to the city morgue. He wanted to hand over this information personally to Dr. Philip Boyette, the medical examiner, who didn't care about the identity of the corpse he was about to examine. By God, Simon thought, now I can force him to pay attention. Simon had known since he saw what was left of her that she was Anne Bloodworth, and now the rest of the world was going to know it, too.

Dr. Boyette, masked and gowned in pristine green scrub clothes, was extremely annoyed to be interrupted in the middle of an unusually gruesome autopsy by a jubilant Professor Simon Shaw. He stood in the outer office of the morgue autopsy rooms, prepared to dress the young man down for creating such a commotion that the receptionist had been compelled to summon him from the autopsy room, scalpel still in hand—that is, until Boyette looked at the documents Shaw had brought.

"I'll be damned," Boyette said. "Where did you turn up these?"

"From the Pinkerton archive in New York City," Simon said. "Her father sent the description and the dental chart to them a few days after her disappearance. The archivist just faxed them to me this morning."

"Are you sure they're the real thing?"

"Look," Simon said. "Cutting open bodies is your job. History is mine. These are authentic documents. I'll vouch for Bloodworth's handwriting and signature personally. And the dentist was practicing down the street in Raleigh at the time. We can probably verify his signature, too."

"I'll be damned," Boyette said again. "Well, let's go look. Want to come?"

"I said that cutting open bodies is your job. I'll accept your word for whatever you find," Simon said.

In fact, Simon was beginning to taste a little bile in his mouth just thinking about the scenario in the next room. So he got directions to the nearest Coke machine and chugged his second of the day. By the time he returned to the anteroom of the morgue, Boyette was waiting for him.

"It's her," Boyette said. "No question about it. There are a couple of teeth missing, but otherwise the dental records match perfectly. I found the broken arm, too."

"Can you say she was murdered?"

Boyette shrugged his shoulders. "After so many years, real physical evidence of the cause of death is impossible to detect, but for heaven's sake, she was nineteen years old and shot in the back of the head. And buried secretly in her own backyard. Of course she was murdered. Officially, we'll call it 'death by misadventure.' "

"The question now is, who killed her, and why?" said Simon.

"We'll probably never know," said Boyette. "But look, if you can wait until I finish up, we can talk. My report will get to the police department eventually, but there's no reason I can't tell you now what I've found. It's public information."

Simon was willing to wait as long as necessary.

When Boyette returned, he was dressed in street clothes. He led Simon into his office, which was as prim and excessively neat as he was. Simon was not sure why the medical examiner made him feel the way chalk scraping against a blackboard did, but he did. If only his mustache was a little fuller or his matching Cross writing implements didn't line up across his breast pocket so martially, he might be a little less grating on one's nerves. At any rate, Simon thought he had converted Boyette to his mission.

"Here," Boyette said, handing Simon two sealed plastic bags. One contained a pair of reading glasses with half lenses and black rims. They looked exactly like ones you could buy in the Rite Aid today, except the rims were metal, not plastic. In the other bag was a small pebble.

"We found the glasses loose in the quilt when we unwrapped it," said Boyette. "The bullet was inside the skull, just as I thought it would be."

"This is a bullet?" said Simon. He looked at the object more carefully, rolling it around with his fingers inside of the bag.

"It's been inside a corpse in the ground for seventy years," said Boyette. "It was deformed when it hit the skull to start out with. But it's a bullet all right. Large-caliber one, too."

"Do you keep these?" Simon asked.

"No way. Police property. Got to send them to Sergeant Gates. Chain of evidence and all that."

He took the plastic bags away from Simon and put them in a large manila envelope, sealing it carefully with paper tape, which he dated and initialed. Then he addressed it to Gates.

"The police department is right across the street," Boyette said. "But interdepartmental mail takes three days to get there."

"Let me walk it over," Simon said. This would give him an excuse to talk to Gates, if he was in, and maybe see Julia, although he didn't know where her office was.

"Why not," said Boyette, handing Simon the envelope. "Just make sure you initial and date it, too."

Simon walked across the street to the Public Safety Center, an enormous concrete structure that housed all of the Raleigh police and emergency-services offices, and the Wake County jail to boot. With the help of a uniformed person manning an information desk in the lobby, Simon found his way to the investigative-services area and finally to Gates's tiny cubicle. Not only was the sergeant in; Julia was with him. They were in the only two available chairs, so Simon perched on the arm of Julia's. The only other furniture in the office was a file cabinet, and most of Gates's desk was taken up by his computer. The bulk of the man himself made the room seem even smaller. There was no window, either.

"I'm sorry this place is so uncomfortable," Gates said. "I think it's intentional—makes us want to get out of the office and into the field, where we're supposed to be anyway."

"Boyette called and told us about the results of the autopsy. I've been trying to convince the sergeant to proceed with an investigation," Julia said.

Julia was wearing another prim lady-lawyer suit, complete with severe blouse and tie. At least this outfit was midnight blue, a color that suited her better than gray. Simon much preferred her in denim and T-shirts.

"Come on, Julia. This is wearing me out," said Gates. "You know we can't spend any money investigating this. We don't have the budget to indulge your curiosity. Be happy we got an identification so this poor woman can have a decent burial."

"But you will open a file?" asked Simon.

"Of course," said Gates. "We have to do that."

"What about the bullet?"

"We can determine the caliber here," Gates said.

"I think you should send it to the FBI," Julia said.

"In your dreams," Gates answered. "Do you know how much that costs?"

"What are we talking about?" Simon asked.

"The FBI operates an information bureau called the Criminalistics Laboratory Information System," Julia said. "One of their databases is the General Rifling Characteristics file, which can be accessed to identify the manufacturer and type of weapon that may have been used to fire a bullet. You send the bullet to them, they analyze it and then send it back with a complete report."

"I wish you would stick to Miranda warnings and leave the police work to me," Gates said.

"They also have some other files—firearms and stolen-property lists—that they could check to see if the bullet was fired from a known firearm."

"They would never have a record of a gun this old."

"You don't know that. The weapon could have had a history for years after this crime occurred."

"This is very interesting," said Simon. "And they charge you for this?"

"The fibbies charge for everything," said Gates.

"How about if I pay for it?" asked Simon.

"Out of the question. We can't have private citizens making decisions for the police department."

"Look," Julia said. "No one will ever know. You have the authority as investigating officer to send the bullet to the CLIS. You'll get the report back. You'll put it in the file. The invoice will get paid by the accounting office, just like a thousand other invoices. You haven't done anything wrong."

Gates groaned. "The chief will kill me."

"He'll never know," said Julia. "Besides, you just say that in your professional judgment, this was a necessary step to take before closing the file. You're in the clear. Trust me—I'm your lawyer."

"It was a dark day when you came here to work, Julia. All right, I'll send the damn thing out. I have to admit, I'm curious, too."

"Okay, so we send the bullet off for analysis, and we open the file today," Julia said. "Then what?"

"I think it's our historian's call," Gates said.

Both of them looked at Simon expectantly.

"Well," said Simon. "I'm not exactly sure. I've been so obsessed with getting the body identified, I haven't given any thought to where to go from here."

66

Simon was running out of research ideas. He had completely searched the newspapers and the Bloodworth papers. Julia had found Peebles's report, which seemed to be the only document in police files. The offices of the local detective agency hired by Charles Bloodworth had burned, presumably with all its records.

"It's possible that there's more information at Pinkerton," Simon said. "All I asked Mark for was the letter, which I knew existed. I'll ask him to make a complete search, but it will take some time."

"If this was a modern crime, the next step would be obvious," Gates said.

"What?" asked Simon.

"See who shows up at the funeral," said Gates.

AS IT TURNED OUT, ANNE HAWORTH BLOODWORTH'S FUNERAL was packed. Her next of kin, a cousin of some kind who lived in Charlotte, expressed horror at the thought of claiming the mostly decomposed body of a relative she had never known, so the Preservation Society took on the responsibility. After all, the society leased and operated the house and grounds, and someone had to see that the previous owner was buried with respect. Anne Bloodworth had been the scion of an old Raleigh family. The newspaper put the discovery of the body on the front page. Her funeral evolved into an event, and everyone who was anyone attended.

The Historic Preservation Society, whose membership coincided largely with that of the Junior League, never did anything halfway. The funeral and reception were held in the formal rooms of Bloodworth House, which was beautifully decorated with pink and white camellias, peonies, and roses from the college gardens. Tastefully, the coffin of the deceased, whose appearance was beyond the repair of any embalmer, remained in the hearse outside. The crowd gathered around her black-draped picture in the dining room while the minister conducted her funeral.

The rector of the Church of the Good Shepherd, which Miss Bloodworth had attended in her day, rose to the occasion.

Although Simon was half Jewish and had been raised in a determinedly secular home, he was always stirred by the encouraging words of the funeral service of the Episcopal prayer book.

"I am the resurrection and the life, saith the Lord; he that believeth in me, though he were dead, yet shall he live; and whosoever liveth and believeth in me, shall never die," the minister began.

At every Christian funeral service Simon attended, he added his own silent prayer that whatever God existed would take pity on those good people who didn't know what to believe, and give them a shot at redemption, too. He thought of his parents in this context always. When he was so miserable after his wife had left, the Christian side of him had demanded some action, and he had begun to send some short messages—although they could barely be called prayers—in the vague direction of the deity: humble messages requesting whatever aid and solace might be available to him. Most of these were forwarded in the small hours of the morning. He wasn't sure if he had received any reply, but he didn't think so. He knew that the experts were divided about what form an answer would take, but it seemed to him reasonable that he would know it when he saw it.

His Jewish side accepted that better minds than his had puzzled over the question of the afterlife for an extremely long time, even, if the paleontologists were to be believed, since before man had officially evolved into *Homo sapiens,* and that he ought not to make himself crazy wondering about it, especially at night when he needed his sleep. Since right now was the only life Simon knew for sure he had, he had decided that he'd better make the best of it.

The minister continued: "I know that my Redeemer liveth, and that he shall stand at the latter day upon the earth: and though this body be destroyed, yet shall I see God: whom I shall see for myself, and mine eyes shall behold, and not as a stranger."

Let's hope so, thought Simon.

The minister delivered a brief eulogy. He had bothered to find out something about Anne Bloodworth from Simon, and it made the funeral seem almost personal, though not a soul in attendance had ever met her.

The *News and Observer*'s front-page story on the discovery and identification of the body had made Simon a minor local celebrity. His experience after he won the Pulitzer taught him that the blitz of phone calls, letters, and handshakes would end quickly, and he could return to blissful obscurity. However, that did not prevent him from enjoying himself thoroughly for the duration. He was the center of attention during the reception after the funeral. He was surrounded by the mayor, the president of Kenan College, who patted his arm with a proprietary pride, and the chairwoman of the historical society, as well as other hangers-on, including the press from several out-of-town papers. Simon answered all their questions with enthusiasm, but, cautioned by Sergeant Gates, he never said a word about his interest in solving Anne Bloodworth's murder. He did, though, agree to write an article on Anne Bloodworth for *N.C. History* when he could get to it.

"You would think the man was a rock star or something," Alex Andrus said to Marcus Clegg. The history department was out in force, since the historical society had endowed a teaching position and Walker Jones wanted to show the flag. "It frosts me how he manages to get the attention he does."

"Grow up, Alex," Marcus said. "Simon gets noticed because he does remarkable things. He's just better than most of the rest of us."

"That's your opinion."

"If the police had asked me to help identify an old decayed corpse, I wouldn't have bothered, not in a million years. This poor woman will get a proper funeral and a gravestone with her name on it because of Simon. He deserves whatever attention comes his way for this."

Simon finally detached himself from his admirers and joined the delegation from the history department. Andrus turned on his heel and walked out the door.

"I don't want to ask," Simon said.

"He's jealous because you got your name in the paper," Marcus said. "Forget it."

"I wish I knew what I could do to make peace with him."

"That's easy," Marcus said. "Just don't ever do anything noteworthy again. I expect that will be difficult—for you, that is. Let's eat. That's what funerals are for."

The two men attacked the buffet, which was loaded with the perennial foods of southern social functions—shrimp, ham biscuits, chicken salad, baked Brie and chutney, fresh strawberries to dip in chocolate, and pecan tartlets. The predictability of the food didn't make it any less delicious, and Simon was loading his plate for the second time when he and Marcus ran into Julia and Sergeant Gates grazing on the strawberries.

"Not too busy today, Sergeant?" said Simon.

"I'll have you know that this is official police business," Gates said. "We're checking out the attendance at the victim's funeral. Miss McGloughlan is, of course, here in her capacity as legal adviser to the police department."

"Actually," said Julia, "we heard they were having shrimp and strawberries, and this rather neatly coincides with our lunch hour."

Simon introduced the two of them to Marcus Clegg.

"What's this about a murder investigation?" asked Marcus. "There wasn't anything in the paper about that."

"We're half-kidding when we say that," Simon said. "We'd like to find out more about what happened to Anne Bloodworth, but we're not sure we can."

"Keep it under your hat," Sergeant Gates said. "I'm afraid the powers that be at the police department wouldn't be pleased with me."

"I'm not sure what the chairman of my department would think about it, either," said Simon.

"Hey," said a young voice. "You guys have monopolized the strawberries long enough. Let some of the rest of us get some."

The speaker was Bobby Hinton. He was wearing a black armband and carried a half-full buffet plate.

"Sorry, Bobby. We'll get out of your way," Simon said.

The group moved outside to the porch, where they could stuff themselves while enjoying the weather. North Carolina had entered that lovely phase in late May after most of the pollen had been washed away in yellow rivers down the city's storm drains, and before the wall of heat and humidity descended on them in July. Then it would be too hot even to go swimming, and air conditioning would become a necessity of life comparable to bread and water. Now the little group stood comfortably on the porch, looking out over Hillsborough Street and the grounds of the college.

The group ate in silence for a few minutes, then collectively paused for conversation.

"In a few weeks, we won't want to be outside," Gates said. "We'll all be inside hovering over the air-conditioning vents."

"I sometimes wonder if summer is worth it," Julia said. "I mean, in July and August, you can't walk from your house to the car without breaking a sweat."

"You business types wear too much clothing," Marcus said. "Human beings were made to wear T-shirts and shorts in the summer."

"And baseball caps," Simon said.

"And sandals," Marcus said.

"I could see me showing up at work looking like that," Julia said. "I would probably get fired."

"I don't know, Julia," Gates said. "I think the police department would thoroughly enjoy you in shorts. We could pick a day when the chief is out of the office."

"I'll do it if the guys wear shorts, too. *Some* of you must have decent legs," Julia said, looking pointedly at the bottom half of Gates's massive self. His legs were the size of good-sized tree trunks.

"Me in shorts is a sight to behold," Gates said. "But I get your point. Sorry."

Simon was impressed that Julia had treated Gates so gently. He could not have meant to make so obvious a sexist remark. Simon watched Julia finish what was on her plate. She still wasn't dieting, thank goodness. One strand of her auburn hair was tangled in an earring, and Simon longed to reach out and smooth it free.

Julia caught him looking at her. She smiled at him. Simon knew he had been caught out. He desperately wished they were alone so that he could ask her out. But they weren't alone, and his mind blanked on small talk.

He was rescued when Bobby Hinton blundered into the small silence. His plate was heaped four inches high with food.

"What's with the black armband, Bobby?" asked Marcus.

"Oh," said Hinton, waving his fork in the air and waiting to swallow a mouthful of chicken salad before he spoke. "I'm the official family representative. My mother was really taken off guard by all this. She didn't want to get involved, so she asked me to come."

"I had no idea you were related to the Bloodworths," Simon said.

"My grandfather was a nephew of Adam Bloodworth's—his sister's son," said Hinton. "When Adam died, my grandfather inherited. This house and everything involved was a headache for the estate, so it was donated to the historical society. They restored it, and Granddad took a tax deduction."

"So your mother is the official next of kin," Gates said.

"That's right. Of course, she never knew the woman. When the society offered to claim the body and bury it, she was very relieved."

"Do you know anything about what happened back then?" asked Julia.

"Haven't a clue," Hinton said. "Who cares anyway?"

"We're just kind of interested in how she died," Julia said.

"She was shot, wasn't she?" Hinton asked. "How could you possibly find out the details after all this time?"

"Think, Bobby," Simon said. "You must know a family story about her disappearance. It would have been a big deal at the time."

Bobby Hinton thought.

"Well," he said. "My grandfather told me that Charles didn't have any sons, so he brought Adam in to learn how to run the family business. It was sort of understood that he and the girl would get married, but then she backed out."

"Really?" said Simon, remembering that Adam Bloodworth had insisted in the newspaper that the marriage was still on.

"I think that's the story. Of course, Adam would have been up the creek if she had married someone else, because then maybe he would have been out of a job. But then she disappeared and later was declared dead. So he inherited the whole shebang after all."

"Maybe Adam killed her?" Marcus suggested. "Because she broke off the engagement and he was out in the cold?"

"He had an alibi," Julia said. "He was on a fishing trip."

Simon noticed that Sergeant Gates had put down his plate, taken a small black notebook out of his pocket, and was methodically taking notes. He had the old-fashioned habit of licking his pencil every few minutes.

"Mr. Hinton," Gates said. "Do you have any idea who Adam Bloodworth went fishing with that night?"

"For God's sake," Hinton said. "How on earth would I know something like that!"

"Part of your family lore, maybe?" said Julia.

"I haven't got the faintest idea," said Hinton.

"Would you humor us a little, Bobby?" asked Simon. "Call your mother and see if she could add something to your recollections."

"She'll think I've lost my mind, but okay," Hinton said. "You could never prove anything after all these years anyway."

"Maybe not, but I'm going to try," Simon said.

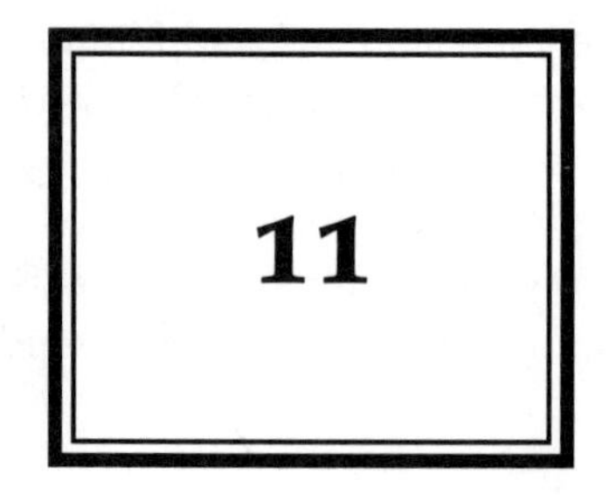

THE GOOD INTENTIONS OF THE PEOPLE WHO WENT TO ANNE Bloodworth's funeral did not extend to the more macabre activity of following the hearse to the cemetery for internment. There were, after all, no refreshments served during this aspect of the occasion. Only Simon, Julia, Bobby Hinton, the president of the historical society, and the minister stood at the grave site as Anne Bloodworth's coffin was lowered into the ground. There was, of course, a Bloodworth burial plot, and she was interred next to her parents. Some efficient person would see that she had an appropriate gravestone.

Simon heard a small scraping sound behind him. He turned, and saw that his little group was not alone after all. About twenty feet behind him were two black women, one elderly and one younger. The scraping noise had been made by the older woman's cane on the cement walk. While Simon watched, she sat down heavily on a concrete bench, scraping the cane on the sidewalk again, louder this time. Simon saw her exhale heavily as she settled herself. Both women were dressed up. The older woman was wearing an old-fashioned dark shirtwaist dress with a small print, a dark straw hat, and black orthopedic shoes. Her hair was almost completely white, and she was very thin. Her companion, whom Simon speculated was a granddaughter, was dressed in a stylish turquoise blue suit and matching shoes. She sat on the arm of the bench, with a hand on the old woman's shoulder. They were voyeurs, Simon guessed, visitors to the cemetery on some personal mission who stopped to watch the funeral while the old woman rested. Well, why not,

Simon thought. We're all voyeurs in this instance.

At the appropriate point, the minister instructed a very uncomfortable Bobby Hinton to throw earth on the coffin. "Unto Almighty God we commend the soul of our sister departed, and we commit her body to the ground; earth to earth, ashes to ashes, dust to dust; in sure and certain hope of the Resurrection unto eternal life, through our Lord Jesus Christ."

When the service ended, Bobby Hinton was visibly relieved. He wiped perspiration away from his eyes and pulled off his black armband.

"I need a cold beer," he said. "I didn't know this was going to get so intense!" He turned and walked quickly, very quickly, toward the parking lot and his car. He was followed by the minister and the president of the historical society. Simon heard the scraping of the old black woman's cane as she and her companion also left.

For some reason, neither Julia nor Simon moved. They watched silently as the grave was filled with dirt and the grave diggers smoothed the mound with the backs of their shovels. Simon helped them cover the grave with the flower arrangements that had come to the cemetery with the hearse. There were enough to cover the grave. The two biggest were from the Historic Preservation Society and Kenan College, but there were several from individuals. Simon wondered who would send flowers to the funeral of a woman who had been dead for seventy years.

The grave diggers piled their tools on a small wagon pulled by a converted golf cart and drove off. They were listening to old rock and roll from a boom box balanced on the dashboard. Simon could hear the beat of "Pretty Woman" reverberating long after the melody and vocals faded away down the road.

Simon and Julia looked out over the huge city of dead people. Old magnolias shaded its rolling hills from the hot, clear sun. The endless vista of markers was spotted with small Greek temples, little stone houses, and monoliths that gave the cemetery a skyline. Asymmetrical groups of gravestones were crisscrossed by paths that reminded Simon of streets and alleys in a neighborhood. Each plot was like a house with an address, inhabited by entire families and an occasional friend who had nowhere else to go. Simon had explored the graveyard many times, and he knew it even had its ghettos—the old black section and the Jewish corner. As in any southern cemetery worthy of the name, Confederate soldiers, both known and unknown, were proudly massed in troops and regiments, with their officers out front.

The cemetery was right smack in the middle of town, so the noise and bustle of daily life gave the impression that its residents were still somehow participating. Lawn mowers roared, dogs barked, traffic streamed by, and the band at the high school across the street was practicing for graduation.

"This is strange," Julia said. "Graveyards are supposed to be depressing. But I'm not depressed. I feel like we should have a picnic or something."

"I know what you mean," Simon said. "When I come here, I always feel like I've walked into a neighborhood block party."

"It makes death seem a little less cold. All the families are together, and lots of the people buried here must have known one another."

"Do you have time to take a walk around?"

"Just for a few minutes. I work for the people, you know."

Simon led Julia toward the military section of the cemetery. They had to carefully pick their way around countless stones—not just headstones but also squared-off stones that surrounded plots and small markers without inscriptions that popped up in odd locations. They both tripped before Simon decided to get on a path.

They walked through the flower-draped marble arch that was the entrance to the Confederate cemetery. Simon was always fascinated by the sheer determination of the Daughters of the Confederacy to memorialize its unknown dead. It was a continuing process—many of the markers were new and the plantings around the graves were beautifully maintained.

Simon supposed that it had been a comfort to southern families in the 1860s to know that the son they never heard from again was being cared for by strangers not far from some bloody battlefield.

"This is incredible," Julia said. She walked down the rows, stopping to read each inscription. "I always assumed that people who died in battle were just sort of tossed into mass graves, if they were buried at all."

"Not at all," Simon said. "Of course, bodies couldn't be sent home in those days—no refrigeration. So they were buried locally, and families were always notified where the remains were, if at all possible. And locating and identifying remains from the Civil War, and other wars, too, was a process that went on for years. They're still bringing bones back from Vietnam."

"It seems like a lot of trouble," Julia said. "After all, dead is dead."

"Not to the people left behind. They don't forget. That's what this is all about."

Simon led Julia into a small marble replica of a Gothic church. It was about twenty feet square, and every possible surface of its walls was lined with tablets listing the local dead of past wars. There were hundreds and hundreds of names.

"Not only do survivors want to remember; they want some way to immortalize. So we have places like this, where people like you and me can wander around and read the names of people who are no longer remembered by anyone alive." So that just for a few seconds a beloved's name cast in cold metal might cross the consciousness of a breathing person, Simon thought.

Simon suddenly felt profoundly depressed. Standing in the cool shadows of the mausoleum surrounded by ghosts had overwhelmed the benefits of modern chemistry. He remembered that his parents were dead, his wife had left him, and he had no children. If he died tomorrow, how long would it be before his friends and family forgot him? How long before the only thing left of his life was an award-winning book on a library shelf? And how long before that book was culled from the collection by a librarian making space for new books?

He remembered the words of Isaiah: "All flesh is grass, and all the goodliness thereof is as the flower of the field. . . . The grass withereth, the flower fadeth: but the word of our God shall stand for ever."

Simon shot out of the little building, forcing himself out of the cool shadows into the hot sunshine. Astonished, Julia turned from reading a tablet dedicated to seven men who had died on a battleship in the Pacific as Simon abruptly vanished from her side. She saw him sit down outside on the base of a marble angel, which was just settling on a grave, its wings outstretched in landing. Simon was breathing as though he had run a mile very quickly.

The oddness of this behavior added to Julia's concern about her interest in Simon. He was not her type. He was shorter than she was, and he looked Jewish. He didn't own a suit, or he surely would have worn it to the funeral instead of the khaki pants and blue blazer he was wearing. His shirt and tie looked as if he'd ordered them from a catalog years ago. Every other time she had seen him, he was wearing blue jeans. To her, he seemed intelligent and personable, but she had heard he had emotional problems. He probably didn't make any more money than she did. And if he was so brilliant, why was he working at a small college when there were three major universities just a stone's throw away?

She walked out of the mausoleum and sat down next to Simon at the foot of the angel.

"Sorry," Simon said. "I just felt a little claustrophobic."

"It's okay," Julia said.

"Listen, do you like baseball?"

"I guess so. When I was a kid, my dad used to take me to see the old Washington Senators. I haven't been to a game in years, though."

"Would you like to go see the Durham Bulls play tomorrow night? It's one of the last games before they move to the new stadium. The college has a box."

"Yes, sure. That would be fun." A minor-league baseball game would not be Julia's choice for a first date, but she had to admit she was tired of movies.

"I'll pick you up at six-thirty. We can eat there."

Great, Julia thought. Hot dogs. Maybe she should rethink this.

Simon was intensely relieved. He hadn't asked anyone on a date since graduate school, and it was easier than he had expected. The baseball game was a good idea, too. They could talk, yet they'd still have something to do if they ran out of conversation. He hoped she really did like baseball.

"I've got to go," said Julia. "It's getting late. I can just imagine what my desk looks like. It's probably too much to hope no one notices I took a three-hour lunch."

"Just tell them you were scoping out suspects at the victim's funeral."

Julia watched as Simon's expression changed suddenly. He grabbed her hand so hard that her rings hurt her fingers.

"My God!" he said. "I am an idiot!"

Julia began to wonder if she should think of a way out of their baseball date.

"The people who came to the funeral!" he said.

"What on earth are you talking about? And you're hurting my hand."

Simon released her. "Sorry," he said. "But remember, Julia, what Sergeant Gates said when we were talking in his office? That in a modern-day homicide investigation, the next step would be to see who came to the victim's funeral? He said it again at the reception."

"Sure," Julia said. "That's because the people closest to the victim, who might know something, are likely to be there. Sometimes the perpetrator is, too. But he was just joking."

"How old would Anne Bloodworth be if she had lived? She was nineteen when she died in 1926. She would be eighty-nine years old now. There are surely some people alive in Raleigh who knew her."

"Well, maybe."

"You know that old black woman whom we saw at the internment? She could be eighty-nine."

"Come on, Simon!"

"Why not? The story about the funeral was in all the papers. Anyone who wanted to could just come on out to the grave site. That woman was all dressed up, and she deliberately sat right there on that bench for the whole service. Then she left with everybody else."

"You know, you could be right."

"And then there are the flowers."

"The flowers?"

"The flower arrangements at the grave site—the ones from individuals. I wondered who would send them. People who knew her, her friends, of course; who else?"

"It's possible," Julia said.

"I am an idiot," Simon said. "Come on."

"Where are we going?"

"Back to the grave site to get the names of who sent flowers and the florists. I'm going to try to find these people and see what they remember about what happened on April ninth, 1926."

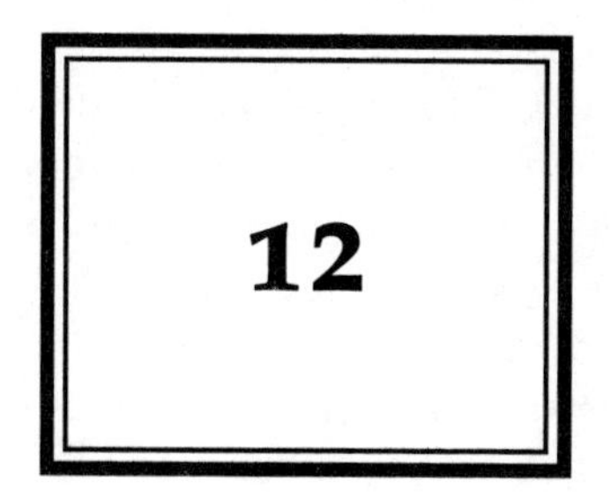

12

ALL THE WAY HOME, SIMON TRIED TO FIGURE A WAY TO GET IN touch with the old black woman whom he had seen at Anne Bloodworth's funeral. The only thing he could think of was to advertise in the paper. "Will the two black women who watched Anne Bloodworth's funeral at Oakwood Cemetery on Tuesday please get in touch with Dr. Simon Shaw of Kenan College. You may hear something to your advantage." Who could resist such a Holmesian offer?

Simon parked his car at his house and walked to campus. He had fifteen minutes until class started and he wanted to work off the nervous energy he had built up since realizing that he had some new leads in his research into Anne Bloodworth's death. He and Julia had scrambled over the grave, looking at the cards on the flowers. He had five names, all women, from two different florists. He would contact the florists tomorrow and try to pry the addresses and phone numbers of their clients out of them.

About a block from campus, Simon forced his conscious mind to put Anne Bloodworth aside and think instead about North Carolina Colonial history. If he wasn't careful, his students were not going to get their money's worth, and he didn't need to give Alex Andrus any more ammunition just now.

Simon got home after class around six o'clock. Despite his hearty lunch, he was starving. Close inspection of his refrigerator and pantry revealed that his cupboard was bare except for cat food and raisin bran. Neither appealed to him just then, so he decided to venture out to the local Yuppie grocery store for gourmet takeout from the deli.

As Simon backed his Thunderbird out of his driveway, he closed all the windows. There had been a carjacking at the shopping center recently, and he didn't want to tempt any potential car thieves while he was in the grocery store.

Driving the narrow streets of Cameron Park was always a challenge. Residents insisted on parking their cars in the street instead of conveniently in driveways or alleys, so there was often room for just one car to pass. Everyone very politely took turns letting one another by at the narrow spots. Children on their way to and from the local elementary school had a way of darting out of side streets without warning. Naturally, the college kids taking shortcuts through the neighborhood drove much too fast and didn't pay attention to children or to the width of the streets. The repair trucks that visited frequently to patch up the neighborhood's ancient utility lines always created traffic havoc. Simon came upon a big city truck parked on the diagonal as he went around the corner. There was no warning flag or sign, and Simon had to brake quickly to avoid hitting the traffic cones that blocked off the street. Two uniformed men with a serious jackhammer were breaking up the roadway while the street flooded with water. Simon swore under his breath, turned into a driveway, and headed in the opposite direction. A two-block trip had just turned into a ten-block detour around the neighborhood.

As he pulled to the side of the street to let a minivan loaded with children pass, Simon felt curiously light-headed, and his head began to ache. This was ridiculous. How could he be that hungry after having two helpings of the buffet at the funeral?

Simon pulled out into the street again, just in time to miss a dog darting across the street and fetching up on a curb two inches from a newly planted red maple. Now his heart was pounding as well as his head. What the hell was going on here? He was just going to the grocery store, and he had narrowly missed having two accidents. Well, he had read that most accidents happen less than a mile from home. Make that two blocks, in his case. This just reinforced his determination to walk or to ride his bike more.

There were no other vehicles in sight, so Simon left his car on the curb for a minute to collect himself. His heartbeat slowed down, but his head still hurt. He backed carefully off the curb, avoiding the bright red tricycle behind him. He set off again, driving less than fifteen miles an hour now.

Simon was very sleepy, but he didn't question it. He watched with detachment as he passed a blur of houses, trees, and alley entrances. His breathing became difficult, and his chest hurt. At the same time, his instincts and his judgment stalled. He went through a stop sign. The street curved to the right up ahead, but he continued on straight, dead into a stone retaining wall. He heard an awful crunching noise, his windshield grew a thousand spidery cracks, and the soft white folds of the air bag exploded out of the steering column as his body lurched forward. The engine was still running.

He wasn't aware of anything until he heard two voices.

"Maybe we should wait for the paramedics," said the first voice.

"I don't think so," said the second voice. "We should get him out in case the car blows up."

"It's not going to blow up, you dweeb. There's no fire, and no gas leaking. But maybe we should pull him out anyway."

Someone opened the car door on the driver's side, and Simon saw two young teenage girls, one dark and one blonde. Teen angels, Simon thought absurdly. The dark one tried to undo his seat belt, but it was jammed. The blonde pulled out a Swiss army knife and cut through the belt. Then she grabbed Simon under the armpits and pulled him free of the remains of the air bag. The dark one disentangled his legs and the two carried him about ten feet from the car, then lowered him onto the grass near the two bikes they had dropped. They were strong girls, Simon thought. But then, they were both bigger than he was.

The open air and cool grass began to clear Simon's head. What in God's name had happened to him?

"Don't worry, mister, the paramedics will be here soon. The lady across the street called nine-one-one," the brunette said.

Simon tried to speak, but he couldn't come up with the words to match his thoughts.

"Do you think he's drunk?" asked the blonde.

"I'm not drunk," Simon said. "I think I'm sick." It was the only explanation for his behavior he could think of that matched how he felt. His chest still hurt.

The authorities arrived in the form of two fire engines, an ambulance, and a police car. A small crowd began to gather. Sergeant Gates climbed out of the police car with a uniformed officer.

Simon was sitting up and coughing repeatedly while the medics examined him.

"How do you feel?" asked one of the paramedics.

"My chest hurts," Simon said. "I can't breathe very well."

"Do you have heart problems, diabetes? Any in your family?"

"No," said Simon.

"Do you take any medications? Do any recreational drugs?"

Simon hated to answer this question in front of Gates, who was standing just a couple of feet away with his arms crossed. The policeman who had come in the patrol car with him was taking photographs of Simon's car.

"I take an antidepressant," Simon said. "I've got some other prescriptions, but I haven't taken anything else today. That's all."

"How did you feel before the accident, while you were driving?" Gates asked.

"What are you doing here?" Simon said.

"Just happened to be in the area. Now how did you feel before the wreck?" Gates asked again.

"I was sleepy, and I couldn't think."

Gates, the policeman, and the medic looked at each other knowingly.

"Have you had any trouble with your car's exhaust system recently?" the policeman asked.

Simon answered that the car was fine, as far as he knew. At that point, the medic strapped an oxygen mask over his nose and mouth, making talking difficult. The medic looked in Simon's eyes with a small flashlight and checked him for broken bones. Simon noticed that Gates had gotten down on his hands and knees and was looking under his car. The policeman was interviewing the two girls. Gates stood up, then looked back toward Simon. He had a very serious expression on his face.

"Well," the medic said. "I don't think that there's anything wrong with you that a hundred percent oxygen for a while won't cure."

"What is it?" Simon mumbled through the mask.

"Carbon monoxide poisoning," the medic said.

Simon tried to process this startling information as he was loaded into the ambulance. He could have been killed, or killed someone else. Gates looked in the back of the ambulance just before it drove off.

"I'll check in on you at the hospital later," he said. "Whom should I call?"

Simon gave him Walker Jones's home number. Somehow, he didn't think he'd be working tomorrow.

"What about my car?" asked Simon.

"I'll take care of the car," Gates said.

"IT'S LIKE THIS," THE EMERGENCY ROOM DOC SAID. "WHEN YOU breathe, oxygen molecules hook up to your red blood cells and get transported all over your body. When they get to their destination, the molecules are released, and the red blood cells head back to the lungs for more oxygen. However, the carbon monoxide molecule hooks up to a red blood corpuscle and never lets go. When enough red blood cells can't carry oxygen to your body because they've been hijacked by carbon monoxide, you suffocate."

Wonderful, thought Simon. He was lying in a cubicle in the local emergency room, where the paramedics had deposited him.

"Get that car fixed," the medic had said to him earlier while his partner briefed the doctor. "You could have hurt someone, not to mention yourself."

"I didn't know anything was wrong with it," Simon said. "It was not my intent to drive around a residential neighborhood in a semiconscious state and hit a stone wall."

"It's a good thing those girls pulled you out," said the medic. "Or you would have gotten an even bigger snifter of the stuff."

Simon had spent a long hour lying on a narrow bed in the emergency room before any doctor saw him. His was obviously a pretty boring case. The nurse had taken his pulse, blood pressure, and temperature. The oxygen mask had been replaced with a thing that hooked under his nose and into the wall. At least he could talk. The doctor had come in, read the medics' report and the nurse's notes, grinned at him, and left. Finally, he had returned to lecture him on the life cycle of red blood cells.

"Fortunately for you," the doc said, "red blood cells don't live very long before they die and get replaced. You'll need to stay overnight on oxygen. You should feel better by morning."

Simon didn't want to stay in the hospital, but he knew the doctor was right. He still felt awful.

"What was wrong with your car?" the doctor asked.

How should I know? Simon thought. I'm here in the emergency room waiting for my red corpuscles to die. I haven't had a chance to have any lengthy conversations with my mechanic.

"I don't know yet."

"Better get it fixed."

No. I just thought I'd drive it again first and see what happens.

"We'll get you admitted right away," the doctor said.

"Thank you," Simon said.

Right away in hospital parlance clearly meant something completely different from the dictionary definition. First, he had to wait for the admissions person to come and take down volumes of insurance information. She also wanted to note down the number of his AmEx card, which Simon found worrisome. Then he had to wait for them to find a bed on the appropriate ward, which appeared to be the pulmonary unit. There were a number of beds available on other wards, but apparently one of these just wouldn't do. Then he had to wait for a wheelchair. Finally, he had to wait for an aide to come and push him up to his room. It was not acceptable for him to walk there himself. The admitting officer implied that the possible scenarios that could result from his self-ambulation were horrific. He could fall down, get hurt, or even die, and his family might sue the hospital. She didn't accept the possibility that he might make it.

Eventually, Simon was escorted up to his room by an extremely nice-looking young woman. He was then forced to undress and put on one of those hospital gowns that don't cover anything. A nurse put another oxygen thing under his nose. Simon had to admit that he could breathe better now.

"I thought I read somewhere that these things were going to be redesigned," Simon said about the gown.

"What fun would that be?" the nurse said.

Simon asked her about food. He was starving.

"Dinner was over hours ago. I'll bring you some ginger ale and crackers. Breakfast in the morning usually gets up to this floor about quarter to six."

The nurse deserted him, with an air that indicated that he didn't need much attention and wasn't going to get any. Simon lay in his bed and began to worry. What was wrong with his car? What was Gates going to do with it? Would he be able to work tomorrow? Should he call his own doctor and tell him he was in the hospital with carbon monoxide poisoning? What if his red blood cells were unusually long-lived? Would he be able to go on his date with Julia tomorrow night? Just how much damage could Maybelline do if she didn't get let out or fed this evening?

Simon was contemplating trying to work the hospital phone system when his delivering angel walked in. His friend David Morgan had never looked better to him. He was his usual potbellied, underdressed self, and he carried a huge McDonald's bag in one hand and Simon's only pair of pajamas in the other.

"If you die," David said, "can I have your Otis Redding boxed set?"

"No. I'm taking it with me."

"You don't look all that bad. What happened to your car?"

"If another person asks me that, I'm going to scream. I don't know what's wrong with the car. Something, obviously. What's in the bag?"

"Sodium, caffeine, fat. Smells good, doesn't it? Gosh, if I'd known you were hungry, I'd have brought you some. This is mine."

Before Simon could protest, David grinned and tossed him the bag.

"These, however, will cost you," he said, holding Simon's pajamas aloft. "Pay up or go bare-assed all night."

"This is not funny," Simon said. "Give those to me right now."

David gave him the pajamas, and Simon quickly put them on. Then he dug into his Quarter Pounder with cheese, fries, and large Coke. David sat in the chair next to Simon's bed and watched him eat.

"Honestly, how do you feel?" David asked.

"Better," Simon said with his mouth full. "I just have to stay for the night. Until my poisoned red blood cells die."

"Please, spare me the gory details."

"When you got my pajamas, did you let my cat out, by any chance? And how did you get in the house?"

"I remembered your strange habit of leaving the back door unlocked," David said. "And yes, I let the cat out, and back in, and fed her, too. Nasty creature."

"How did you know what happened?"

"Sergeant Gates called Walker Jones, and he called me. Walker said to tell you, by the way, that he'll cover your class for you tomorrow."

David left a half an hour later, after promising to go by Simon's house in the morning and tend to the cat. Right after he left, Julia called him.

"This is kind of an extreme way to get out of our date tomorrow, isn't it?" she asked. "Are you all right?"

"I will be," Simon said. "I'm lucky I wasn't killed, or didn't kill someone else."

"Do you want to postpone tomorrow?"

"Absolutely not. I might gasp every now and then, but I think I'll be fine. How did you know I was here?"

"From Sergeant Gates. I was still at the office when he came in to file a report."

"Do you know what he did with my car?"

"It's been impounded. It's locked in the county lot. They'll release it to you when they're done with it."

Simon didn't much like the sound of this.

"Why would Sergeant Gates impound my car? I need to get it repaired."

"You haven't talked to him?"

"No. Why?"

Julia was silent for a few seconds. Simon couldn't help but think she was trying to get out of an uncomfortable situation.

"Look," she said. "He's a very thorough policeman. He must have had a reason."

"I can't imagine what it could be."

"Let's just say that, generally speaking, carbon monoxide poisoning attracts his attention. Don't worry about it. You can probably have the car tomorrow."

After Simon hung up the phone, he had the distinct impression that Julia knew something that he didn't know about his own accident. It was a feeling he did not like at all, not just because he didn't want to be in the dark but also because he didn't want to think that she would hide anything from him.

Simon wondered where anyone had gotten the idea that a hospital was a restful place. The only people who could rest here were in the morgue. It was unbelievably noisy. People walked around all night, talking as if they were on the streets of New York City in the middle of the day. Their sex lives and grudges against supervisors were the main topics of conversation. The doctors, nurses, orderlies, and janitors all dressed the same—in jeans or wrinkled slacks with lab coats that didn't fit. Simon figured that the ones carrying stethoscopes were medical personnel, but he wouldn't have bet his life on it. The only concession to night was that the overhead lights in the rooms were turned off.

Television was the drug of choice for everyone—patients, doctors, and nurses. Every bed had a little TV set above it, all tuned to different channels. Situation comedies prevailed, so raucous laughter and applause burst inappropriately from rooms full of sick people. People who were unconscious or asleep were not spared. Nurses would automatically turn on any set in any room they entered. Exhausted interns would slip in, change the channel, and sedate themselves for a few minutes before the next crisis. George Orwell got it backward, Simon thought. Instead of Big Brother watching us, we're watching Big Brother.

A new nurse walked into Simon's room. The evening shift, he assumed.

"Don't you want the TV on?" she said.

"No," Simon answered. "Absolutely not."

"Get some rest, then."

"How could anyone sleep here? This place is like Grand Central Station," Simon said.

"I could bring you a sleeping pill."

"Please do."

Even under the influence of a sedative, Simon didn't sleep very well. The oxygen thing under his nose irritated him, and his room turned out to be next to the helicopter landing pad. About one in the morning, a huge helicopter landed with a noisy whir and rotating blue-and-red lights that filled his room. Simon rose about a foot out of his bed. He thought he'd had a close encounter of the third kind—contact with alien space invaders. He got to his window just in time to see the helicopter, which had a big red cross on its side, discharge some poor soul on a stretcher. He went back to bed, but it was a long time before his adrenaline stopped pumping. Another helicopter landed about four. This one had military insignia on the side and three stretchers.

There was no way Simon could go back to sleep. So he waited until morning, which was about 5:30 on this ward. That was when the nurse came in and took his temperature, pulse, and blood pressure.

When she was finished, he asked her to take the oxygen tube out. It was driving him crazy, and his chest barely hurt anymore.

"I can't do that without doctor's orders," she said. After she left, Simon removed it himself. When breakfast came, all he got was a little box of cereal, milk, and coffee. Simon devoured it in about one minute. He was still hungry, and he could smell hot food somewhere.

"Could I get more to eat?" he asked the aide when she came into his room to pick up his tray.

"You got cereal because you weren't here in time yesterday to fill out a menu," she said.

"That's not what I asked," Simon said. "Can I get any more?"

"Let me see if there's an extra tray on the cart," she said. A few minutes later, she came back carrying another breakfast.

"The man in four-oh-seven died last night," she said. "You can have his."

The guy in 407 must have had a good appetite until the end, because he had ordered scrambled eggs, toast, bacon, and yogurt. What was it that John Steinbeck had said? That you couldn't get a decent dinner or a bad breakfast anywhere in America. Simon enjoyed every mouthful of this breakfast, and he appreciated that he was alive to eat it.

After breakfast, Simon got up, got dressed, shaved, and brushed his teeth. He used the disposable razor and disposable toothbrush that was in the cute little toiletry package they gave him when he was admitted. Then he was ready to go home. It was 7:30 in the morning.

Simon rang the call button, and a nurse came in.

"When can I leave?" Simon asked.

"Let me go see if anyone's written any discharge orders," the nurse said.

God, let there be discharge orders, Simon thought. The nurse came back.

"No orders," she said. "You'll have to wait until the pulmonary team has rounds. Then they'll decide if you can leave."

"Hold on," Simon said. "The doctor in the emergency room said I could leave today."

"Well, he can't do that. You were automatically transferred to the pulmonary team when you were admitted," she said. "They haven't even seen you once yet."

"Listen," Simon said, "I'm an American citizen. You can't hold me here if I want to go. I haven't been charged with anything. I have my rights."

"It's hospital policy," she said.

"What time does the pulmonary team make rounds?" Simon asked.

"Oh, early afternoon sometime," the nurse said. Then she left.

Like thousands of others before him, Simon wondered if he was a mouse or a man. If he was a mouse, he would stay patiently in his room until the powerful forces of the American health-care establishment allowed him to leave. If he was a man, he would walk out right now.

Simon stayed. He worried that he might still have something wrong with him he wasn't aware of that would kill him as soon as he got home. Then everyone at his funeral would say, "If only he had stayed until the pulmonary team had made rounds, he could have had that innovative lifesaving surgery and still be alive, listening to CDs and drinking beer."

"You don't look too bad to me," his own doctor said from the doorway. "Considering that you spent the night in this madhouse." Ferrell was leaning up against the doorway, hands in his khakis.

He wasn't wearing a white coat, but he did have a stethoscope wound around his neck. It gave him that requisite look of authority all doctors acquired before they left medical school. Simon wondered if they took a course in it.

"God, I am glad to see you," Simon said.

"I'm sure you would have told me eventually that you were hospitalized with carbon monoxide poisoning," Ferrell said.

"The guy in the emergency room said I was okay, and I didn't want to bother you after hours."

"Couldn't figure out the phone system, huh?"

"Can you get me out of here?"

"Let's see," Ferrell said. He walked over to Simon's bedside, warmed the stethoscope with his hands, and listened intently to Simon's chest.

"I don't hear anything to worry about. No wheezing, no fluid buildup. You won't feel great for a couple of days still, but you'd be better off in your own bed than here."

But instead of leaving, Ferrell sat down in the chair next to his bed, as if he was planning to visit for a while. Simon thought he seemed more serious than usual. He sat tensely, with his legs crossed and both hands gripping the chair arms.

"Aren't you going to discharge me?" Simon asked.

"Probably," Ferrell said. "How do you feel really?"

"A lot better than last night."

"I mean, emotionally."

Oh, hell, Simon thought. I'm not in the mood for this.

"A lot better, really."

"Sleeping better, eating better?"

"I've been eating like a horse."

"Two breakfasts, I see," Ferrell said, looking at the two trays stacked on the bedside table.

"I only got cereal on the first one. Listen, I've got a date tonight. It's okay to go, isn't it? I won't faint or anything?"

Dr. Ferrell relaxed visibly and grinned at Simon.

"You've got a date tonight?"

"Yeah. I want to go, but not if I'm going to be sick."

"I think you'll be fine. Better let her drive, though."

"She'll have to. I don't have a car that's running."

Ferrell rang for the nurse. When she appeared, he asked for Simon's chart so he could write discharge orders.

"You can't do that," she said. "He was assigned to the pulmonary team last night. They're the only ones who can discharge him."

Simon had never heard anyone say no to a doctor before. He waited for Ferrell to explode. To Simon's surprise, he didn't.

"I am Dr. Shaw's family physician. He's my patient. Please get me his chart."

"But the pulmonary team—" she began.

"I've fired those guys," Simon said. "They have terrible bedside manners."

She gave in. "All right," she said.

"It's not the staff's fault," Ferrell said later while writing in Simon's chart. "These specialists think they're the only people in the world who can tell if you're breathing."

Ferrell gave Simon a ride home on the way to his office.

"By the way," Simon said as he got out of the car, "how did you know I was in the hospital?"

"That detective friend of yours called me," Ferrell said. "He said he was looking into your accident."

"Oh," Simon said.

He watched Ferrell drive off in his ten-year-old gray El Dorado. He wondered why on earth Gates had thought it necessary to call his doctor. For that matter, what interested the detective so much about Simon's little accident? Surely he had better things to do.

Once home, Simon entered that middling state of convalescence where one doesn't feel well enough to do anything much but is too bored to rest. He took a long shower and washed his hair. He discarded the clothes he had put on yesterday morning and changed into clean jeans and a knit shirt. He fed his cat. He opened a Coke. He checked his answering machine. Walker Jones, Judy Smith, and Marcus Clegg had left concerned messages. Julia said she assumed his car was still out of order, so she would pick him up at his house at six, unless she heard differently from him. That was all. It was ten o'clock in the morning. He had nothing to do until it was time to go to the ball game with Julia. The eight hours he had to pass until then loomed lengthily ahead of him.

Then he caught sight of his blue blazer where he had thrown it over a chair before he set out for the grocery store the day before, and he remembered the florist cards he had collected at Anne Bloodworth's grave site. Here was something he could do.

He took the cards upstairs to the library, collected the phone and the phone book, and turned on his CD player. He sat cross-legged on the floor and spread the four cards out in front of him. One read "All our love, Lillie and Sallie." Another simply said "Bessie." Simon figured that his chances of locating three old ladies in Raleigh named Lillie, Sallie, and Bessie this morning were nil. Another card was signed "Mrs. Irene Parker." The final one gave Simon hope. It read "With fond memories, Blanche Caviness Holland." It was a full name, and the salutation implied that Blanche Holland had known Anne Bloodworth personally.

Simon took a chance. He opened up the phone book. There were a zillion Hollands, but no Blanche or B.C. She could be listed under her husband's name. She could live with a relative, or in a rest home. Or out of town. Simon set her aside and looked for Irene Parker. There was a Mrs. I. V. Parker listed on Cowper Drive. Simon took another chance, and a woman answered the telephone. Simon explained who he was and why he had called, and the woman didn't hang up on him.

"I am Irene Parker," the woman said. "But I didn't know Anne Bloodworth. My mother did. They were fast friends, and my mother wondered her entire life what had happened to Anne. Mother died ten years ago, but when I saw the article in the paper, I knew she would want me to send flowers, so I did."

"Did your mother ever talk to you about Anne Bloodworth's disappearance?" Simon asked. "Anything you remember could be helpful."

"Not really. I just know she vanished. My mother and all her friends thought she had run away."

"Really? Why?" Simon asked.

"Because her father wanted her to marry her cousin, and she didn't want to—at all. And after old Mr. Bloodworth died, they all thought she would come back to town, or at least contact her friends. She didn't, so Mother suspected she must be dead. And she was right."

Simon asked her if she knew Lillie and Sallie, or Blanche Caviness Holland.

"Lillie and Sallie, I can't place. Mrs. Holland was old Dr. Caviness's daughter. She and mother were in the same bridge group for years."

"Do you know where she lives, or what her husband's first name is?" asked Simon.

"Sorry," Mrs. Parker said. "I didn't know she was still alive. I lost touch with all Mother's friends after she died."

Simon thanked her for her help, and she promised to call him if she remembered anything else.

Simon was excited. He had found out that Anne Bloodworth did not want to marry her cousin—to the extent that her friends thought she had run away, and stayed away. That seemed like an extreme act for a young woman in 1926. There was clearly one serious stress within the Bloodworth family. And he had talked to a person who was related to someone who had known Anne Bloodworth. This gave him hope that he could locate a living witness to her drama.

Simon called the florist who had delivered the flowers from Bessie, Sallie, and Lillie, and Blanche Caviness Holland. He was not nearly as cooperative as Mrs. Parker, nor was he impressed by Simon's mission.

"There is no way I would give you the names or phone numbers—or anything else, for that matter—of my customers. You could be anybody. You could be trying to sell them real estate," the florist said.

"But I'm not," Simon said. "I'm a history professor at Kenan College, and I can prove it."

"I don't care who you are," he said. "People don't expect their merchants to hand out information about them to strangers."

"If one of these women is a friend of Anne Bloodworth's, she will be happy to talk to me."

"Exactly how am I supposed to know that?"

"Please," Simon said. "Could you call them up, tell them what's going on, and if they're interested in talking to me, give them my phone number?" The florist grudgingly agreed, but he didn't sound as if he was planning to give the task much priority. Simon was frustrated. The Holland woman was obviously alive and functioning, and he desperately wanted to talk to her.

Simon could think of only two more things he could do that morning. First, he called the newspaper and placed a classified advertisement asking for the elderly black lady who attended Anne Bloodworth's funeral to call him. The person who took his order acted as if she placed ads like this every day.

"If you offer money for information leading to the identification of this person, you'll probably get a better response," the ad lady said.

"Okay," Simon said. "How much money do you think?"

"A hundred dollars," she said promptly.

This detective business is getting expensive, Simon thought. He wondered if bribes were deductible.

The woman read his ad back to him. "One hundred dollars reward for information leading to the identification of the elderly black woman who attended Anne Bloodworth's funeral. Call Professor Simon Shaw at five-five-five–six-eight-eight-four."

Simon hoped the title of professor would make him sound safe and reliable, the kind of person a little old lady wouldn't hesitate to telephone, despite the oddity of his request.

Then Simon called his friend Mark Mitchell at the Pinkerton archives. He wasn't in, but Simon left a message asking Mark to send him anything that might be left in the Bloodworth files. Somehow, he thought this would be a dead end. Surely Mark would already have sent him anything he had.

It was now 11:30 A.M. Simon was hungry. Unfortunately, he had never made it to the grocery store, so his choices were still raisin bran or cat food. He chose raisin bran, and ate two bowls.

Now it was 11:45 A.M. Simon was losing his mind. He had just about decided to go to work and teach his class in spite of his doctor's orders when his doorbell rang. It was Sergeant Gates.

"Hi there," Simon said. "Come in and sit down. Want some raisin bran for lunch? It's all I've got."

"No thanks," Gates said. He came in, but he didn't sit down. He stood right inside Simon's door, restlessly jangling his car keys.

"Do you feel well enough to go somewhere with me?" Gates asked. "We need to talk about your accident."

"Speaking of my accident," Simon said. "I have a few questions to ask you, too."

"In time," Gates said. "Right now, you need to come with me. If you feel okay, that is."

"You certainly have your serious side," Simon said as he climbed into Gates's unmarked police car. "Can I have a hint what is going on?"

"I'm not trying to be secretive," Gates said. "It's just that you need to see your car before I can explain anything. Be patient."

The county lot where impounded vehicles were stored was on government property on the outskirts of town. The entire area was virtually treeless and crisscrossed with chain-link fences and non-descript one-story brick office buildings. The lot shared acreage with the police-and-fire-training center, the Department of Motor Vehicles, and was across the street from the youth prison. There was not a tree or a blade of grass anywhere, except for a line of brilliant pink azaleas that paraded inexplicably down the median of the access road. As they drove past the prison, Simon saw a knot of listless teenagers pressed up against the chain-link fence, watching the traffic.

Since it was lunchtime, uniformed men and women were lounging around outside the buildings, eating sandwiches out of paper bags and drinking soft drinks. They were all wearing sunglasses. Simon wished he had his. The unrelieved noonday sun was glaring straight down and hurt his eyes even inside the car. It was a harsh scene, and Simon felt his spirits wane a little.

Gates drove up to a gate in one of the many fences and flashed his badge at a guard, who opened it and waved him through. Once inside, Gates stopped and pulled out a diagram filled with rows of typescript.

"We've got hundreds of cars here," Gates said. "Every one is marked on this map. I've got to remind myself where yours is located."

Simon looked out over a paved field full of automobiles, most with the orange sticker pasted on the windshield that meant it had been abandoned. Then among the metallic blacks, grays, and blues, Simon saw the sun glint off a rosy hood about ten cars down.

"I swear," Simon said, "I see a pink automobile."

Gates tucked the diagram into his inside coat pocket and eased his car forward until they were even with the hot-pink Cadillac. It was pink inside, too, and had huge speakers in the back and a plastic naked lady hanging from the rearview mirror.

"Is that a drugmobile, or what?" Gates said. "Talk about a walking advertisement for cocaine. You should have seen the courier. He was wearing a white suit and a white hat with a pink feather in it. Incredible."

"So, do you arrest everyone you see driving a pink car?"

"Unfortunately, no. That's not probable cause to arrest anyone. The Constitution protects your right to drive a pink car without being hassled by the police."

Simon listened for a hint of cynicism in Gates remarks, but there wasn't any.

"But," Gates said, "you can bet the Highway Patrol tails a car like this all the way up I-Ninety-five, hoping the guy will make one teensy little mistake. He did. He tried to leave a self-serve gas station without paying. The guy is hauling half a million dollars' worth of cocaine from Florida to New York City, and he tries to steal twenty-five bucks' worth of gas. What a loser."

"So after you arrested the guy, you searched the car?"

"We had to have probable cause for that, too. We can't search a vehicle for drugs when it's stopped for a non–drug-related violation. In this case, the guy was frisked during protective search and he had drug paraphernalia in his pocket. That gave us probable cause to search the entire car, and what we found counts as admissible evidence. It wouldn't be, say, if we had opened his trunk just because he was driving a pink car and looked like a bad guy right out of *Miami Vice.*"

"Sounds complicated."

"It can be. The police are very restricted when it comes to search and discovery. Julia gives us a seminar on proper procedures about once a week. There always seems to be some new twist."

"So what happens to the car?"

"It's government property now; it'll be sold. Know anyone who might be interested?"

"Not offhand, but I'll ask around."

Gates had started moving down the row of cars again.

"There's your Thunderbird," he said.

The damage to his car wasn't as bad as Simon had feared. Even though he had been too woozy to put on the brakes, he hadn't been going very fast, and the stone wall was curved at the point of impact. The front fender on the driver's side was crumpled, the left headlight was smashed, and the hood was popped. The rest of the car looked okay.

"I think the engine is all right," Gates said. "I ran it for a while. Who knows about the drive train—you might get lucky."

"Of course, there's the matter of where the carbon monoxide poisoning came from," Simon said. Gates didn't say anything.

Simon walked around the car and looked inside it.

"Where's all my stuff?" he said, noting that his CDs, sunglasses, and other personal possessions were missing.

"All in a sealed box up at the impound office. You can pick it up when I take you home if you like. We'll release the car to you whenever you say. Just call the office here and tell the guys what wrecker company will pick it up."

"Thanks," Simon said. "But I still don't understand what all the fuss is about."

Gates went back to his car and opened the trunk. It was filled with cop stuff—Simon saw traffic cones, a couple of big tackle-type boxes bound up in plastic tape, a broom, and a shotgun. Gates extracted a powerful flashlight from the clutter, walked back to Simon's car, and knelt down next to the Thunderbird. He shined the light under the car.

"Look at this," he said.

Simon got down on his hands and knees and looked. It took a few seconds for his brain to process what he saw. A piece of hose had been inserted into the tailpipe of his car and taped in place with duct tape. The hose ran along the pipe a short way and then was jammed into the drain hole in the trunk and taped there, too. The exhaust from his car had entered the trunk and from there seeped into the interior of the car, where Simon inhaled it and then drove into a stone wall.

"Dear God," Simon said. He was unable to think clearly, and suddenly he didn't feel very well. He sat down on the ground and tried to collect his thoughts. No wonder Gates had investigated the accident so closely.

"I don't have to tell you that this is a very serious matter," Gates said. "Whoever did this could be charged with attempted murder."

"Dear God," Simon said again. "Who would want to do such a thing?"

"You tell me," Gates said.

"I have no idea. It can't have been personal."

"Let's get out of the sun and find someplace where we can talk," Gates said.

They drove out of the impound lot and parked at the brick building next to it. When they went inside, it was cool, quiet, and dark. It was still lunch hour.

Gates commandeered a small conference room and went to get Simon's personal effects. Simon sat at the small cheap table in an old office chair that had been bought around 1950. The green plastic seat was torn and the springs sagged. The walls of the room were painted an institutional green and the linoleum floor was gray with age. There was an out-of-date state calendar on the wall with a picture of the legislative building on it. There were no curtains on the windows, just institutional blinds with slats about two inches wide. The closed blinds directed the strong sunlight down into bars of light on the floor. There wasn't a magazine or anything else in the room to distract him from thinking about the fact that he had almost died. His mind refused to progress to the thought that someone had deliberately tried to kill him.

Simon wanted to go home and not have the conversation he was about to have with Sergeant Gates. Better yet, he wanted to go back in time to a safe place—a really safe place. Say his parents' cabin in the mountains, where it would get so dark in the holler that he couldn't see his hand in front of his face in the middle of the night when the hooty owls woke him up. Then he would turn on his Boy Scout flashlight and find his way into his parents' room and get in bed with them. There he would feel absolutely safe and sleep soundly until morning. It was a time when nothing went wrong that his parents couldn't fix and when the people he loved didn't leave him.

Gates came into the room with a cardboard box under one arm and a Coke in the other.

"I figured you could use something cold," Gates said. "Isn't this your poison?"

Simon gratefully drained half of the Coke that Gates handed him.

"You know," Gates said, "that stuff dissolves nails."

"There are worse addictions," Simon said.

Gates sat down and pushed the box and a release form over to Simon. Simon just looked at the paper.

"You need to sign that to show that you received all the personal contents from your car," Gates said.

"Oh," Simon said. He took the pen Gates handed him and signed the form.

"I wish you would check the box first," Gates said.

"I'm sorry," Simon said. "I'm just not thinking very clearly right now."

Simon looked through the box. The only things he cared about were his CDs and sunglasses, and they were there, along with a lot of other junk—maps, an ice scraper, a yellow pad with a pen clipped to it, a handful of pennies, nickels, and dimes, his college parking card, and three packets of sugar. He took out the sunglasses and hooked them in the neck of his polo shirt.

"It's all here," Simon said.

"Good," Gates said. "Now, let me fill you in on what I've learned about your accident. Then I've got some questions for you, and I expect you have some questions for me."

"Okay," Simon said.

From the time he had seen the hose threaded through his Thunderbird's exhaust and into the trunk, Simon felt like he was watching a grade-B detective flick for the second time from the back row of a movie theater. It was hard for him to concentrate on Gates. How could he be sitting here, about to be questioned by a police detective about an incident that could have cost him his life? When was the show going to end and the lights go up?"

"Are you okay?" Gates asked.

"I guess so," Simon said. "This is hard to take in."

"You're still in shock," Gates said. "Believe me, I had a motive for springing this on you the way I did. I wanted to see the expression on your face when you saw that apparatus under your car and realized what it meant."

"And what did you see?" Simon said.

"Disbelief, anger, a little fear," Gates said. "All the reactions one would expect from an innocent man."

"Innocent?" Simon said. "What do you mean, innocent?" The implication forced Simon to reenter reality. He sat up a little straighter and drained his Coke. He wanted to take a headache pill, but he didn't want Gates to see him do it. "Surely you don't think I did this to myself?" Simon asked. "You think I tried to kill myself?" The thought pulled the knot in the back of his neck a little tighter.

"Actually, no, I don't," Gates said. "Not now."

"But you thought about it. Why?"

"You yourself told me you were taking an antidepressant," Gates said. "And the first person I talked to this morning was Alex Andrus. He implied that you might have tried to commit suicide. He said your wife had left you and that you were in the midst of a professional crisis, as well."

Simon felt the room begin to tilt slightly and he concentrated on bringing his emotions under control and the moving room to a halt.

"Spit it out, son," Gates said. "You look like you're about to explode."

"Alex Andrus is pond scum," Simon said finally.

"He is not a big fan of yours, either. But let me start at the beginning."

"Please do."

"When I arrived at the scene of your accident, both the paramedics, and I realized that your symptoms were indicative of carbon monoxide poisoning."

"That's why everyone kept asking me if there was anything wrong with my car."

"That's right. We assumed that you had an exhaust leak somewhere. I looked under the car. The tampering was obvious. So I impounded the car and our evidence guys went over it with a fine-tooth comb."

"And what did they find?"

"Not much. No fingerprints on the rough surface of the hose, which, by the way, matched a hose I found in your carport with a length cut out of it. The only other places where fingerprints of the perp might logically have been found—the exhaust pipe and the undercarriage of the car near the trunk drain—had been wiped clean."

"I can't think of any reason why anyone would do such a thing." Simon was gripping the sides of his chair so hard that his fingers were growing numb. He forced himself to relax, releasing his grip and breathing deeply. It didn't help. He found himself with his arms and legs crossed tensely, as if he was protecting his body from attack.

"Let's not get ahead of ourselves," Gates said. "Anyway, then we ran the engine for a while with the hose in place, and sure enough, plenty of carbon monoxide filtered into the passenger compartment. The air conditioner was on, wasn't it? All the right buttons were pushed."

"Yes."

"The volume control on the stereo was on seven. Kind of loud. It about blasted me out of the seat."

"Under normal conditions, I can listen to Eric Clapton and drive at the same time. I have a Ph.D."

"Be serious," Gates said quietly. "This is an official inquiry."

"Isn't there supposed to be a bright light shining in my face or something? Aren't you going to book me?"

"We can arrange that, but I'd rather not. Look, I know you're the victim here, but I need answers. If you don't feel well, we can do this another time."

Simon felt fine, except that he was very angry. His heart was pounding and his face was hot from the blood that had rushed to it.

"I'm sorry," Simon said. "I'll be serious."

"Okay," Gates said. "Now, when was the last time you saw your garden hose?"

Simon stared at him. He had to be kidding.

"Gosh, I don't know. I usually check the whereabouts of my garden hose several times a day, but I guess I've just been busy recently. Do you mean, on the way to the grocery store did I see my garden hose with a chunk cut out of it and wonder about it? No, I did not. Sure do wish I had. Could have saved ourselves a lot of trouble, doctor's bills and taxpayers' money and all that."

"I asked for that," Gates said. "That question came out wrong. Let's start again. Do you remember the last time you used your hose, and where it was at the time?"

"Nor did I cut a chunk of said hose and thread it into my car and try to kill myself in such an incompetent way, in full view of the entire neighborhood."

"I don't think you did."

"What did Alex Andrus tell you?"

"Is this what all this rage is about?"

"Yes, goddamn it."

"I don't blame you for being angry. You can take on Andrus later. Now, cooperate with me, or I'll take you downtown and get that bright light and a few minions and a stenographer and we'll stay there until we're done. Or I'll take you back to the hospital and make them examine your head."

Simon leaned his elbows on the table and put his head in his hands for a few seconds. Then he sat up.

"Okay," he said, "the last time I noticed my garden hose was when I watered my front yard a few days ago. I don't remember what day. Then I rolled it up and threw it behind a bush."

"Where the water spigot is?"

"Yes."

"I found it a few feet away in the carport. Together with a roll of duct tape. Was that yours?"

"I honestly don't know. Probably. I used some a few days ago to hold my lawn mower together so I could cut the grass. I guess I left it in the carport."

"Okay. So you drove home from Anne Bloodworth's funeral, parked in your carport, and walked to your four o'clock class."

"Right."

"You walked home, arriving when?"

"I'm not sure. Maybe around six o'clock."

"You went to the grocery store when?"

"Around quarter after six."

"You weren't headed in the right direction."

"The streets were blocked by utility trucks," Simon said. "I had to go around the block."

"Then you had the accident. That means your car was tampered with between quarter to four and six o'clock. The guy who did this—whoever he was—had some nerve. He cut up your hose and got under your car in full view of the street."

"He could have come in from the back, from the alley."

"Yes, but he still would have had to work right in the carport," Gates said. "He took a big chance. Mind you, it would have taken only a few minutes to cut the hose, get under the car, thread the hose into the exhaust, poke it through the drain hole, and tape it in place. Still, it's a miracle no one saw him."

"It's unbelievable," Simon said. "I still can't figure out why someone would do such a thing."

"We'll talk about that in a minute."

Gates referred to his notes. "I hung out around your neighborhood yesterday evening. I saw some weird characters."

"*Colorful* is the word."

"Does colorful include the guy with the raincoat who mumbles to himself and the woman dressed in the ball gown and sneakers?"

"They're regulars. Harmless."

"And all those guys with yellow plastic bags labeled CENTRAL PRISON wandering around?"

"They're not wandering around. They get on the bus when they get released and get off at Hillsborough Street. Then they go to Cameron Village and spend their fifty bucks or catch another bus. Contributes to the ambience of the place. The Republicans in the neighborhood give us more trouble."

"There are enough alleys, garages, storage sheds, and lean-tos around the houses on your block to hide the entire James gang. And I checked the police logs for major crimes over the past two years in a four-block area surrounding your street. One rape, three arson attempts, break-ins—"

"The rape was a once-in-a-million-years thing; the arsonist was a guy who went a little crazy when his girlfriend left him. He was very careful to torch only garages. The break-ins . . . well, it's an urban neighborhood. It's as safe as anywhere else these days. What's your point?"

"My point is, considering the location of your home, vandalism becomes a possibility."

Simon seized on this. He hadn't much liked the idea of someone trying to kill him personally. Killing him impersonally was much more acceptable, psychologically speaking.

"You think it was some kind of prank?"

"It was such an incompetent way to try to kill someone, it's hard to believe there was homicidal intent. For one thing, the hose could have worked its way out of the exhaust pipe. You could have had the windows or the vents open and never known it was there. And finally, you could have just fallen asleep and hit something, which is what happened. For all those same reasons, suicide doesn't work, either—a guy with your brains could surely come up with a better idea."

"Why would someone risk being arrested just for an anonymous prank?"

"Look at it this way. Some petty con's been released from prison, he's real angry—maybe he was expecting his girlfriend to meet him and she didn't show—and all he's got in the world is fifty bucks and a yellow plastic bag with a razor and a few odds and ends in it. On his way to the bus stop, he passes a nice house with a real nice car in the driveway—things he'll never have in his life. Nobody's home or on the street. He takes out his rage on you and your property. That's what malicious mischief is all about. Except we could charge this guy with something a lot more serious. But if this was not directed at your personally, it'll be impossible to find him. There's no witness, no prints, no MO, and no motive. The guy vented, got on a bus, and is long gone."

Simon felt himself relax a little.

"So," he said, "you don't think I tried to kill myself? And you don't think someone deliberately tried to murder me?"

"I'm ninety-nine percent sure on both counts. Which is about as good as it gets in this business."

"And?"

"And I would suggest that you be careful. Let me know if anything suspicious happens in your life."

"You said I could ask you questions when you were finished."

"Absolutely."

"What did Alex Andrus say to you about me?"

"You're really obsessed, aren't you?"

"He's trying to ruin what's left of my life."

"Okay. After the ambulance left for the hospital and your car was impounded, I went to the office and made some phone calls. I wanted to talk to your colleagues and get a feel for your life. I talked to Walker Jones first, then Andrus, then Marcus Clegg, and finally your secretary. Andrus was the one who suggested to me that you had tried to kill yourself. No one else even hinted at it."

"I bet that's not all he said."

"He holds a grudge, that's for sure. I called Jones again. He said that you had been somewhat despondent when your marriage broke up, and that Andrus was using it against you out of professional jealousy. I asked him if he thought you could have tried to kill yourself. He said he wasn't a psychiatrist but that he didn't think so, and he was absolutely certain that you wouldn't endanger anyone else by driving around your neighborhood impaired. Your secretary had given me your doctor's name. When I called him, he was adamant that you were not suicidal."

Then, Simon thought, the doc had come around to his hospital room the next morning to check on him, to see if his evaluation of Simon's mental status had been correct. Knowing Ferrell, if he had any doubts at all, Simon would probably be up on the hospital mental ward making baskets right now. And all this had gone on while he was blissfully ignorant about the cause of his accident, and while his friends and enemies were talking to the police about the most personal details of his life. It made him feel very vulnerable.

Gates went on with his story. "I visited Mr. Andrus in his office this morning, before I picked you up. I told him that he was the only person I could find who had a grudge against you, and I asked him if he had an alibi for that afternoon."

Simon was shocked. "You did what?"

"I scared hell out of him." Gates grinned. "Partly, I did want to know where he was, since he seemed to dislike you so much, but also I wanted to scare him. Maybe he'll be careful to stick to the facts the next time he speaks to a law-enforcement officer. I don't much like the idea of being used to damage someone's reputation."

"Did he have an alibi?" Simon was fascinated. He couldn't imagine that Andrus would have the physical courage to assault him, even indirectly. Alex was sneaky, not violent.

"Yes, he did. He fell all over himself telling me that he was drinking beer with a student of his, Bobby Hinton, at Hinton's apartment. I checked it out later; he was there from four until six-thirty."

"I suppose," Simon said, remembering her evasions over the telephone when he was in the hospital, "that Julia knows everything."

"Well, yes, actually," Gates said. "She does have official access to all police reports, so when she asked me what happened, I told her."

How convenient, thought Simon. He wouldn't have to waste time telling Julia his life story on their date that night. She would be well acquainted with the whole sordid mess already.

SIMON AND GATES WALKED OUT OF THE DRAB GOVERNMENT building and into the bright sunlight. Simon was in some ways more cheerful than he had been when he entered it an hour ago, now that the threat to his life had been reduced to common vandalism, but he was also angry. He was tired of being a victim, sick of not being able to control events that were driving his life from one day to the next. He didn't know exactly what or whom he was angry with—God, Providence, Alex Andrus, his ex-wife, or just his run of lousy luck, but he was angry. While Gates got his car, Simon put on his sunglasses. The knot in his neck had slowly tightened around his head, until his temples throbbed from the constriction, and he took a painkiller. Just one, so that he could still control his faculties. He would be damned if he would go home and wait for whatever life planned to spring on him next.

"Do me a favor," Simon said as Gates's car swung out of the gates of the government complex and headed back into town, "take me to Kenan instead of my house."

Gates looked at him suspiciously out of the corner of his eye as he drove.

"Why?" he asked. "I thought you weren't supposed to teach your class today."

"Am I still being questioned?"

"Of course not."

"I've got things to do."

"They can't wait?"

"Nope."

The two drove in silence until Gates pulled into the Kenan campus behind Simon's building.

"I think I'll just cruise around the block a few times," Gates said. "That way when I hear there's been an ADW at Kenan College, I'll be handy."

"What's an ADW?" Simon asked.

"Assault with a deadly weapon," Gates said.

"I don't have a violent bone in my body," Simon said.

Gates watched Professor Simon Shaw walk up the tree-lined brick walk toward his office. He longed to follow him and witness the fireworks, but then he would be honor-bound as a sworn officer of the law to stop Simon, and he didn't want to. He chuckled to himself as he drove down the street to the local McDonald's. He would get himself a chocolate milk shake and hang around for a few minutes, in case he was needed.

JUDY LOOKED UP from her computer terminal in surprise as Simon walked into the history department.

"Hi there. I thought you were supposed to stay at home today," she said. She couldn't see his face behind his sunglasses. "Are you all right?"

"I'm fine," Simon said. "I got restless. I think I'll take my class after all."

"Okay," she said. "I'll tell Dr. Jones."

"Thanks," Simon said. "Is he here?"

"Actually, no. He's over at the administration building for a meeting."

"Good. Is Alex in his office?"

"Sort of. Actually, he's using the facilities right now."

"Thanks," Simon said. He walked casually down the hallway and through a set of swinging doors into the men's bathroom.

Judy smacked the intercom on his desk. "Marcus," she said, "you need to get out here fast."

Simon walked into the bathroom just as Alex was finishing his business. Simon didn't give him time to zip up his pants before he grabbed him by the collar and belt and slammed him against the wall between two urinals.

"Jesus, Simon, what are you doing? Let me go!" Andrus said.

"You're slime, Alex," Simon said.

"Look, I didn't mean—"

"Of course you did," Simon said. "Let me tell you something. You tell any more lies about me and I'll sue you for slander and libel. I'll file a formal complaint with the dean. Whom do you think the college would rather have on this faculty—me or a second-rate guy like you? You'll be lucky to get a job teaching English as a second language on the fourth floor of the post office by the time I get done with you."

"Okay, I'm sorry. Let go of me!"

"Sorry isn't enough. Get a life of your own. Stay out of mine."

Just then, Marcus Clegg came through the swinging doors.

"Marcus, tell him to turn me loose!"

"No way," Clegg said. "I'm just here to prevent the shedding of blood, nothing else."

Simon released Andrus.

"Put your dick back in your pants and get out of here. I don't want to see you again today."

Alex did as he was told.

"Boy, has he had a bad day," Marcus said. "First that policeman asked him for his alibi for your accident, then Jones tells him he's going to put a reprimand in his file, and then you throw him around the men's room."

Simon got around to taking his sunglasses off, hooking them in the neck of his shirt.

"I shouldn't have done that," Simon said. "I think the last time I got physical with someone, I was eleven years old. What a juvenile thing to do."

"Nonsense," Marcus said. "Don't you feel better?"

"Yes," Simon said. "I do." He noticed that his headache was gone. "What was that you said about a reprimand?"

"Jones was livid when he realized that Alex had told the police that you're mental."

"What a charming expression."

"So he told Alex he was going to put a negative letter in his file, but if he managed to keep his big mouth shut, he might take it out before his contract comes up for renewal."

Simon wondered what Alex would, or could, do if he lost his job at Kenan. He almost felt sorry for him.

Simon was preoccupied when he walked past Judy's desk, so he didn't see her grin and give him the thumbs-up as he passed by. Since he had told everyone he was taking his afternoon class, he had to prepare for it. For the rest of the afternoon, he reviewed his notes on the Halifax Resolves. At five minutes to four, he went upstairs to his class, where his students detected a tone of voice that caused them to sit up straight and take copious notes.

POLICE LEGAL COUNSEL JULIA MCGLOUGHLAN SAT IN THE chair opposite Sgt. Otis Gates's desk in the Detective Division of the Raleigh Police Department, reading the report on Professor Simon Shaw's automobile "accident." She finished and carefully rearranged the papers in a neat rectangle before closing the file.

"Well, what do you think?" asked Gates.

"I don't see a thing in here that points toward homicide, or suicide, either. I think you're right—I think the incident was malicious mischief by an unknown person. Nothing else fits."

"I know."

"But you're not convinced?"

"I have"—Gates held his thumb and forefinger about a quarter of an inch apart—"about this much doubt, and I don't like it."

"You know what I think. I think you like Simon and you've gotten to be friends with him, so you're not being objective."

"You're probably right. Personal involvement is never a good idea. Speaking of which, aren't the two of you going to a ball game tonight?"

"Yes, but we're just friends, too," Julia said. "And speaking of ball games, I've got to go home and change. See you tomorrow."

After Julia left, Otis Gates got up and closed the miniblinds between his small glass cubicle and the rest of the department. Everyone knew that meant he wanted a few minutes peace to think. Gates sat down at his desk and lit one of the three Marlboros he allowed himself a day. He dragged on it happily. He opened the bottom drawer of his desk and took out two battered drumsticks, with "Otis" woodburned on the shafts. With the cigarette dangling from his lips, he played the rhythm section from that classic gospel song he had heard Aretha Franklin sing twenty-five years ago at Fillmore West. He supplied the words and melody from memory. "When you're down and out, when you're feeling blue . . ." He closed his eyes and visualized her in a white satin dress with big yellow roses at her magnificent bust, singing her heart out. "Like a bridge over troubled water, I will lay me down." What a belt the woman had.

Gates began to taste filter, so he regretfully opened his eyes, put his sticks away, and crushed the cigarette stub in an ashtray. He carefully wiped the ashtray clean with a paper towel over the wastebasket. Then he put Simon's accident file into the stack of files labeled OPEN. The last thing he did was open the miniblinds before giving himself to his job again.

AFTER HE FINISHED WORK THAT DAY, SIMON GOT HOME WITH barely enough time to shower, shave, and feed Maybelline before Julia McGloughlan pulled up in front of his house and honked.

She was driving an old black two-door BMW with creased leather upholstery. He slid into the passenger seat next to her.

"Are you sure you want to do this?" she asked. "Aren't you exhausted? If I'd been through what you have, I'd be in bed curled up in a fetal position under the influence of Ernest and Julio's best."

"Actually, I'm not tired at all. Must be adrenaline," Simon said. "Or maybe caffeine and sugar."

Julia pulled away from the curb, backed into a neighbor's driveway, turned around, and headed for the highway and the thirty-minute drive to Durham Athletic Park. She was relieved that Simon hadn't asked to drive. She could avoid her long spiel about how this was her car and why shouldn't women drive men, et cetera—which always sounded defensive and neurotic. It shouldn't matter who drove. It was just that a man wouldn't give up the wheel of his own car, so why should a woman?

Simon, oblivious to all this feminist soul-searching, was comfortably stretched out in the seat next to her, pretending to listen to the Schubert emanating from the classical radio station she was tuned to.

Actually, he was looking at her. She was wearing a sleeveless gold shirt tucked into black jeans, along with well-worn running shoes without socks. Large gold hoop earrings hung to her chin, and sunglasses dangled from a strap around her neck. Simon had resolved earlier not to make too much of this date. The woman had learned the most embarrassing details of his private life from a police file, and he didn't want to know what she must think of him. Now that they were together, though, he couldn't ignore the attraction he felt for her. He wished he'd thought of something else to do. She probably would have preferred a nice dinner somewhere.

When they pulled into the outskirts of Durham, she asked for directions to Durham Athletic Park. Simon guided her downtown, past the high school, and into the maze of factories and warehouses that comprised the tobacco industry of Durham. They negotiated parking along the shoulder of a narrow, weedy side street where the odor of menthol permeated the air. Then they walked two blocks to the baseball park, which was wedged into a triangle between buildings painted royal blue out of respect for the team that had played there since 1939.

Simon and Julia waited in line for tickets with dozens of other couples, some young, some old, and some in between, all dressed in jeans or shorts and Bulls T-shirts. It seemed as if all the couples were holding hands or snuggling, and Simon was self-conscious. What did thirty-something people do on a first date, physically speaking?

His lack of adult dating experience just added a new dimension to his self-consciousness. Reserved seats cost six bucks each. With food and beer, he would be lucky if he spent thirty dollars tonight. What a cheap date. And he had forgotten his stadium seats. Even in the reserved section, the old concrete bleachers would numb their butts in five minutes flat. He wondered if Julia would give him another chance after this fiasco.

In a reserved lady-lawyer way, Julia bopped to the rock 'n' roll that was blaring from the park's loudspeakers as they walked down the narrow concrete steps to their seats, which were just on the third-base side of the netting that stretched over the bleachers behind home plate.

"What a fantastic place," she said, sitting down and looking around. "I had forgotten what a happening a baseball game is. This is a great spot for foul balls. I should have brought my glove. And I need a Bulls baseball cap. Have they got them for sale anywhere?"

Simon's spirits revived.

"Wait right here. I'll be back."

Simon went up the steps into the concessionaires' domain and bought a Durham Bulls baseball cap, a T-shirt, two cheap foam seat cushions, two souvenir programs, and two beers in plastic cups. He returned to their seats with his booty.

"Let me repay you for this stuff," she said as she put on the T-shirt and cap.

"No way," Simon said. "This fabulously expensive evening is my treat."

They drank their beers and settled back to watch the show. Simon thought there was nothing so satisfying as the view from behind home plate looking out over the baseball diamond when the ballplayers fanned out onto the field. That combination of visual spectacle, the sounds of the crowd and the calliope, and the perfection of a warm, clear Carolina evening produced an indescribable sense of well-being in him. Simon doubted that even fifth-century Greeks watching the chariots wheel into the hippodrome at Olympia with the Temple of Zeus as background had experienced such harmony. It was probably ridiculous to compare the oratory of the ballpark announcer to Pindar reading his poetry between the discus and the marathon, but Simon made the comparison anyway—just to himself.

Most sports fans love the game they once played, and for Simon the thwack of the ball on the bat and the thunk of it in a glove brought back dreams of glory. Simon had played high school varsity baseball, but his college career ended ignominiously. He could catch, throw, and run, but he only weighed 130 pounds, and that was after Thanksgiving dinner. The coach thought he'd get killed on the field, so Simon warmed the bench until he got tired of wasting his time. From then on, he was just a fan.

"How's the food here?" Julia asked.

"Is that a hint?" Simon asked.

"I'm famished," she said.

"The food's incredible—flying burritos, pizza, hot dogs, ribs, fries. Real fries—the kind with the skins still on."

"Oh God," she said. "I'd be happy with just the fries."

"We have to have ribs, too, to keep up appearances," Simon said. He negotiated the narrow steps and aisles and walked to the Dillard's Bar-B-Q stand at the far end of the left-field bleachers. He waited in line with about two dozen other hungry fans. The smell of roast pig, barbecue sauce, and homemade french fries overwhelmed his other senses and his reason. By the time he reached the head of the line, he had lost all dietary restraint. He carried back cardboard platters heaped full of ribs, fries, cole slaw, and magnums of sweetened ice tea. Simon sometimes felt guilty eating pork, but his conscience vanished when he took his first succulent bite, dripping with the eastern-style barbecue sauce that was mostly vinegar and hot sauce.

They both happily cleaned their plates. Julia insisted on making the trip to the trash can, and she came back with two more beers.

During a lull after a Bulls home run, Julia brought up the subject that was on both their minds.

"I'm sorry that last night when I called you at the hospital I couldn't tell you anything about your accident," she said. "I just couldn't, no matter how much I would have liked to. Sergeant Gates hadn't finished his investigation yet. He hadn't talked to you. It was a confidential matter."

"It's okay, really," Simon said. "I understand that professional ethics were involved."

"But you're irritated anyway."

"Not with you, or anyone else, really. It just gives me a queasy feeling that all these people I know were talking about me to a policeman and I didn't have a clue. It makes me feel uncomfortable."

"You couldn't be told anything until after Gates talked to you."

"Why? Because I was suspected of attempted suicide and you didn't want to tip me off? Gates wanted to surprise me with what he knew, in hopes I would slip up and admit it?"

"Well, yes, exactly."

"He surprised me all right. Shocked the hell out of me is more like it." Simon remembered the rush of adrenaline that had almost knocked him down when he saw the apparatus under his car, and the way the room had tilted when Gates told him his psychological stability had been questioned.

"Do you agree with his conclusions?"

"Vandalism is the only thing that makes sense to me. Alex Andrus has a serious grudge against me, but he would be too scared of the consequences if he got caught."

"The way it was done convinces me," Julia said. "What a stupid method. First of all, it wasn't likely to work. And the hose under the car was so obvious. So I don't see how it could be a serious attempt on your life, by you or anyone else."

"I can't think why anyone would want to hurt or threaten me."

"You'd be surprised what some people would murder for," Julia said. "There are probably a dozen people within five miles of here who would kill you for five bucks if you were in the wrong place at the wrong time."

"Still . . ."

"Say you ran into a panhandler near your house. He asks you for money, and you turn him down. Maybe he's mentally ill anyway. He hangs around the neighborhood so he knows where you live. He's furious with you and the world, so he plays a terrible trick on you."

"He's a sociopath."

"That's right. Or let's say you're a very unpopular guy. Everyone who knows you thinks you deserve to die. Or you're a good person, but you are innocently thwarting someone. Like that assistant professor who tried to convince Sergeant Gates that you were mentally ill—he wants something you have."

"But he has an alibi."

"That's right. Which gets to my main point—you can't start with consideration of motive when you're investigating a crime. You have to figure out how the crime was done, who had the opportunity to do it, and voilà, the motive will become apparent."

"This is interesting. My colleagues accuse me of being too emotionally involved in my research all the time. So I have been trying to figure out why anyone would want to kill a nineteen-year-old woman in 1926, when I should have been coldly and unemotionally gathering facts."

"Absolutely. Of course why is more fun than how and when. On TV, the detective always walks into the crime scene and hollers out, 'Who had a motive?' In real life, the police are wary of motive as a starting point. What they want to do is to eliminate everything that couldn't have happened, then analyze the rest."

"Did you pick all this up in law school?"

"No. From a famous London consulting detective."

"Who?"

"Sherlock Holmes, idiot. It's from *The Sign of Four.* 'When you have eliminated the impossible, whatever remains, however improbable, must be the truth.' He also said that it is a 'mistake to theorize before one has data.' And we have damn little data to theorize from."

"That may change," Simon said. He told her about the classified ad he'd placed in the newspaper, his conversation with the unfriendly florist, and his plan to find some lucid contemporaries of Anne Bloodworth.

"If the florist doesn't cooperate," Julia said, "maybe I can do something official to shake their phone numbers loose."

"Like what?"

"I have no idea, but I'll think of something."

The Bulls won the game in a most satisfying manner. They scored six runs against the Kinston Indians, which meant the famous mechanical bull in the outfield got to spew smoke and fire, to the delight of the fans. There was also a fifth-inning triple play and a seventh-inning grand-slam. The ballpark lights came on precisely at dusk, and the cool night fell just as the ninth inning began. Simon could not have ordered a more perfect minor-league evening.

Once they had picked their way carefully through the ballpark traffic and navigated the maze of one-way streets in downtown Durham, Simon and Julia drove home uneventfully. The modern freeway lined with streetlights and exits could have been anywhere in the United States, but Simon knew that rural North Carolina lay just past the glass buildings and fancy hotels of Research Triangle Park. Out in the county, almost every house had a tobacco allotment or a livestock barn next to it, and the whole town went to church on Sunday mornings. Double-wides sat on lots next to huge brick houses built by guys who made a fortune feeding chickens for Perdue or Holly Farms. No one cared, because if God had wanted the county zoned, he'd have done it himself during that first week. Out in the country, men came home from their day jobs and picked tobacco or fed the pigs. The women drove school buses in between doing their regular chores and going to the church to set up and cook for the Wednesday-evening service and supper. They spent their vacations selling barbecue and fried dough at the state fair every year in a booth marked with the name of their town and the words FIRST PRESBYTERIAN CHURCH so they could raise the money for a new church roof or an organ. This was where you couldn't get elected dogcatcher unless you were a Democrat, your daddy was a Democrat, his daddy was a Democrat, and everyone bragged that they voted a straight Democratic ticket. Mysteriously, though, the Republicans had carried the state during national elections since 1960. No one seemed to be able to figure that out.

The rural North Carolinians, with their immense capacity for work and their absolute confidence about right and wrong, were different from their town cousins, who, together with carpetbaggers of various stripes, lived in the cities and university towns. Simon needed to remember that. The Raleigh of Anne Bloodworth's time would have been much more like this than the city it was today.

"Do you like working for the police?" Simon asked.

"Yes, very much," Julia answered. "More than I should. I really ought to concentrate on finding a place in private practice."

"Why?"

"Oh, more money, more prestige. I had an excellent academic record. Contracts was my specialty. I took the job with the police department because nothing else was available when my clerkship ran out."

"Why didn't you go somewhere else?"

"A guy."

"Oh."

"I've been engaged twice."

"We're pretty even. I've been married once."

"The thing is, I really like the work. I feel that I'm helping real people, that I'm on the side of the guys wearing white hats instead of whoever walks in the door with that month's overhead in his pocket. And I like the atmosphere. It's much more exciting and interesting than the work my friends in law firms are doing."

"If you like it so much, don't leave. I can't think of anything worse than not enjoying your work."

"According to my mother, my stepfather, various law professors, and two past boyfriends, I'm not living up to my potential. I ought to aim higher."

"I'm an underachiever myself," Simon said. "I do what I like. I highly recommend it."

"That's right," Julia said. "You should be at Harvard or Yale or someplace, shouldn't you?"

Simon groaned. "I would never fit in. I'm hopelessly politically incorrect. I drive an American car. I love rock and roll. I like to eat a steak occasionally. Every now and then, I think a Republican says something sensible—not often, mind you, but sometimes. Also I think faculty, not graduate students, should teach."

"You've lost me."

"There is no greater bastion of conformity than the fashionable American university today. Everything from the type of shoes you wear to the music you like to the foods you eat and the way you teach has to meet a standard tougher than the handbook of the Junior League of Chattanooga."

"Every profession has its uniform and its code."

"Not to the point of absurdity," Simon said. "When I was in graduate school, I opposed a plan to open a separate student lounge for minority students. I actually think Americans ought to work together, eat together, and room together, not break off into little groups defined by whose great-grandfather abused whom."

"Wow. I detect strong opinions here."

"And I was told by some nitwit first-year grad student who was trying to make a name for himself that I was 'no liberal.' Can you believe it? And everyone else in the department went along with it because they were afraid—they had real fear—of being out of political fashion."

"So, you accept underemployment to escape academic politics?"

"And you're thinking of leaving a job you love because it's not prestigious enough to suit your friends."

"Touché." Julia laughed. "Does that mean we're both hopelessly screwed up?"

"Not any more than anyone else, and less than most, probably," Simon said.

Simon had meant to ask her to have coffee at home with him, but he realized, first, that he didn't have any decent coffee in the house and, second, that he was exhausted. The adrenaline or caffeine or whatever had fueled him for the last thirty-six hours was completely depleted. He'd had a good time, but now he wanted to go to sleep.

Julia pulled over in front of Simon's house but didn't turn off the engine. Apparently not being asked for coffee wasn't going to bother her any.

"I had a really good time," she said.

"I did, too," Simon said. "Can I call you?"

"Sure," she said.

Simon leaned over and kissed her gently on the cheek before he got out of the car. She drove off, thinking that she liked him very much. He was bright, he could talk about something other than his job and money, and he wasn't demanding. He would be fun to pal around with. Of course, he was entirely inappropriate for her otherwise. She kind of wished he hadn't kissed her.

Simon liked Julia, too, but relationships were far from his mind just then. He actually stumbled as he walked up the steps to his house. He leaned against the doorjamb of his bathroom while he urinated, and he didn't bother to brush his teeth. He got partially undressed, falling into bed in his Jockey shorts and socks. He didn't stir all night, even when Maybelline walked on his back on her way to curl up between his legs.

Simon would have slept later the next morning if the city recycling van hadn't stopped outside his house to grind up the entire block's accumulation of bottles and cans. As it was, by his standards it was very late when he woke up, almost ten o'clock. It took about twenty minutes from the time he became conscious to force his eyes open. The process was like a submarine slowly surfacing from a great depth, with the longest stretch right before breaking the surface. Simon sat on the edge of the bed and tried to focus. His eyes were gummy and his mouth tasted like cheap paper towels. A dull ache in the back of his head stretched down his neck and across both shoulders. Well, why not, he thought. After all, he'd been in a car accident two days ago, and yesterday hadn't exactly been restful, either. He told himself firmly that he'd had plenty of sleep and it was time to get up and do something constructive. To do that, he needed a hot shower, a cold shower, a shave, and lots of coffee.

A half an hour later, he was sitting at the International House of Pancakes with David Morgan, whom he had encountered when he walked in the door. The IHOP was a favorite gathering place for students, truckers, taxi drivers, and other denizens of Hillsborough Street. Most of them wore their hair in ponytails and wouldn't be caught dead eating bran muffins. Except for the waitresses, they were all men.

A nearly toothless waitress brought them an insulated pitcher of coffee.

"What'll you have, hon?" she asked. "We're out of sausage, by the way. The Neese's man hasn't come yet." She cocked a skinny hip and looked at David.

"I'll stick with coffee," David said.

"I'll have a large orange juice, with three scrambled eggs, bacon, and a short stack," Simon said. "No syrup—lots of strawberry jelly."

"You know, you dig your grave with your fork," David said, slurping his mug of nonimported, non–freshly ground black coffee.

"Strong words from someone who lives on Swanson TV dinners," Simon answered. "What was it last night, fried chicken or turkey and stuffing?"

"I'll have you know, I didn't touch the apple cobbler. The tray is still on my kitchen counter if you want to check," David said.

"I'm sure it is," Simon said. "What are you doing here in the middle of the morning, anyway?"

"Waiting for the damned front-loader I hired an hour ago to turn up. It should have been here by now."

"What do you need a front-loader for? I thought excavating machines were against your religion."

"To move the pile of dirt and debris we stacked up on the north edge of the excavation," David said.

"Why, pray tell, do you want to move it?"

"We located an old brick pipe leading from the cistern straight to the pile, which is about ten feet tall at this point. We've got to move it if we want to find out where the pipe led."

"What could it be?"

"Anything. An icehouse, a laundry room, some kind of workshop. You need water for blacksmithing, for example."

"Someone would pump it up from the cistern and dump it into the pipe," Simon said. "Saves a long walk carrying a couple of buckets. The pipe must slope some."

"Exactly. Only a few degrees, but enough to move water along."

"Nineteenth-century pipe? Or eighteenth?"

"Nineteenth. The cistern was probably built around the time of the Civil War. The creek and all the storm drains in your neighborhood feed into it, so it never goes dry."

The skinny waitress put a steaming platter in front of Simon. She dumped a dozen tiny boxes of strawberry jelly next to the plate. Simon painstakingly opened half of them and scraped the contents onto his pancakes. Then he dug in. David watched him eat for a while before he spoke again.

"There is something else," he said.

"What?" Simon said, his mouth full.

"I found a new artifact associated with the Bloodworth burial."

Simon's next forkful stopped before it got to his mouth.

"What was it?"

"A suitcase of some kind."

Simon put his fork down on his plate.

"A suitcase?" he asked. "What kind of suitcase? What was in it? How do you know—"

"Just give me a chance," David said. "When Julia McGloughlan said something to me about watching out for other items that might be related to the body, I got curious. So I began to excavate the area around her body at the depth at which she was found. I located the bag several feet from her."

Simon went back to his breakfast. He knew that David was saving up the best for the end of the conversation, and he didn't want to spoil his fun by rushing him along.

"It was an old carpetbag," David continued. "Most of the fabric is gone, but you can see the pattern on a few scraps. The handles and the clasp are still there, though. Brass."

"It could have nothing to do with Anne Bloodworth," Simon said.

"But it does," David said.

"Out with it. I promise to be properly excited."

"The bag had the initials AHB inscribed on the clasp."

"Damnation," Simon said through a mouthful of breakfast. "She was leaving town!"

"I knew that you would come to some wild conclusion. There's no evidence of that at all. The bag could have been buried much later, or earlier, for some other reason."

"Why would anybody want to bury an old carpetbag? You said yourself it was associated with the body. Anne Bloodworth was going somewhere far enough away and for long enough that she needed luggage, and after she was killed, the murderer had to conceal the bag, too. Nothing else makes sense."

"You know this kind of speculation makes me nervous. I like facts."

"Come on, you wouldn't have told me this if you didn't think it was important. Can I see it?"

"The bag? Of course. It's at the Bloodworth house office—in the safe."

THE PRESERVATION SOCIETY'S office was in a late addition that housed the Bloodworth kitchen. It had been added at the back of the house and didn't look right even when painted the same colors and trim as the rest of the house, and it really should have been torn down. But the society needed a place in the house to use as an office for its docents. Rather than convert an historical part of the house, they had stripped the kitchen and put in a couple of desks, a coatrack, two telephones, a metal cabinet that locked, and a Coke machine.

David unlocked the cabinet and removed what looked like a dirt clod with tree roots clinging to it. The mess was sealed in a big plastic Ziploc bag. Simon sat down at one of the desks and examined the sodden mess for a long time. Decayed brown leather handles were attached by brass rings to a spine with a hinge at each end. The brass clasp still firmly held the two halves of the spine together and to what was left of the fabric of the bag. David had rubbed the part of the clasp with Anne Bloodworth's monogram until it was bright, and the initials were simple and clear. The fabric body of the carpetbag had decayed, but Simon could still make out its pattern of red cabbage roses with green leaves. The carpetbag was the duffel bag of its time—made of leftover carpet remnants, it was cheap and strong. Its mouth opened wide to accommodate almost any kind of baggage its owner wanted to carry. Simon carefully held up the spine to calculate how big the bag was. It was about two feet long and would have held a lot.

For most people, the decayed carpetbag was just another artifact. For Simon, it was much more. It had belonged to a human being, and it represented the act of someone leaving somewhere to go someplace else. It had meaning; it had figured in a murder. Simon knew that Anne Bloodworth had had this bag with her when she was shot, knew it as well as he knew his own name. He wasn't worried about the details missing from his scenario. He knew the truth of it. And he was more determined than ever to decipher the mystery of Anne Bloodworth's death.

"Some of us have real jobs," David said, disturbing Simon's reverie.

"Sorry," Simon said. "Listen, can I have this? I'd like to give it to Sergeant Gates."

"Can't do it," David said. "There are restrictions on disposing of artifacts from an archaeological site. The bag is the property of the Preservation Society."

"But it could be important to a murder investigation," Simon said.

"You're incorrigible. Let me lock it back up. You can tell the police about it, and if they think it's evidence, of course they can have it."

17

"THINGS ARE REALLY DIFFERENT AROUND HERE," JUDY SAID TO Simon when he stopped by the faculty mailbox on his way to his office. "Alex went into his office this morning and closed the door. We haven't heard a peep from him since—no whining, no moaning, no complaints. You must have really scared him."

"I should think so," Simon said. "I'm a scary person."

"Seriously, he's not the same man."

"Good. Let's hope it stays that way."

"And you have a zillion messages," Judy said, handing him a thick stack of pink message slips.

Simon took his mail, his messages, and a cold Coke into his office and closed the door. He sat in his chair and put his feet up on his desk, popping the top of his Coke. For the first time in a long while, he felt as if he was in some kind of control of his life. He knew this feeling was an illusion, but he welcomed it anyway. Maybe he would even go to the grocery store later.

His mail was all junk, and the telephone messages were mostly concerned with his car accident. There were two calls from his insurance agent and one from the garage that was working on his car, probably about settlements and estimates. There were calls from Julia and from David. They were hours old, so he crumpled them and threw them in the wastepaper basket. The last one was from the florist, who said he had the information Simon had requested. Simon's feet landed on the floor with a thud, he chugged his Coke, and headed out the door.

"Hey," Judy said as he passed her, "you just got here. Where are you going? When should I tell all your admirers you'll be back?"

"I don't know. Before class, I guess," Simon said. Then he remembered that he didn't have a car. He turned back to Judy's desk with a question about car-rental agencies. She was dangling a set of car keys from her hand.

"Marcus left you his old Mustang," she said. "He said you could have it as long as you wanted it but that if you so much as scratched it, he would have your hide."

Marcus's 1967 Ford Mustang convertible was his pride and joy. His father had given it to him when he was sixteen, and he had maintained it impeccably ever since. The car was Carolina blue, with a white interior and a white vinyl top. It was probably worth a fortune. Simon knew he should be flattered that Marcus had entrusted it to him. He wished he hadn't. The Mustang had two great flaws as far as he was concerned: no air-conditioning and an AM mono sound system. He wished he had thought to rent a car yesterday. He could never let Marcus know he wasn't appreciative, though, so he resigned himself to his hot, windblown, tinny fate.

The gas gauge was close to empty, so he pulled into Brooks Amoco. It was probably the last gas station in the universe that gave full service. Simon patronized it faithfully.

"This is Mr. Clegg's car, ain't it?" the attendant asked. "It's a beaut."

"Yes," Simon said. "He's lent it to me for a while. Do you know what he puts in it?"

"I'll fix you right up," the attendant said.

"Thanks."

After inserting the nozzle of the gas pump into the car, the attendant moved around to the front to clean the windshield.

"You're looking better," he said.

"Excuse me?" said Simon.

"You was lower'n pig iron in water for a while there," the attendant said. "You know, your wife stopped here for a fill-up on her way out of town."

Good grief, thought Simon.

"I've had two of 'em leave me. It's hell. They take everything you own and the courts let 'em. My first didn't get much 'cause I didn't have much, but my second got a nice double-wide that sits on my daddy's property, all the furniture, my brand-new truck, and two hundred and fifty bucks a month, just 'cause we had a couple of kids."

Simon made sympathetic noises. In fact, Tess had taken almost nothing when she left. Everything she considered hers was packed onto and into a very small car. All the years he thought they were sharing a life, she was just camping out.

"Believe me, you'll get over it," the attendant said. "Get you another woman, too. Just don't marry her or get her pregnant. Then she can't leave with your stuff."

THE FLORIST WAS just as ill-tempered as the last time Simon had talked to him.

"Some woman at the police department called me," he said. "Said I should cooperate with you. Said you are some kind of a consultant working with them or something. Said they might be able to get a search warrant if I refused."

"I appreciate it. I really do," Simon said.

"I had better things to do," he said. Rummaging around under the counter, he pulled out a notepad, ripped the top page off, and handed it to Simon.

"Whoever bought the flowers that were sent from Bessie paid cash," he said. "Blanche Holland paid for hers by check. Her name and address and phone number were on the check. I called her and she said she would be happy to talk to you. The arrangement from Lillie and Sallie was ordered over the telephone and charged to a Lillian Blythe. We had her phone number because we always ask for it—in case the credit card's no good. Mrs. Blythe said she'd talk to you, too."

Simon carefully folded the note with the women's names and phone numbers on it and put it in his wallet.

"Thanks again," he said.

The florist ignored him.

"THIS IS BLANCHE HOLLAND," SAID THE VOICE ON THE OTHER end of the phone. The voice was elderly but strong and lucid. She had a cultured old Raleigh accent.

"Mrs. Holland, I'm Simon Shaw," he began.

"Yes, I know. The historian from the college who is interested in Anne Bloodworth's death. I read about it in the newspaper. She was my very dear friend. I would be happy to talk to you about Anne if you think it could be useful to you."

"Is now a good time?"

"That would be fine." She gave Simon directions, and a few minutes later, he pulled into a modern block of condominiums that had been built near a fashionable old section of Raleigh. The condos had been planned for upwardly mobile Yuppies, but instead, many of the aging owners of nearby mansions promptly sold their big homes and moved in. Mrs. Holland's unit was on the ground floor. A well-tended plot of impatiens and hosta bordered the short slate walk that led to the front door.

Mrs. Holland must have been watching for him, because she opened the door before Simon had a chance to knock.

"I'm glad to meet you," she said, waving Simon into the immaculate living room. "I've been thinking about Anne ever since I read the article in the paper. I've had to take sleeping pills to get any rest at all."

Mrs. Holland was, as they say, old as dirt. Her hair was absolutely white and her skin was deeply wrinkled. Her hands were blotched with age spots and the knuckles were swollen. She wore bifocals. But somehow, she didn't seem that old to Simon. Her hair wasn't done like an old person's; it was cut short in a natural elfin style. Her glasses, which hung from a chain around her neck, were round wire rims. She was wearing, of all things, jeans, a ribbed knit tunic, and black Keds.

"I've got some tea steeping. It's Earl Grey. I hope you can drink it."

"Yes, please," Simon said.

The interior of the condo was bright and uncluttered. The modern pecan furniture looked new, and the sofa and chairs were upholstered in a colorful chintz. Across from the sofa in an entertainment center were a big TV, VCR, and CD player. Miniblinds and ivory lace curtains were at every window, letting in plenty of light. Two porcelain cats lay sleeping under a table. Mrs. Holland brought in a tray with the tea and a plateful of cookies.

"I like your place," Simon said.

"Thank you," she said. "When I moved, I couldn't see bringing the big old heavy pieces of furniture from my house here. I split everything up between my children and grandchildren, including all my silver. Good riddance, too. Let someone else polish it."

"I'm sure a big house would be a burden," Simon said.

"I feel sorry for the young couple who bought it. They don't know what they're getting into. All those twelve-foot ceilings that collect cobwebs and brass fixtures that have to be polished—not to mention the utility bills. There's no domestic help to be had these days, either. Which is a good thing, mind you. When I was a young matron, our maid, houseman, and cook were practically slaves. We expected them to live with us and be at our beck and call. I didn't so much as get a glass of water for myself until the Depression."

"Sounds like you don't think much of the good old days," Simon said.

"These are the good old days," she said. "But you came here to talk about Anne. What a shocking thing. After all these years of wondering about her, to find out she was murdered and buried in her own backyard! Mind you, I was pretty sure she was dead."

"Why?"

"We—our crowd, that is—thought she had run away to avoid marrying Adam Bloodworth. We expected to hear from her after she turned twenty-one, or after old Mr. Bloodworth died. When we never did, we were afraid that she was dead. But murder was something that didn't cross our minds. In our day, young people died of influenza, not gunshot wounds."

"Tell me about her."

"There was something different about Anne. Oh, we all considered ourselves to be modern young women. We danced the Charleston and bobbed our hair and thought Charlie Chaplin was the bee's knees. And we read F. Scott Fitzgerald and Sinclair Lewis and Theodore Dreiser. But we also wanted to go to parties and meet eligible young men. Anne didn't really care about her social life. She did all the right things—joined the Cotillion and made her debut—but she was just going through the motions. She was more interested in her college classes. And she was very active in the League of Women Voters, even though she wasn't old enough to vote yet."

"Maybe she wasn't interested in her social life because she was already engaged."

"She had no intention of marrying Adam Bloodworth. That was an arrangement made by her father. He had this massive business empire and was determined to keep it in the family. Women weren't supposed to run businesses back then—at least not railroads—so he brought Adam in and decided Anne should marry him. Anne went along with the engagement because she had to live under the same roof with the two of them, but she kept putting off the wedding. Her plan was to keep putting it off until she was twenty-one and could break it off officially. She was due to get a little something from her mother's estate, so it wouldn't matter if her father cut her off. Oh, there was nothing really wrong with Adam—he was quite attentive, in fact. He always sent flowers and gave nice gifts. But he and Anne had nothing in common."

"Running away seems rather extreme."

"Anne had another sweetheart. She wouldn't tell anyone who he was. We called him Mr. X. She showed us some of his love letters. He was very literary and romantic. Somehow, I suspect he wasn't in our crowd; otherwise, we could have figured out his identity. I think, or I thought, that her father was suspicious and pressed her to marry Adam immediately. So she ran away."

"Her father must have been very difficult."

"Not really. She was his daughter—he was just trying to take care of her, make her future secure. She was supposed to do what he said. He wasn't much different from my own father. It was Anne who was different."

"So when she disappeared, you thought she'd run off with Mr. X?"

"That was our fantasy. Within a few years, we knew it wasn't true, because we would have heard something from her."

Simon told her about the empty carpetbag that had been found at the excavation.

"Something terrible must have happened to her that night," she said.

"Do you think Adam Bloodworth could have killed her?"

"Good heavens! What a thought!" Mrs. Holland poured another cup of tea for herself. She passed him the plate of cookies loaded with chocolate chips and pecans.

"Please eat these up," she said. "I made them myself."

"I've already had three," Simon said. "They're wonderful."

"Made with real butter. I gave up watching my diet when I turned eighty." She took a cookie and dipped it into her tea.

"Could Adam Bloodworth have killed Anne?" she repeated. "I don't know. It's hard to imagine. Why should he?"

"He wound up with the business, didn't he?"

"He couldn't count on that. And if Anne ran away with another man, I think Charles Bloodworth would have relied on Adam even more. And I don't believe he loved her, except as a sister. I just don't know. In those days, only poor white trash killed one another. Besides, I seem to recall that Adam could prove his whereabouts."

"A fishing trip."

"That part, I don't remember. And anyway, we were not thinking that she was murdered. Couldn't it have been a tramp, or a burglar or something?"

"The police think that's unlikely," Simon said. "The body was arranged so carefully, almost ritually."

"I have wondered so many times in my life what happened to

Anne. We grew up down the street from each other; we saw each other almost every day. We were what one used to call 'bosom friends.' At my wedding, I found myself looking for her. She was going to be my maid of honor. It's like when my baby sister died. No matter how many years go by, there's always a face missing at the dinner table."

"I know," Simon said. When he had accepted his Pulitzer, for just a second he had searched the audience for his parents' faces.

A horn sounded outside.

"Oh Lord," Mrs. Holland said. "That's my taxi! I have to leave for my bridge date."

She opened the door and called out to the driver.

"Five minutes, Joe!"

As she picked up her purse, Simon asked her if she could tell him anything about Lillie Blythe and a Sallie, or a Bessie.

"Lillie Blythe would be a good person for you to interview. Like lots of old people, her memory of the past is excellent. Her present existence is pitiful. I haven't seen her in years. Sallie was her sister. She's dead. Bessie—let's see. Oh! I know! She was Anne's maid. They were around the same age. Bessie's mother was the Bloodworth cook. Their last name was White, I believe. Bessie got married later, and I can't remember her married name. After old Mr. Bloodworth died, Bessie and her mother opened a restaurant on Hargett Street. They were wonderful cooks. Bessie's mother made a banana cake with caramel icing that was to die for. I pined for a piece many times after they left. And all I had to do was to go to their restaurant. I never did it because it was in the colored part of town. Isn't that stupid?"

Simon walked outside with her and opened the door to Joe's taxi. Joe looked nearly as old as Mrs. Holland, but his black face wasn't as wrinkled. His eyes were enormous behind lenses that were thick as the bottom of a Coke bottle.

"I'm running late, Joe," she said.

"You always running late, Mrs. Holland," Joe said. "You never could break off a conversation."

Mrs. Holland reached out of the taxi window and grasped Simon's hand tightly.

"If you find out anything about what happened to Anne, anything at all, would you please let me know?"

"Absolutely," Simon said.

"You-all talking about Miss Anne? I saw where somebody from the college found her body," Joe said. "My daddy worked for Mr. Bloodworth down at the depot."

"That's right!" Mrs. Holland said. "Joe, do you know what happened to Bessie White?"

"She married Ben Watling's boy Freddie; they farmed out near Apex when it was still country. I used to see her sometimes at the city market on a Saturday. Freddie died during the war and she married somebody else and moved back to Raleigh. They ran her momma's restaurant for a while after she died. I can't remember Bessie's second married name, though. His people were Methodist, and mine have always been Baptist, so we didn't run together."

"I think she's still alive," Simon said. "Flowers came to the funeral in her name. In fact, I think she might have been at the burial."

"Could be," Joe said. "The Whites were all long-lived. I can ask around, see if anyone knows what happened to her," Joe said. "If she's still alive, she'd be old. Almost ninety."

Simon gave him a card. "If you find out anything, will you call me?"

"Sure," Joe said. "Bessie sure could make lemon meringue pie. My wife got the recipe from her, but it never tasted the same."

SO, SIMON THOUGHT, ANNE BLOODWORTH WAS A BLUESTOCKING. She attended a four-year women's college and planned to graduate. She belonged to the League of Women Voters, just one of the women's clubs, leagues, and missionary societies that waged war on the considerable social ills at the early part of the twentieth century. By Anne's day, they had passed women's suffrage and Prohibition into law, and women had turned their attention to law and order, lynching, child labor, and prostitution. These women were a formidable lot. They didn't much like what America's preoccupation with business and moneymaking had done to society, and they intended to do something about it. It was a big job. Life was prim and prosperous on the surface but rotten with poverty, crime, and the double standard at its core. Al Capone was just one of the nasty products of the era. And Anne's father, Charles Bloodworth, railroad baron that he was, would have represented the Establishment in spades. Dinner-table conversation in the Bloodworth home must have been very lively.

Lillie Blythe's name had nagged at Simon ever since the florist had given it to him. He thought he'd heard of her before in another context. He stared at her address, and then he remembered. Her house was on Rose, a small two-block street buried deep in his own neighborhood. Once when he was collecting signatures for a zoning petition, he had made the mistake of knocking on her door. She had seemed pleasant enough at first, but her conversation revealed the frightening mental chaos of old age, and Simon had beat a hasty retreat as soon as he could. She attracted all the neighborhood speculation that elderly recluses usually do. Rumors about her abounded, especially among the kids, who carefully avoided walking by her house on their way home from school. She supposedly had a loaded gun in every room and would shoot anyone who set foot on her property. Raccoons, squirrels, and stray cats lived in her house, it was said, lured by the food and water she left out for them every day. She played opera all night—usually *Carmen*—on an ancient hi-fi. Every now and then, her neighbors would wonder if she was dead or alive. Just as they would be about ready to call the police to check on her, she would emerge from her house, carefully dressed in an outfit from the Eisenhower era, complete with demure hat and gloves, and go to Cameron Village to do her shopping. Sometimes she pulled a cart behind her to bring back her groceries, and sometimes she returned in a cab.

Simon did not look forward to interviewing Lillie Blythe, but he didn't see how he could avoid it. She might know something critical. After all, if she had been mentally competent enough to read about Anne Bloodworth's funeral in the newspaper and to order flowers, then she must have periods of lucidity. Maybe Simon could catch her in one.

Mrs. Blythe was pleasant enough to Simon when he called her on the telephone. He wasn't sure that she really understood the purpose of his visit, but she did invite him to come by that afternoon.

Rose Street was so short, it almost qualified as an alley. Narrow and winding, it hadn't been asphalted in years, and the original cobblestones showed in patches. If any place in Cameron Park was haunted, this was it. At first glance, the house looked like it belonged in a fairy tale; it sat on a huge wooded lot. Its roofline, front door, and window arches were rounded. The house was a wreck, though. The porch was piled with junk—old lumber, Victorian fretwork that must have fallen off over the years, window screens, and the rotten remains of some wicker porch furniture. The roof was decorated with fallen leaves and branches. An old paneled station wagon with broken windows and four flat tires was parked next to a Quonset hut. Once a garage, it had now fallen in.

The yard was a new-growth forest. Saplings and volunteers

sprouted all over the place. Grass would have been impossible under the layer of leaves that hadn't been raked in years. Kudzu had begun its inexorable work, growing over a side yard and covering a patio on its way to tear down the house. Simon could see the lumps on the patio where the wrought-iron furniture had been carpeted with the stuff. If the kudzu got any kind of a grip on the foundation, it would take blowtorches to stop it.

Mrs. Blythe had stacked piles of wood across the walkways to the house and painted them white to discourage trick-or-treaters many Halloweens ago. The barricades couldn't stop anyone serious about getting to the house, but they made it look fortified and forbidding.

Simon picked his way around the piles of wood and climbed up the crumbling stone steps. He rang the bell but didn't hear it sounding inside. So he knocked twice, loudly.

Lillie Blythe answered the door almost immediately. She wore a neat blue dress with a wide skirt and white Peter Pan collar and cuffs. The dress was faded and threadbare, although clean and ironed to perfection. She wore stockings, black pumps, and a pearl choker. Her blond hair showed an inch of gray at the roots and was styled like Doris Day's forty years ago. She could have stepped out of a Frigidaire advertisement in the pages of *Life* magazine in the 1950s, except maybe for the cigarette that dangled out of her mouth and the dowager's hump that caused her to lean forward slightly. Her skin was remarkably clear and unlined. She had obviously spent most of her life indoors.

Simon was so busy taking in her appearance that he didn't say anything.

"Yes?" Mrs. Blythe said. "Can I help you?"

Simon introduced himself. To his surprise, she remembered who he was.

"Please come in," she said, opening the door wide and gesturing into the dark interior. Simon entered with the same apprehension Pip must have felt when he was summoned by Miss Haversham. But instead of cobwebs, dirt, and decaying wedding cake, Simon saw boxes piled everywhere.

Mrs. Blythe's living room was stacked at least five feet high with boxes sealed with packing tape. From the labels, Simon could see that the boxes had originally held everything from Jack Daniel's to lamp shades. There was no clue what was packed in them. The living room was so crowded that it could be negotiated by only two narrow paths, one that disappeared down a central hallway and one that went into a dining room. From where he stood, he could see that the dining room table and floors were stacked with boxes, too. What he could see of the wallpaper and furniture had been aged to a uniform gray-brown, with an occasional splotch where a pattern had once been. The house was very clean. There were no cobwebs and decayed wedding cake here.

"Come into the kitchen," Mrs. Blythe said. "I'm afraid that there isn't room to sit in here. When one gets old, one does tend to collect things."

Yes indeed, thought Simon. He followed her down the path that led into the central hall, which was lit by a chandelier with just one functioning lightbulb. There were boxes here, too, stacked along the wall and lining the sides of the staircase to the second floor.

He definitely did not want to walk into her kitchen. But he did, and he saw the clues to what Mrs. Blythe stored in her boxes stacked on the kitchen table. Crocheted blankets, shawls, and pillows were piled on a big old kitchen table in a breakfast nook with a bay window. Mrs. Blythe must spend all of her time crocheting at this table, he thought. An old wing chair stood at its head, and near to hand were a lamp and baskets of yarn and other supplies. Simon reckoned if all the boxes in the house were full, she had been crocheting almost constantly for many, many years.

The kitchen was clean, too. There was no grime on the old stove or refrigerator, and the counters looked clean enough to eat on. The stove was a gas one. Simon didn't much like the idea of an open flame in that house.

Vines almost obscured the view from the large window near the kitchen table. One tendril had worked its way inside through the window frame, crept along the floor, and twisted around the leg of the wing chair. Simon could imagine that someday the vine would cover the chair and Mrs. Blythe, too. The image disturbed him deeply, and he had to fight the urge to leave and disregard whatever Mrs. Blythe might know about Anne Bloodworth.

She led him over to the table, where she sat down in the wing chair. The ivy twined perilously close to one foot. Simon took a straight chair next to her.

"Please excuse this mess," she said. "I'm afraid crocheting is my passion. This piece," she said, holding up a lovely, intricately patterned shawl, "is for my sister Sallie's girl. She's having a baby soon. She gets so cold when she's expecting."

It was at least eighty degrees outside, and Sallie's girl was probably a grandmother by now.

"It's very nice," Simon said.

"Thank you. Time does crawl by now that my boys have gone to college. And my husband travels so much in his work. I just have to do something to keep busy. All this," she said, gesturing around the table, "is for the church bazaar next month. My things always sell so well there."

Simon wondered if it would be possible to get her on the subject of Anne Bloodworth, and whether it would be productive if he did.

She picked up her hook, threaded yarn deftly over her fingers, and began to add a row to the shawl. Her hands moved easily and confidently.

"I know you're here to talk about Anne," she said. "I'm not surprised that she died violently. When you socialize outside your class, that's what happens."

Simon could not believe his luck. "Are you talking about her beau, Mrs. Blythe?"

"Of course. This is what this is all about, isn't it? She was in love with someone who was completely inappropriate for her. She couldn't even tell her friends who he was. Called him Mr. X—what nonsense. It's no wonder her father tried to hurry up her marriage to Adam. He was probably afraid she would make a fool of herself and never recover socially."

"Do you think she was trying to run away when she disappeared?"

"I suppose so. She was so influenced by those college people, and by all those suffragettes in the clubs she belonged to, she thought she could do anything. She gave no thought of her responsibility to her father. She was his only child and heir, and she had obligations. Adam Bloodworth was the perfect match for her.

They would have had money and social position. But she didn't care about that."

"Do you know who Mr. X was?"

"I would be the last person she would tell. But I do know she met him at college. She couldn't help but drop a few clues about him. All the other girls in our crowd thought it was thrilling to have a secret lover. His letters were so romantic, they said. I would say, 'What's the point if he can't afford to give her a ring?' "

"Couldn't he?"

"If he could afford to marry her, why didn't they get engaged like regular people? Because he didn't have any money or expectations, that's why. So they had to sneak around behind everyone's back. I used to tell her she watched too many Greta Garbo movies."

"What do you remember about her disappearance?"

"She had given the help the night off so they could go to some movie they wanted to see. It wasn't their regular night off, either. Anne didn't have any idea how to handle servants. She treated that maid of hers as if she were white. Anyway, the servants came back late, after Mr. Bloodworth and Anne were in bed, or so they thought. No one knew she was missing until the next morning. Then the neighborhood was in a complete uproar. I remember sitting by the front window of our sitting room, watching everyone look for her. I've never seen so many men and dogs in my life. Even the boys from State College and the volunteer fire department from Fuquay-Varina showed up to help search. It took two years for our camellias to recover from the trampling they got. Then, of course, everyone seemed to think she had left town. But she didn't get far after all, did she?"

"No, she didn't. Where was her cousin during all this?"

"Adam was supposedly fishing all night up at Whitaker Mill, and he showed up at the house hours after all the fuss started. I didn't believe it then, and I don't believe it now."

"You don't? Why not?"

"He was absolutely fastidious. He took germs very seriously. Anne told me that he washed his hands with carbolic every day. I cannot envision him baiting a hook."

"So you think he could have killed Anne?"

"I didn't say that. I think he didn't have a good alibi, so he made one up, quickly."

"Did other people accept it, or did most people think as you did?"

"Those niggers in Little Rock, they're out of line, don't you think?"

"Excuse me?"

"You let colored people go to school with white people and pretty soon they'll want to marry one another," she said. "It seems to me that if they use the same books, they're getting the same education. Separate but equal—that makes sense to me."

Now Simon understood why she dressed like June Cleaver. This woman was still living in the fifties.

"Imagine President Eisenhower sending in federal troops like that, to a sovereign state," Mrs. Blythe said. "The states have the right to run their own affairs. It says so in the Constitution. That's what we fought the Civil War over."

Somehow, Simon didn't think it would help to mention the fact that the South had lost the Civil War.

Simon tried to get Mrs. Blythe back on the track of Anne Bloodworth's disappearance in 1926, but he only managed to get the subject changed to *Sputnik* and the Russian menace.

Mrs. Blythe escorted Simon out of her decaying house, past the boxes of crochet destined for the church bazaar. Should she ever decide to deliver them, she would have to hire Mayflower to do it.

20

"I THINK YOU CAN TRUST WHAT SHE SAID ABOUT EVENTS IN THE distant past," Marcus said. "The present would be another story."

"She's not living in the present," Simon said. "She's somewhere in Eisenhower's second term. She kept talking about *Sputnik* and the Little Rock school crisis."

The two men were sitting in the faculty lounge of the history department, where Simon had gone to drink a Coke and unwind after his interview with Mrs. Blythe. There he had found Marcus grading blue books at the long table in the middle of the room.

"What would make her like that?" Simon asked. "Alzheimer's disease?"

"Without having talked to the woman," Marcus said, "I think there must be some other syndrome at work, rather than the common senile dementias of old age. I would guess that something psychologically traumatic happened to her, which caused her mind either to return to the 1950s or kept her from leaving them."

"So if she lives in a time before the event," Simon said, "she doesn't have to deal with it."

"That's right. Her mind protects itself. It's a coping mechanism. Not what most psychologists would consider a very healthy one, though."

"Whatever happened to her must have been terrible."

"Terrible for her. Not necessarily for someone else. She sounds like a person who is very rigid in her attitudes. Rigid people always have more trouble adapting to change than flexible ones."

"How do you think I'm doing?"

"Excellently. Your psychology is so normal that I could use you as a control when I'm training my rats."

"Be serious."

"I am serious. It's normal to be unhappy if something miserable happens to you. What's not normal is to get stuck permanently in 1957."

"Could anything be done for her?"

"I would never suggest it if she was my patient. Maybe thirty years ago, psychotherapy or medication would have served some purpose. Now it would just be cruel. If you were able to bring her out of the past, think how disoriented she would be. Leave her alone."

"But you do think her memory of 1926 is trustworthy?"

"As much as anyone's would be."

Simon bummed a yellow legal pad from Marcus and sat with him at the table, reconstructing his interviews with Mrs. Holland and Mrs. Blythe. Usually Simon took a tape recorder to interviews. He preferred to concentrate on reaching a rapport with his subjects rather than on taking notes. But Simon hadn't wanted to make these elderly ladies uncomfortable by arming himself with a tape recorder. Fortunately, he had an excellent memory, and he was able to reconstruct the conversations almost verbatim.

Simon taught a semester course in oral history every other year. He never got tired of watching his students' reactions when they participated in one of his favorite exercises. He would ask them to read several popular accounts of the Pearl Harbor crisis, then to interview eyewitnesses who lived in the community. One old gentleman, who was a retired civilian employee of the Navy Department, could be counted on to make such pungent and shocking observations about Franklin Roosevelt that his young interviewers were left stammering. Then Simon would ask them to write a paper about the differences between the printed sources and the oral testimony they had collected. This little experiment always separated the historians from the dilettantes. If they were historians, the students became addicted to diaries, letters, and old people, like chocoholics who had to have Ghirardelli every day. If they were dilettantes, they changed their major.

So it wasn't a surprise to Simon to find, after just two conversations with real people, that the newspaper accounts skimmed the surface of the story of Anne Bloodworth's disappearance. Now he wanted desperately to find Bessie. If she really had been Anne's maid, her knowledge could be crucial. There was still no answer to his newspaper ad, and Simon wished he'd offered a lot more than a hundred dollars for information about her.

When Simon finished his notes, he looked up at the clock and realized it was almost time for his class. Marcus had slipped away long ago, leaving him a brief note propped facing him on his empty Coke can. "No neurosis," it read, "is possible with a normal sex life (Freud)." Simon carefully folded the note in half and put it in his jacket pocket. Then he wrote a reply. "Nullum magnum ingenium sine mixtura dementiae fuit (Seneca)."* Grinning, Simon stuck the note in Marcus's mailbox on his way to class. Let him work on that one for a while.

*"There has not been any great talent without an element of madness."

21

SIMON, JULIA MCGLOUGHLAN, AND OTIS GATES MET AT THE neighborhood bar at 5:15 for a conference on the Bloodworth murder case. Simon had made copies of his interviews for Otis and Julia. They read the pages carefully while sipping on their beers, and Simon drank his and stared at the old black-and-white pictures of various North Carolina State football teams that covered the walls.

The bar had been built in a blessed time before ferns, piped in classical music, and pastel prints. A jukebox blasted out rock 'n' roll from the golden sixties and seventies. The knotty pine walls were stained the color of mahogany from years of cigarette smoke. The old-fashioned pinball machines rang, crashed, and lit up. Pool was played night and day in a side room, at five dollars a rack, no one under eighteen allowed. Burgers, buffalo wings, steak, spaghetti, fries, and iceberg lettuce salads were the only items on the menu. There was nothing at all trendy about the place. It was packed all the time.

Sergeant Gates took up an entire side of the booth and still oozed a little over the edges of his bench, while Simon and Julia sat together on the other side of the booth. Simon was glad to see Julia was drinking beer. He wouldn't have been devastated if she'd ordered white wine, though. No one was perfect.

Gates looked over his reading glasses at Simon.

"This is interesting," Gates said. "It tells us a lot about Anne Bloodworth. She was intelligent, independent, and had no intention of marrying her cousin. She was in love with someone else. Just about everyone in her circle thought she had run off with him when she disappeared."

"That may be why the hue and cry over her disappearance died down so quickly," said Julia. "No one was very worried about her."

"Exactly," Simon said. "In fact, there was probably a lot of effort spent on covering up. Bloodworth wouldn't have wanted anything about a lover in the newspaper. There was that one reference about rumors that she had run off with a lover, but Adam Bloodworth denied it."

"So her father makes a big show about looking for her by hiring Pinkertons and putting ads in newspapers all over the world, but he doesn't really care about her being found—because of the scandal," Julia said.

"He's protecting her from embarrassment," Simon said, "not to mention his own and his cousin's."

"You can bet, though, that if all these girls knew about Mr. X, lots of other people in the community did, too," Julia said. "Especially after she vanished. One of those girls was bound to have told her parents. After that, there would have been no stopping the rumor."

"Rumor is different from scandal," Simon said. "One is speculation and the other is often true."

"Only after they didn't hear from Anne in a few years did her friends begin to worry about her safety. And her father was already dead," Julia said. "He would have been the obvious person to reopen an investigation. But since he couldn't, we're the first people to do anything about it in seventy years."

"Hold on, you two," Otis said. "You're letting your imaginations run off with you. The only new fact that surfaces in these interviews is confirmation of the secret beau. Everything else is just guesswork. We come back to the same problem. The girl might have intended to run away. The suitcase certainly adds some weight to that conclusion. But she didn't. She was shot in the head and buried on her own property. We still have no idea who did it."

"I don't think so," Simon said. "I think all the evidence points right at Adam Bloodworth."

"How do you figure that?" Gates said.

"It's clear that it was common knowledge that Anne Bloodworth was not going to marry Adam Bloodworth, and that she had another beau."

"Agreed," Gates said.

"Adam stood to lose everything if he and Anne didn't get married. He had been brought into the family and the business for that express purpose. If Anne jilted him, what would happen to him? If she died or disappeared, he would be the obvious person for Charles Bloodworth to turn to. And that in the end is what happened. Seven years after Anne Bloodworth vanished, three years after her father died, Adam had her declared dead. He inherited everything."

"I think we've discussed motive before," Julia said. "Motive is meaningless without opportunity. You can't single out an individual for suspicion just because he may have benefited from someone's death. You've got to prove it through physical evidence, and we haven't got any."

"And declaring her dead seven years after she vanished would be a very reasonable thing to do," Gates said.

"I guess what really makes me think he's guilty is that his alibi is so lousy," Simon said. "Adam was supposedly out of the house, having gone fishing, but apparently he wasn't the fishing type. Did he go alone? If he didn't have any fishing buddies along with him, what kind of alibi is that?"

"And," Julia said, "the servants were not in the house, so they wouldn't have known where he was."

"What about the elder Bloodworth?" asked Gates. "He was home."

"He would cover up for Adam," Simon said.

"His daughter's murderer?" Gates said.

"No, of course not. He wouldn't have known that she had been murdered. He thought she'd run away. And he'd want to protect Adam, who was the only relative he had left."

"So if Adam killed Anne, he did it right there on the property, while Charles Bloodworth was in the house? And the old man didn't hear or see anything suspicious? That doesn't make any sense," Gates said. "And there's Peebles. He seems like a pretty good cop to me. His report is very matter-of-fact. He says Adam had an alibi. He repeats the fishing story. I don't think a cop would accept something like that without corroboration, even in 1926."

"Even if it came from two very rich and very influential men? I mean, if Charles Bloodworth said Adam was out of the house fishing, wouldn't Peebles automatically accept that?"

"Maybe," Gates said. "But I'm still inclined to think Adam's story was somehow verified, and we just don't know how yet. I don't think social status alone would save Bloodworth from suspicion in her disappearance, even at that time."

"And besides," Julia said, "the whole community knew about Mr. X. Even if the police ignored the love affair, the detective agency wouldn't."

"We'll never know what the agency uncovered," Simon said. "Those records are all lost. But speaking of Mr. X, any thoughts on him?"

"He must have been really unacceptable," Julia said, "if even Anne's girlfriends didn't know who he was. That implies that they wouldn't approve of him themselves."

"Yes, but in 1926 more men would be considered unacceptable for someone like Anne Bloodworth than would be today," Simon said. "The guy could have been completely respectable by our standards—like a doctor whose parents were farmers or immigrants, for instance."

"Mrs. Blythe said she met him through her college," Julia said, "but wasn't Kenan a school for women then?"

"They could have met at a lecture or a tea or who knows what all," Gates said. "Don't forget State College was right down the road. Unacceptable men were everywhere, I would think."

"So," Julia said, "Anne Bloodworth was running away with Mr. X; she was caught in the act by Adam Bloodworth, who shot her and buried her in the backyard. Then he fabricated an alibi, which was corroborated by Charles Bloodworth, who wanted to avoid a scandal. Then what did Mr. X do? Wander off and pine and write despondent poetry for the rest of his life? Why wouldn't he go to the police the next day and say Anne never made it to their rendezvous? Instead, he didn't say a word to anyone, just let the world think she was safe with him somewhere."

"Maybe Adam killed Mr. X, too," Simon said.

"Then where's his body? Or a missing person's report? Whoever he was, he wouldn't vanish without someone noticing," Julia said.

"Maybe she wasn't going to meet him; maybe she was just running away in general," Gates said.

"That's possible, I guess," Simon said. "But I think she was too smart to take off without a plan."

"The truth is," Gates said, "we don't have enough apples to make a pie. There are just too many missing pieces to this puzzle. The damn case is seventy years old. The principals are all dead, and the eyewitnesses who are still around think Elvis is alive."

"Seventy years is no time in historical terms, Otis," Simon said. "Your great-grandparents were slaves. My mother's family experienced the Holocaust. Those two facts alone affect the two of us profoundly every single day. Who knows what impact Anne Bloodworth's death had. Or what the impact of her existence would have been if she'd lived."

"I think I'm getting a headache," Gates said. "All I know is, I've got a forty-seven-page psychologist's report on an arson suspect in my briefcase, grass in my yard a foot tall, and tonight my two boys are playing ball at the same time seven fields apart. That's about all I can handle in one evening." Gates got up from the table to leave. "I don't want the two of you to think I'm not interested," he said. "I am. Murder is murder. But I need facts to proceed officially. Keep in touch."

Gates left, without allowing Simon to pick up his check.

"Am I imagining things, or did I irritate him just a little bit?"

"Your speech about the significance of history was just a tad preachy," Julia said. "But don't worry about it. You've just bonded with the victim. Gates knows that. He's done it himself."

"What?"

"Homicide investigators get cases that they just can't let go of," Julia said. "The victim is unidentified, or there is no evidence, or it leads nowhere. Long past when a normal person would give up, the cop carries that file around with him—for years and years. He's bonded with the victim. The search for justice has become personal. You have an interest in the past that attracts you to Anne Bloodworth's case. Sergeant Gates has enough in the present to keep him busy. But don't worry—if we can still turn up facts, he'll be interested."

Sergeant Gates had taken up a lot of the physical and psychological space in the booth, and after he left, Simon was conscious that he and Julia were alone and sitting very close together. He wondered if he should get up and move over to the other side. She didn't seem uncomfortable—with her spoon, she was carefully steering some spilled beer through the trough of a name cut deep into the wood of the booth. Simon was acutely aware that he had nothing at all to do. He envied Otis Gates.

"Would you like to stay and eat dinner?" Simon asked. Instantly, he could have kicked himself. His question probably insulted her by assuming she had no plans, either. He should have asked her out for the weekend instead.

"I would love to," she said. "But could we eat someplace else? I've had my quota of hamburgers this week."

Simon and Julia wound up two blocks away at the new Indian restaurant in town. The place was in an old gas station, but the food was wonderful.

Julia ordered aloo tikki and lamb kofta with naan and chutney. Simon had samosas and chicken curry. He ordered extra basmati rice, which he loved. He and Tessa used to go to the Indian supermarket and buy a five-pound bag every month. What was left of the last bag was still sitting in his pantry. He hadn't cooked any since she had gone.

Fortunately, Julia was a sharer rather than a hoarder, so they happily ate off each other's plates as well as their own, washing everything down with Indian beer.

"Time travel," Julia said while spearing a bite of samosa off his plate.

"What?" Simon said. He had to wait until she finished chewing for his answer.

"Science fiction," Julia said. "We were talking earlier about going back in time, and I was just thinking that there's a lot of literature based on time travel."

"H. G. Wells," Simon said.

"And Jules Verne. Not to mention *Star Trek* and the space-time continuum."

"The what?"

"You know, some space event happens and the *Enterprise* is catapulted back in time and the crew accidentally affects some little thing that would change the course of history so that they'd be slaves of the Romulans when they go back, so they have to fix it. And they don't have access to their technology and Spock or Data has to use a toaster and a curling iron to make the transporter work, and so on."

"That does sound familiar. Except I think the space-time continuum is from *Back to the Future.*"

"Same thing. But I thought science fiction was supposed to be based on elements of truth," she said. "Time travel is impossible."

"Oh, I don't know," Simon said. "You just have to think of time in a non-Western way. We think time is linear, a straight line that continues on forever. Instead, picture it as a river with eddies and whirlpools and curves and bends. Then you can imagine that the river doubles back on itself in places, and you can cross over a little spit of land and wind up in the past."

"I don't think my brain can quite grasp that," Julia said.

"Law school probably ruined you for real thought," Simon said.

"Probably so."

"Look at it this way. Suppose you had to clean up your grandmother's house after she died. You wind up in the attic, and you find a trunk full of letters and photographs and other stuff that you spend the whole afternoon reading. You become so engrossed that you lose yourself completely in her story, and you also lose complete track of time in the present. Haven't you spent time in the past, and lost some of your own present? Isn't that time travel?"

"That's stretching it, don't you think?"

"Let's suppose you find out something about your family you never knew before. Something astounding. Say you discover that your father wasn't really your father, but a stepfather. Your real father is in jail for murder or embezzlement or whatever. Wouldn't finding that out change your past and your future? You aren't who you thought you were, and what are you going to do about this father who's still alive? Visit him in prison at Christmas, or what?"

"Could I find one hundred shares of original Standard Oil common stock in that trunk and be rich beyond my wildest dreams, too?"

"Why not?"

"Then I'm all for it."

"Speaking of science fiction, have you seen *Independence Day*?"

"No, but I'd like to."

"Let's go," Simon said.

WHILE STANDING IN line at the theater for popcorn and sodas, Simon and Julia ran into Bobby Hinton and his date. She had one of those southern double names that started with Mary. She was dressed in preppy clothes, from her tortoiseshell headband right down to her Pappagallo flats. Bobby Hinton coordinated well in khaki slacks, polo shirt, and Bass Weejuns without socks. They both had the kind of tan one couldn't get if one worked for a living.

"Well, how's the investigation going?" Hinton asked.

"It's interesting," Simon said. "We're accumulating some contemporary information. Some of Anne Bloodworth's friends are still alive."

"You're kidding," Hinton said. "I wouldn't have thought of that. Is my illustrious ancestor still one of your suspects?"

"Absolutely," Simon said.

"He's got motive, but that's about it so far," Julia said. "Real facts are in short supply."

"Let me know what you find out," Hinton said. "I'd be interested. It's not everyone whose relative is part of a mysterious murder case."

"Did you learn anything new from your mother?" Simon asked.

"What? Oh, no. Just what I told you at the funeral," Bobby said.

Independence Day turned out to be a great date movie. Simon wasn't sure if thirty-year-old men were supposed to get off on holding hands, but, apart from the sexual frisson, he liked the warmth of contact with another human being again.

22

WHEN THEY GOT TO HIS PLACE, SIMON MADE ICED HAZELNUT coffee for them. Julia browsed his CD rack and put on Ray Charles. They went out to Simon's small porch and talked about music and books and movies while the ceiling fan turned slowly overhead and june bugs crashed into the porch screen.

Ray Charles's cover of "Still Crazy After All These Years" faded into silence.

Maybelline strolled proudly onto the porch and leapt into Julia's lap.

"Why do you call her Maybelline?" Julia asked.

"Because she can't be true. She'll go with anything with gonads."

Julia eyed the cat critically. "It looks to me like she's not having safe sex, either. She's pregnant."

"No kidding," Simon said. "That's great."

"You must still be feeling the effects of all that carbon monoxide," she said. "No one wants his cat to have kittens."

"I wouldn't mind."

"You could still have her fixed."

"I wouldn't dream of it." Maybelline had started to knead Julia's lap, so Simon picked her up and put her on the floor.

"Pick out some more music and I'll get us some more coffee," Simon said. "It's decaf."

Julia watched him walk into the kitchen. She could not even

imagine her two ex-fiancés, or any other man she had ever dated, taking care of kittens.

Julia was trying to decide between Lyle Lovett and Rubenstein playing Chopin when Simon walked up behind her and slipped his arms around her.

"Lyle Lovett," he said.

"Okay," she said.

She put the disc into its slot. As she pressed the play button, Simon pulled her closer to him and held her with crossed arms and rubbed her hips with his hands. She breathed deeply and covered his hands with hers. He had to tiptoe slightly to nuzzle her neck and kiss her hair. His hands moved up to cup her breasts. Julia pulled his hands away and turned to face him. She was steeled for anger and frustration, but she saw only disappointment in his face.

"I'm sorry," Simon said. "Did I offend you?"

"Not at all," she said. She tried to make her voice sound casual, as if she didn't know that Simon wanted to make love to her. "It's just time for me to go home. I have to work tomorrow."

"Okay," he said. "Let me get my keys."

It was just a few blocks to the parking lot of the bar where Julia had left her car. Simon opened her door and made sure she was in her own car with the doors locked. He didn't try to kiss her good night. Julia realized that she felt awful.

"I didn't hurt your feelings, did I?" she asked.

"Of course you did," Simon said. "But I take rejection extremely well. I'll even come back for more. Will you go out with me again?"

"Of course. I'd like to."

"Okay. I'll call you."

Simon watched Julia drive her noisy old BMW out of the parking lot and into the empty street. Damn, he thought, damn and damn and damn. He wondered how long he should wait before calling her again, or if she really wanted him to. She could just have been being polite. He could have sworn that he had felt a response when he touched her, though.

When Julia was out of Simon's sight, she put one hand on her face to see if it was as hot as she thought. She was still shocked. Her response to his touch was so profound that she had run away from him long before the situation had really called for flight. She hadn't even let him kiss her. Yes, Simon was cute, intelligent, funny, and gracious. And he hadn't acted like a thwarted child when she asked to go home. But sexy? No way. Too small, too bookish, too unambitious. But he had provoked a physical response in her that was beyond her understanding. She must have just been taken off guard. She really hadn't expected him to try to sleep with her so soon.

After the fiasco with the banker, Julia had decided that her next serious relationship would be *the one.* She wanted to get married and have kids, and she wasn't getting any younger. She didn't have time to waste on a man who wasn't appropriate, as Simon obviously wasn't. He was nice, though, and she didn't want to hurt him. She wondered if he would call her, and if he didn't, how she would go about making friends with him again. Compulsively, she counted all the streetlights on the right-hand side of the road until she arrived at her duplex. There were thirty-three, if you included one in the parking lot.

Simon walked back into his house. A few lights were on, the door to the porch was open, and the ceiling fan still turned the hot air slowly. Two iced coffees, both full, sat where Simon had left them on the table near the CD player. Lyle Lovett was singing "All My Love Is Gone." The house seemed a lot emptier than the absence of one person could explain.

Simon hummed along with Lyle while he cleaned up, turned off the lights, and locked the doors. He was disappointed but not unhappy. He knew that attraction is a more complicated issue for women than for men. Julia needed time to worry their relationship to death before she made any decisions about it. He was willing to wait and see what happened.

WHEN HE GOT TO WORK THE NEXT DAY, SIMON FOUND A MESSAGE on his desk from Joe Bagwell at the Safety Taxi Company. Simon called him immediately.

"I don't drive much myself anymore," Joe said. "I dispatch mostly. I just drive a few regulars, like Mrs. Holland. She and I talk about old times, mostly about how glad we are those old times are over. Anyway, my daughter and my sister's boys drive three cabs for me now."

"Is this a bad time?"

"There's not going to be a good time," Joe said. "Things are always wild around here. Listen, I found Bessie White, but I don't know if her people are going to let you talk to her."

"Don't say that. I've got to talk to her."

"She's real old, and she was very upset about the newspaper story. Finding the Bloodworth girl dead and everything. Her granddaughter is afraid she might have a heart attack. But the granddaughter said she'd talk to you herself. Her name is Cofield, Dr. Elizabeth Cofield. She's one of those doctors who read X rays. She works out at the medical center. Said she'd talk to you at her lunch break, but she was real frosty about the whole thing."

"Thanks, Joe," Simon said. "I really owe you. I'd about given up hope of finding her."

"Hey, you," Joe said. "Get your paws off that old tire. You'll get dirty and your mama'll fuss at me."

"What?"

"Not you. My granbaby. I'm keeping her for a while. Hold on.... Doris!" he shouted distantly. "I said Park Road, not Park Drive. You need to listen to me, girl. Sorry," Joe said to Simon.

Simon was thoroughly confused, so he started over.

"How did you find her?"

"It wasn't hard," Joe said. "I recollected that Bessie's second husband, the one named Cofield, was in the Fidelity Lodge with a cousin of mine. It was easy after that. She lives with the granddaughter I told you about, the doctor who reads X rays. In my day, you just had to go to one doctor to get patched up. Now you need one to see for this and one to see for that. No wonder everybody's got to have Blue Cross. Hey, Leroy," he yelled, "if you got that fare to the VA, go on out to Jimmy's Market and pick up Mrs. Wilson. She should be done with her shopping. If you keep her waiting, I'll hear about it at church."

Simon thanked Joe, then hung up and called the radiology department of the county medical center, where he was told that Dr. Cofield had her lunch break at one o'clock and he could meet her in her office.

THE BLUE-HAIRED volunteer at the information desk in the medical center directed him down two halls and two flights of stairs to a dingy basement corridor. The fluorescent lighting overhead buzzed and popped as he walked down the hall, looking at room numbers. When he finally found the office to which he had been directed, it was empty. It was clearly not Dr. Cofield's personal office, but a room where anyone on duty could come and write up notes or have a cup of coffee if they had the time. One desk sat askew in the middle of the room, surrounded by four plastic stackable chairs. It was covered with empty, stained Styrofoam cups and wadded-up balls of paper. The coffeepot sat in the corner, surrounded by spilled sugar, a creamer, and stained plastic spoons. The coffee smelled as if it had been made three days ago. The pot probably hadn't been cleaned in years. Simon sat on the one upholstered piece of furniture in the place—an orange vinyl sofa with rips in it. Dirty stuffing was coming out of it.

Dr. Elizabeth Cofield opened the door and walked in. She was the same woman Simon had seen at the cemetery with the elderly black woman he had hoped was Bessie. He had been right.

"Dr. Shaw," she said, extending her hand to him. "I understand that you want to talk to my grandmother."

"Yes," Simon began, shaking her hand. Her handshake was just barely civil. She withdrew her hand quickly and crossed her arms. She was a tall, good-looking woman, about forty, Simon guessed. Dressed in green scrubs, she had the omnipresent stethoscope around her neck and a radiation badge pinned to her pocket. She was all business, except for her long bright red fingernails and ruby earrings that hinted at the fashionable woman Simon had seen at the cemetery.

"I'm—"

"I know who you are," she said. "I saw your ad in the newspaper. Let me say right off that I understand you are a reputable historian with an interest in an historical incident that my grandmother was involved in, but I simply cannot allow you to interview her. She is quite elderly, and the stress could be dangerous."

"So I understand," Simon said. "Believe me when I say that I don't want to put your grandmother's health in any jeopardy."

"Granma cried her eyes out when she read that article in the newspaper—or rather, when the sitter read it to her. She was very close to the deceased at the time of her disappearance, and she had convinced herself that the young woman was alive and well somewhere in Europe, even when she didn't hear from her for years. She insisted on going to the cemetery when the body was buried, and she talked to herself and cried for two days afterward. I was very worried about her."

Simon didn't know how to deal with this. He certainly didn't want to cause any anguish, but he desperately wanted to talk to Bessie Cofield.

"All I can say," Simon said, spreading his hands open in front of him, "is that I need to talk to your grandmother to get any handle at all on who might have killed Anne Bloodworth. I'm not the only person interested," he continued. "The police are involved, too. This is a homicide. But I'd be deceiving you if I said that the police are investigating it actively. They don't think it can be solved. And I don't have any authority to question anybody myself. I'm just interested. The more people I talk to, the more interested I get."

Dr. Cofield had been expecting someone more difficult. She relaxed her arms a little and cocked her head to one side slightly, thinking.

"Let's sit down," she said. The two of them sat.

"You know how these old black people are," she said. "They're just as attached to the white families they served as they are to their own. My grandmother isn't any different. Anne's mother died when the girl was young, and my great-grandmother raised Anne and my grandmother together in that house. Granma loved Anne like a sister. She must have realized the woman was dead when she never heard from her again, but apparently she concocted an elaborate fantasy that protected her from facing that—all about how Anne probably went to Europe with her mysterious lover, got married, and lived happily ever after. It was such a shock to her to find out she'd been murdered. The sitter called me and I had to leave work and go home to her. She was still screaming and wailing when I got there. The sitter had read her the story in the paper—of course she had no idea of the relationship. I had to give Granma a sedative and put her to bed. She didn't get out of it until I told her about the funeral. Then she had to get up, get dressed in her best church clothes, and go out to the cemetery. I went with her, as you know. She is just beginning to recover. I don't want her to be upset again."

"You're the doctor," Simon said. "Whatever you say goes. I'm disappointed, but I certainly don't want to injure Mrs. Cofield."

Simon's conciliatory manner pleased Dr. Cofield. She studied him for a few seconds.

"Let's compromise," she said. "Would you object to me being present when you talk to my grandmother?"

"Absolutely not," Simon said. "I'd rather you were there, under the circumstances."

"All right," she said. "This is what we'll do. Are you free tonight? Around eight?"

"Certainly."

"Then plan to come. I get home around six. I'll bring it up to her.

If I have any second thoughts at all after I've spent a couple of hours with her, I'll call you to cancel the interview. Okay?"

"Okay," Simon said. "I'll be at home." He gave her his home number, and she drew him a map to her house on a notepad with the name of a drug company on it.

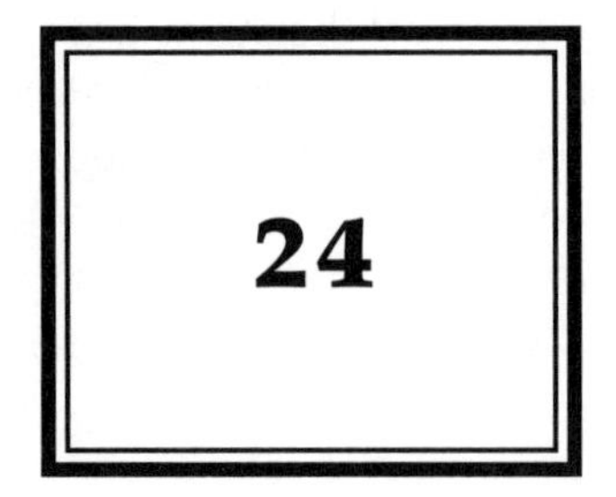

SIMON WAS INTENSELY RELIEVED TO GET BACK TO HIS OWN OFfice at the history department. His father's old desk and wooden file cabinets, the pictures on the walls, his mother's Oriental on the floor, and natural light flooding through the huge windows comforted him and welcomed him back to his own world. But Simon was not himself. He was obsessed with the upcoming interview with Bessie White Cofield. His students' faces, which he always memorized at the start of a semester, were blurry, and he resented their questions, which forced him to abandon his preoccupation with the Bloodworth murder to focus on them. After class, he left immediately instead of talking to his students. "Sorry," he said to one startled student as he fled down the back stairs, "I've got an appointment."

Simon's appointment was with his nerves. When he got home, he couldn't eat. He drank two Cokes and paced the floor while waiting for Dr. Cofield's call. It didn't come.

He left his house promptly at twenty minutes to eight and navigated with one hand clutching Dr. Cofield's map and the steering wheel of Marcus's Mustang and the other trying to knot a knit tie, a task made impossible by the wind blowing. He gave up and flung the tie in the backseat.

Dusk was just beginning to fall when he pulled up in front of the big house in the upper-class black part of town. As a southerner committed to integration, it saddened Simon that life in his hometown was still segregated. He had no idea why blacks and whites lived separately. He suspected that the black middle class couldn't explain why, either. But in towns and cities across the South, busing to achieve school integration had become a way of life instead of a temporary measure. The black community, instead of integrating existing neighborhoods, had built their own.

Dr. Cofield's house was a brick colonial on a quiet shady street. Her yard was perfectly landscaped. A black BMW sedan sat in the driveway. The porch light was on, and interior light gleamed through the screened-in front door.

When Dr. Cofield came to the door, she looked friendlier than she had at the hospital. She was dressed in African-style pants and tunic and wore hoop earrings. Her hair, which had been covered by a hat at the funeral and by a surgical cap at the hospital, was cut in a short Afro. She welcomed Simon warmly and offered him a glass of wine, which he declined.

"This time of night, Granma and I always have a snifter of something," she said, smiling, "for medicinal purposes only." She led Simon through the very modern living room and well-appointed kitchen. The whole house was done in white and neutral colors—white rugs, wheat furniture, white walls, and black accents. Maybelline would make short work of this place, he thought. The kitchen looked good enough to be featured in a magazine, but Simon doubted anyone really cooked there much. It was too clean. There was no spaghetti sauce on the ceiling.

Dr. Cofield stood with Simon for a few seconds in front of a door that seemed to lead to the garage. "Granma seems okay," she said. "She's very calm about talking to you and pleased that she might be able to help. But please try not to agitate her."

Simon promised to be considerate, and Dr. Cofield opened the door. The garage had been converted to a room for the old woman. Bessie White Cofield was sitting in an ancient recliner in the middle of the room, drinking clear liquid out of a jelly glass. She was a very elderly person and had faded mocha skin. Her white hair was pulled back in a bun.

"Good evening, Dr. Shaw," she said. She raised her glass toward her granddaughter. "Did you offer him some, Lizzie?"

"I offered him wine, Granma. Not that stuff you drink. Granma drinks white lightnin'," she said to Simon. "Not much, but regularly. I don't know who her supplier is. He comes when I'm at work. It would probably blind you or me, but she seems to be immune to it."

"I can hear you, Lizzie, you know."

"I know that, Granma. I'm not trying to keep you from listening."

Mrs. Cofield drained her glass and lit what looked like a hand-rolled cigarette. The smell of unprocessed, unfiltered, unmentholated tobacco filled the air. It reminded Simon of the smell of the country store in Boone where he and his parents used to go to buy apples and cider when he was a boy.

Mrs. Cofield's domain couldn't have been less like the main house. In addition to the recliner, there was an old rocking chair, an iron bedstead mounded with quilts and down pillows, several hand-hooked rugs, and dozens of old family pictures crammed onto every available wall space and on every surface. A picture of a black Jesus with very blue eyes looking skyward hung over the bed. A new TV sat on a big pine dresser; its remote was taped to the arm of the recliner with duct tape.

Mrs. Cofield noticed him taking in the room.

"I live here with Elizabeth because she let me keep my own things," she said. "All the others wanted to give my stuff to Goodwill and buy me a new bedroom suite at Rhodes Furniture. What a waste of good money that would be. I probably won't live another six months."

"Nuts," her granddaughter said. "You'll make a hundred easy."

"She also lets me smoke and drink," Mrs. Cofield said. "My other granbabies wanted me to give it up. One of them even said I shouldn't eat fried chicken no more. Lizzie lets me eat anything I want."

"When I'm her age, I plan to smoke, drink, and eat fried chicken, too," Dr. Cofield said.

"What worse could happen to me than already has?" Mrs. Cofield asked. "I buried two husbands and two children. I'm going to join them, this year or next year—what difference does it make? Except," she said, "I never thought I'd hear that Anne died." Her eyes filled with tears. She dabbed at them with her handkerchief.

Simon saw an expression of disgust cross Dr. Cofield's face. Her grandmother saw it, too.

"Don't you roll your eyes at me, missy! You don't know what it was like. My granddaughter, and most of the rest of her generation," the old woman said to Simon, "they think we old darkies are much too attached to our massas."

"I'm sorry, Granma," Dr. Cofield said. "It's hard for me to swallow all this affection for a family who paid you and your mother five dollars a week to run the house and raise a child but who made you use the toilet in the basement."

"And who paid my fees at the colored school and the doctor when we were sick and Mr. Charles left us five thousand dollars in his will so we could open a restaurant after he was gone," Mrs. Cofield said. "It was that restaurant that started this family on the path that took you to medical school."

"This is an old argument, Granma, and neither one of us is ever going to change our opinion, so let's just let Dr. Shaw ask his questions."

"It's all right with me," the old woman said. "You started it." She turned to Simon. "What do you want to know?"

"Tell me about that night," Simon said. "The night Anne disappeared."

"I remember it as if it were yesterday," she said. "It was a Friday night. Mama and I were pining to see *Ben Hur,* so Anne gave us the night off and the money to go. It was wonderful. Afterward we went on down to the City Market to hear Old Man Moe Watson and his string band play. Well, when we got home, the house was quiet. Mr. Bloodworth and Anne were in bed, we assumed. Next morning, Anne didn't come downstairs at eight, like she usually did. She didn't come down and she didn't come down. So at ten, I went up to her room with a cup of tea. It was empty, and her bed hadn't been slept in. At first, I was terrified, but then I realized what had happened. She had sent us away so that she could sneak out of the house and run off with her beau."

"Mr. X," Simon said. "What did you do?"

"Well, I didn't know what to do. In the end, I just went down to Mr. Bloodworth's study and told him Anne hadn't spent the night in the house. Then I asked if maybe she'd gone to a friend's and forgotten to tell me and Mama? Well, he went crazy, just crazy. He said he had kissed her good night at ten o'clock and that she had been in her nightdress—which I wasn't sure I believed."

"Why not?"

"Before going to bed, Mr. Bloodworth was in the habit of drinking a lot of whiskey in his study. I would take the decanter in to him at nine o'clock and just leave it. On Friday and Saturday nights, when he didn't have to go to work the next day, he would drink a lot more. Sometimes he would fall asleep in his chair and Anne and I would have a dickens of a time getting him up to his room. Sometimes we just left him there. He was usually out like a light before the rest of us went to bed. I figured he said that about saying good night to her so he wouldn't have to admit he was dead drunk when she disappeared."

"So Anne knew that on that Friday night her father would be indisposed and that you and your mother would be at the movies, so she could leave the house and meet Mr. X without anybody realizing it."

"When I look back on it, I see it so clear," Mrs. Cofield said. "Two days before that, Anne said she wanted to get out her summer clothes. So we did that and aired them and everything. She had them all laid out on her bed. And she cleaned out her dresser and desk drawers. Said she was spring cleaning. She was fixing to take off."

"Did you tell the police that?"

"No. I didn't tell the police nothing. I wanted to help her." Tears started to drip down her face. "I should have told them," she said. "I didn't know she'd been murdered." She wept quietly for a few minutes.

"Granma," her granddaughter said. "Maybe Dr. Shaw should go now."

"No," she answered. "I want to answer all his questions—every one, tonight. I'm all right." She wiped her eyes again. "There," she said, tucking the handkerchief into her sleeve. "Fire away," she said to Simon.

"I'm interested in Adam Bloodworth," Simon said. "It seems to me he had the best motive to do away with Anne. If she didn't marry him, he would lose the business, wouldn't he? But according to the police report, he was out of the house—fishing. Do you know if there was any proof of that? Was anybody with him?"

Mrs. Cofield chortled. She raised her handkerchief to her face, but her eyes smiled behind it. "That's right, honey, fishing. And I reckon some of the best people in town was with him." She laughed out loud.

"I don't understand."

She looked at him intently, then looked at her granddaughter, then back at Simon. "Oh Lord!" she said. "Thank you for letting me see this day!" She broke out into peals of laughter, rocking back and forth in her chair, until she began to cough, and her granddaughter had to slap her on her back.

"I don't understand this, either," Dr. Cofield said to Simon.

Mrs. Cofield took a long swig of her drink and gasped. "Oh Lord," she said again.

"What is it, Granma?" Dr. Cofield said.

"Gone fishing! Oh Lord, save me! I guess you children wouldn't know, life has changed so much! Fishing, was . . . well, what do you call a word that you use when you really mean something else?"

"A euphemism?" Simon asked.

"Then," Mrs. Cofield said, "*gone fishing* was a euphemism."

"For what?" Simon asked desperately.

"Adam Bloodworth spent every Friday night at Ruby Hart's bawdy house. It was down on Hillsborough Street, in the bottom, between State College and Meredith College. He would drink smooth liquor, play poker, and stay the whole night. This was when sex wasn't free and Prohibition was on."

Simon was stunned. "You're sure about this?"

"Yessir. One of my cousins was Miss Ruby's houseman. He was the one who routed out Mr. Adam, and the police chief, when the patrolman came to tell them about Anne's disappearance. He was there all night, him and a lot of other leading citizens."

Simon's carefully constructed but largely hypothetical case against Adam Bloodworth collapsed all around him.

"Well," he said. "I guess that eliminates Adam Bloodworth."

"It wasn't him. He drove her away, but he didn't kill her."

Simon was so taken aback that he couldn't think. He had hoped that Mrs. Cofield would help him poke holes in Bloodworth's weak alibi, not substantiate a better one.

"I confess I don't know where to go from here," Simon said.

"How about Mr. X?" Dr. Cofield said.

"Do you know who he was?" Simon asked the old woman, who was still chuckling quietly over this misunderstanding.

"No," she said. "Anne never told me. That worried me. She knew that I could be trusted not to tell anyone. I figured that meant she knew I would disapprove of him. I once asked her point-blank if he was married. She said absolutely not. Then she laughed and said to trust her. Used to worry me sick."

"Did you want her to give him up and marry Adam Bloodworth?"

"Lord no, honey. What kind of husband would a man like that make? Go to a whorehouse one night and to his wife the next, and not even try to hide it? She did accidentally let slip that the man taught her at college. She also used to go down to the Manhattan Lunch Counter for lunch every single Saturday, rain or shine. She said she was meeting friends. But one day, I told her I knew it was him. She said yes, he was in the neighborhood 'cause he went to church on Saturdays and met her there afterward. She said to figure that out. I said that was easy—he had to be a Seventh-Day Adventist or a Pentecostal or something like that. She didn't say yes or no. Just went off. It was the next week that she went away."

"Can you think of anyone at all who might have wanted to do her harm?"

"No. Like you said, Adam Bloodworth might have been worried about what would happen to him if he and Anne didn't get married. But Mr. Bloodworth would probably have kept him on. He knew the business, and Anne sure wasn't going to run it. You know what I think? I think she was running away late at night and ran into a bad type. There weren't any shelters or welfare back then to keep people off the streets."

The wandering-tramp theory again, Simon thought. These wandering tramps sure are convenient. He didn't tell her about the careful way Anne's body had been buried, or that her jewelry hadn't been disturbed. He didn't want to upset Mrs. Cofield any more than she already was.

"How did you find me, anyway?" Mrs. Cofield asked.

"Through Joe Bagwell."

"Oh, him. At the cab company."

"That's right. He was picking up Mrs. Holland the day I interviewed her about Anne. He said he might be able to track you down for me, and he did."

"Blanche Holland is a lovely lady," Mrs. Cofield said. "She was that way as a child."

"She has fond memories of you, too. And of your mother's banana cake with caramel icing. She would love to have the recipe."

"Wouldn't everybody," Dr. Cofield said. "I've got the recipe, and I can't make it taste the same. Well, I shouldn't say I've got the actual recipe. It's not written down anywhere. I used to watch Granma make it and I'd try to measure all her handfuls and pinches and such. It just doesn't turn out right."

"I keep telling you, baby," Mrs. Cofield said. "The sugar don't caramelize right on an electric. You've got to have a woodstove to get it to do right."

"The source of the heat should have absolutely nothing to do with it," Dr. Cofield said. "I think you're hiding some secret ingredient from me just to frustrate me. I hope that before you die you take pity on me and remember that I took you in when you got old and let me know what it is."

"Honey, I ain't hiding anything from you. When you get as old as me," Mrs. Cofield said, "you learn that some things, when they're gone, they're gone forever. They don't never come back."

She turned her attention to Simon again.

"Who else have you talked to?" she asked.

"Lillie Blythe," Simon said.

"She's been three bricks short of a load for years," Mrs. Cofield said. "I'd have thought her boys would have locked her up by now."

"She seems to be taking care of herself okay," Simon said. "Except she's got a houseful of crochet."

"She was never a nice person. Not a lady, if you know what I mean."

"A lady," Dr. Cofield said, "says *please* on a hot day when she sends you for a glass of lemonade and a fan."

"What's wrong with that?" Mrs. Cofield said. She turned back to Simon.

"She went crazy in around 1957, when she found out her husband had another family. He was the president of the bank, the one that used to be downtown—where there's a parking lot now. He had a mulatto woman named Helen on the side. Gave her a house and everything. Had three kids. Anyway, when Mrs. Blythe found out, she told him to choose. He chose Helen and went to live with her. After a year or so, the boys went there, too. Had to, to get a square meal and clean clothes. Lillie Blythe hardly left the house after that. Told everyone her husband was away on business and her boys were at college."

"She still does," Simon said.

By Simon's watch, it was almost ten o'clock. He knew he should be going. He started to take his leave, but the old woman stopped him.

"I got something else to tell you," she said. "I don't know if it means anything. But it always struck me."

"What?"

"After old Mr. Bloodworth died—it would be about four years after Anne ran away . . . Well, we all thought she had run away. A lot of the colored help from the neighborhood went to the funeral, and afterward they came over to the house to help Mama and me with the food and the company. We got to talking in the kitchen. We were wondering if Anne would come home soon. After all, she stood to get everything. Well, we were recollecting the day, and Myra Washington told me a story I hadn't heard before. Her son, George, was a doctor—one of three colored doctors in town. She said the morning Anne disappeared, real early—it was still dark—a white man rousted George out of bed. He had a gunshot wound in the shoulder. He was lucky. The bullet had missed the bone and passed right through. There wasn't much blood. George patched him up and gave him some laudanum. George told his mama that the man looked funny. He was young and middling, but he dressed old. His hair was real dark and longish. And he had a funny hat. The man had a suitcase with him, and he said he was going up north and wasn't ever coming back. When I read about Anne being shot, I thought of that story Myra told me."

"Dr. Washington didn't tell the police about this?"

"Of course not. Colored doctors made most of their cash money off white people in trouble. You know, fights, abortions, and such. The whole idea was that the colored doctors kept their mouths shut about such things. This man who came to George was hiding something, and he was getting out of town fast."

"You think he was Mr. X?"

"I don't know," Mrs. Cofield said. "It struck me, that's all."

EARLY MONDAY MORNING, SIMON APPEARED HUMBLY AT SERGeant Gates's cubicle with doughnuts, muffins, and coffee. The sergeant was buried in his PC, and Simon had to clear his throat to get his attention.

Gates looked at Simon's offering suspiciously.

"What do you want from me?" he asked.

"This is not a bribe," Simon said. "It's penance."

"What for?"

"You were right. Adam Bloodworth had a real alibi. He was covering up with the fishing story."

"Wait just a minute," Gates said, reaching for the phone. "I want Julia to hear this."

After Julia joined them, Simon told the story of his meeting with Mrs. Bessie Cofield.

"*Gone fishing,*" Simon said, "was apparently an instantly recognized euphemism for visiting a brothel. That's where Bloodworth was the night Anne had her 'misadventure.' Apparently, half the male population of the town was there to corroborate it, too."

"I'm sure their women were having a good time, putting up green beans or whatever," Julia said.

"Beating rugs," Gates said. "And making the butter."

"Don't forget darning socks," Simon said. "It was the least a good wife could do, since her husband made the living and everything."

"Suckering tobacco," Gates said. "Trying to get two old mules to plow a straight line. Curing tobacco. Lifting bales. Toting barges."

"You two are not getting to me," Julia said, taking another muffin. "I'm just glad I wasn't around in 1926."

"Me, too," Gates said. "If I had been, I would have been looking forward to a summer of picking tobacco."

"I would have been peering out of dirty lace curtains in Irish town somewhere with a bunch of red-haired rug rats hanging on to me and another one on the way. What about you?" she said to Simon.

"I'd have been either walking up the holler with a shotgun looking for squirrels for breakfast or running a pawnshop in Romania," Simon said. "But wherever we were, none of us could get antibiotics."

"This is great fun," Gates said. "But I have work to do."

"Don't you want to hear about Mr. X?"

"Who—Anne's lover? You don't know who he was, do you?" Julia asked.

Simon told them the rest of what he had learned from Bessie Cofield.

"You're still up a creek without a paddle, son," Gates said. "Even if you do identify this guy, there's nothing to say he was the man who visited the doctor or killed Anne Bloodworth."

"I know," Simon said. "But I just can't let go of it. Now that I have some clues, I've got to try to find out who Mr. X was."

Julia walked Simon to the front door of the Public Safety Center on her way back to her office.

"I guess I've thoroughly put off the sergeant," he said. "He looked like he thought I was crazier than ever."

"Don't you believe it," Julia said. "He's interested."

"He didn't look interested. He looked bored."

"Nuts," Julia said. "He took notes, didn't he? He always does that when he's serious about something. He just doesn't want to let on."

She watched Simon walked down the street until he turned the corner. If only he'd apply his energy and brains toward something worthwhile, she thought, he might accomplish something with his life.

26

SIMON WALKED ACROSS THE CAMPUS TO THE HISTORY DEPARTment, where he wanted to put in an appearance and let Judy know he would be at the library if needed. That wasn't likely, but he hoped everyone would think he was working on something having to do with his job.

It was a beautiful day. A half a dozen seagulls, having flown inland from the coast during a storm, were wheeling above the Dumpsters outside the cafeteria. Simon was watching them and wondering how they would get home when he tripped over Bobby Hinton's legs. He was leaning up against a tree, wearing nothing but cutoffs, eating an egg biscuit and drinking a cup of coffee out of a Styrofoam cup.

Hinton pulled off the earphones to his Walkman before he spoke to Simon. "Hey there," Hinton said. "I was trying to catch some early rays. I'm sorry my legs got in your way." He looked up at Simon lazily.

Simon was irritated. Why didn't the kid go on home, or to the beach, or wherever rich kids went in the summer? Simon disliked it when ex-students hung around the campus, unable to let go of college life and move on. In Simon's experience, that often led to trouble. It was usually such people who sold drugs, brought hard booze to parties, and generally fomented problems out of boredom.

"You're not enrolled in summer school, are you?" Simon asked.

"No."

"Working here?"

"You trying to throw me off campus?"

"No. But I could," Simon said. "You're trespassing. And this isn't your backyard. It's the front lawn of a college. We'd appreciate it if you sunbathed somewhere else."

"Oh, right," Hinton said. He got to his feet and collected his stuff. "I wasn't thinking. Making a bad impression on visitors and like that. I'm just so fond of the old place that I think of it as home."

Please don't, Simon thought.

"By the way," Hinton said, "how's the investigation going?"

Simon didn't want to share his work on the Bloodworth case with this twerp.

"Fine," Simon said.

Hinton put on his T-shirt and walked off toward the side parking lot. Simon watched him climb into a Mercedes convertible. Of course. What else would he drive? And naturally, Simon had to pick up his discarded biscuit wrapper and throw it in the nearest trash bin.

After Simon gave his information to Judy, he walked down the hall toward the faculty lounge to see who was in and find out what was going on. But Alex Andrus walked out of his office and stopped him. The muscles in Simon's neck and shoulders tensed as his body instinctively prepared for conflict.

But Alex was decent. In fact, he was positively warm. He very quietly asked Simon if he would lead a module on primary research in his section of World History in the fall. Simon said of course he would. They chatted for a minute about the reenactment of a Civil War battle Andrus had attended in Virginia over the weekend. Simon was astounded at the change in him. Compared with Alex's usual confrontational attitude, this was almost lethargic. Then he noticed Andrus's eyes. In a hallway that was flooded with midmorning light from huge windows, Andrus's pupils were fully dilated. Pharmaceuticals. Poor bastard, Simon thought.

Andrus went back into his office and Simon proceeded to the coffeepot, where he found Marcus Clegg and David Morgan filling up.

"How's my Mustang?" Marcus asked.

"It's fine, thank you," Simon said. "I feel a little self-conscious in it—as if I should be cruising around the high school in shades and a white T-shirt with cigarettes rolled up in my sleeve."

Morgan was ladling sugar into his cup. He delivered several guest lectures in the department of history every year, so he visited the library and the lounge whenever he wanted to.

"Is the IHOP closed today, or what?" Simon asked him.

"It's the end of the month and I'm broke, and I was hoping you'd have doughnuts," Morgan said.

"No doughnuts or muffins or anything else since Professor Thayer complained to Walker Jones that it didn't look professional for us to be eating in here. Also the crumbs attract mice," Marcus said.

"You're joking," Simon said.

"I am not. God, I hope she doesn't get the chair when Walker leaves. She'll probably install a time clock. I don't think I can stand it."

"It's inevitable, isn't it?" Simon asked.

"No, it's not. Not if the faculty is completely opposed."

"The college needs a woman chair," Simon said.

"By the time Walker retires—say in three years—Janna Ornstein will be chair of English for sure, and Pat Brock will have biology if Nigel goes back to England. Which he probably will. His parents aren't well."

"Maybe you can talk Walker out of leaving," Morgan said. "He's only fifty-nine."

"He's got two volumes left of his Hamilton biography," Simon said, "and he thinks he can't finish it unless he retires, or at least goes emeritus. He's probably right."

Simon thought that if the university wanted another chair than Vera Thayer, it would have to look outside the department. Traditionally, the senior tenured faculty member of any department could have the chair if he or she wished. Otherwise, the infighting in the department would be horrific. In the past, Kenan didn't have the prestige to attract an already-successful scholar—it had to grow its own. But Simon thought this had changed, and that bringing in someone from outside would relieve the insularity and inbreeding that was characteristic of a small college.

"Speaking of the anal-retentive personality, I saw you talking with Alex," Marcus said. "He seems very subdued to me."

"Yeah," David said. "I thought he was the guy who was supposed to be so aggressive."

"I think he's taking tranquilizers," Simon said. "He must be really scared of losing his job."

Judy Smith walked in the room and dropped the department's newspapers on the coffee table.

"Judy," Marcus said, "Simon thinks Alex is on tranks. Is he?"

"He's taking something," she said. "I saw a prescription bottle in his office. Diazepam, whatever that is."

"Valium," Marcus said. "Hallelujah. I hope he takes it for the rest of his life."

Simon didn't see any point in kicking Alex when he was down. So he changed the subject. While they drank their coffees, he brought the other two men up-to-date on his findings on the Bloodworth case.

"So now," Marcus said, "now you're going to go to the library and try to find out who Mr. X is. You'll probably get only a circumstantial identification, if that. Then what?"

"I don't know," Simon said. "I guess I'm hoping that I'll find out something that will lead me somewhere else."

"You can't fool me," Marcus said. "I think you're just prolonging your association with that redheaded policewoman."

"Her hair is auburn, and she's not a policewoman. She's an attorney," Simon said.

"Even better. She makes her own money. What are you waiting for?"

"The light to change," Simon said. "It's stuck on yellow."

"What do you think?" asked Marcus after he was sure that Simon was most of the way down the hall on his way out of the building.

"About what?" Morgan answered.

"About Simon and this murder. I mean, it seems to be therapeutic. It's gotten his mind off his troubles and into normal mode again. But I'm concerned he might get depressed again if all this comes to a dead end."

"I don't think we have to worry about that," Morgan said.

"Why not?"

"I think he's going to find out who killed the girl."

ONCE AT THE LIBRARY, SIMON HAD REQUESTED AND RECEIVED a copy of the Kenan Institute annual for 1926.

He leafed through it. To the unschooled, his search would seem like a complete waste of time. But Kenan had been a women's school in 1926. The few men associated with it were probably administrators or teachers. Anne Bloodworth had told her maid that she had met Mr. X at the college. If he was one of these administrators or teachers, his picture should be in the annual. It was as simple as that.

Most of the men in the pages were middle-age, with gray hair and handlebar mustaches. A lot of them were ministers.

Then, on page 37, among the part-time instructors, Simon found him. The dark-haired young man looked directly at Simon out of his photograph. He couldn't have been more than twenty-five. His name was Joseph Weinstein. The few clues that Simon had already collected about his identity coalesced somewhere on the right side of his brain. Weinstein dressed like an old man, he wore a funny hat, he went to church on Saturday, and the features that looked out at Simon resembled his own. The guy was Jewish. Simon leaned back in his chair and whistled. Wow. Double wow. That would really have caused society to sit up and take notice in 1926. No wonder Anne hadn't even told her maid her lover's identity. Simon imagined that Weinstein's family wouldn't have been thrilled with Anne Bloodworth, either. Simon had been reminded many times by his maternal relatives that official Jewishness was handed down in the female line. If this Weinstein guy was Mr. X and he married a Gentile, his family might lose their children to the faith. A love affair between these two would have been a scandal.

Simon once again consulted the 1926 city directory. He found what he was looking for right away. Temple Beth Or was at 612 Hillsborough Street—about three blocks from Anne Bloodworth's house and four from the Manhattan lunch counter. They would have met there after services on Saturdays. Weinstein probably didn't drive on the Sabbath, so wherever they met would have needed to be within walking distance. During the week, they would have seen each other on campus.

And in the lower left-hand corner of the right page, among the other business ads, was a rectangle that read "The Weinstein Brothers: Everything in Junk."

IT WAS NOISY outside on the sidewalk where Simon stood next to the public telephone and dialed Blanche Holland's number because he couldn't wait to get home and call.

"About Mr. X," he began.

"I've been thinking and thinking," she said, "and I just have no idea."

"Could it have been Joseph Weinstein?" Simon asked.

"Who? Oh, Joe Weinstein, the economics and history instructor. I remember him. He was so attractive, in an exotic sort of way, and younger than the other men on campus."

"Could he have been Mr. X?"

"Goodness. Goodness gracious."

"Exactly."

"My word. That would have created an uproar."

"But could he have been Anne's beau?"

There was a long silence on the other end of the phone, and for a minute, Simon was afraid they had been cut off.

"Yes," she said. "Yes. I don't know why I didn't think of it. It answers so many questions."

"Do you know anything about him? His family? What happened to him after Anne disappeared?"

"No. Not really. We would not have encountered each other away from college. He was Jewish, you see. And his father and uncle were junk dealers."

"I know," Simon said.

"I do remember . . ." she said.

"What?"

"I do remember that he wasn't at the college after Anne dis . . . died. I understood that he was teaching somewhere up north. New York City, I think. Do you think that he killed Anne?"

"I have no idea," Simon said. "I just know now that Adam Bloodworth didn't." He explained what he had learned about the younger Bloodworth's alibi.

"One can be so stupid," Mrs. Holland said, "about the weaknesses of human beings."

SIMON GOT HOME AT TWO O'CLOCK, THIRSTY AND STARVING. HE had just enough time to eat something and get to the campus, where he needed to spend an hour figuring out what to say during his four o'clock lecture. Work was definitely interfering with his detecting. Or was it the other way around?

Simon opened his refrigerator door and took out some leftover chicken and rolls and a half-liter bottle of Coke with a screw-off cap that he had been working on for a day or so. There were only a couple of inches left. He swigged about half of it straight from the bottle, then began to tear the chicken apart with his fingers. Maybelline stirred herself from a puddle of sunlight and jumped onto the table. He gave her some scraps of his chicken. If she was preggers, she probably needed the protein. He wondered if his friend Mark Mitchell would trade more potato salad for some legwork on Joseph Weinstein at the New York Public Library. Probably not. Simon thought he could probably fly up between summer sessions and do the research himself. Maybe Julia could go, too. They could see some shows and he could spend some time with his family.

Simon stood up and felt a dizziness come over him. He shook his head, but the dizziness remained. Nausea crept up his throat, and he had to swallow to contain it. Damn it, he thought, I don't have time to be sick right now. He sat down and put his head in his hands, while a chill started in his groin and worked its way up his back and into his shoulders. He looked at the chicken. He had cooked and eaten it last night with no problem. It couldn't have gone bad overnight. He put his head down onto the kitchen table and began to fall asleep, but Maybelline woke him when she rubbed up against his face.

Simon took the cold Coke bottle and pressed it up against his face, which felt hot and flushed. I'm losing consciousness, he thought. I've got to do something. Call an ambulance. He carefully used his hands to push himself up from the table and then reached for his cordless phone. When he did, he saw his three prescription bottles lined up on the kitchen counter where he had left them. All three were empty.

Thanks to the new enhanced 911 system, the emergency dispatcher on the other end of the telephone knew Simon's address, even though he couldn't speak by the time she answered. Within just a few minutes, two paramedics and a policeman walked into his house and found Simon curled into a fetal position on his kitchen floor, deeply unconscious.

"This guy looks familiar. Didn't we pull him out of a car a few days ago, just around the corner?" the first paramedic asked.

"Yeah," the second said. "And this time, he left a note." He pulled the scrap of paper out of Simon's hand. But the note didn't say anything like "good-bye, cruel world," as the paramedic had expected. Instead, it read, "Pump my stomach."

"He must like attention," the paramedic said, handing the note to the policeman, who had picked up Simon's three empty prescription bottles carefully with his handkerchief. "Establish an airway and start an IV and transport," he said. "We can alert the poison-control team on the way to the hospital."

Within just a few minutes, the contents of Simon's stomach, including an undetermined amount of Dalmane, Tylenol No. 3, and Prozac, was being pumped into a glass beaker that looked as if it came from the lab scene in *Frankenstein*.

"Make sure and save that; it'll need to be tested," the emergency room intern said. He looked down at Simon. "He'll be okay. Take him upstairs to sleep it off." He stripped off his gloves and initialed his orders. "Make sure to send him to the psych ward," he said. "We don't want him finishing the job after he wakes up, like the last guy."

When Simon woke up a few hours later, he was thrilled to find himself alive. Mentally, he inspected himself, starting with his feet and moving up to his head, which was splitting. He was very nauseated. When he moved his head or tried to focus, flashes of light moved across his brain. Very slowly, he turned his head to look around. He was definitely in a hospital bed in a hospital room. This was good. And David Morgan was sitting on a chair very close to Simon's bed, reading *American Archaeological Review.* This was very good.

"Hi," Simon said.

Morgan turned to him, putting his journal on top of the copy of *Scientific American* already sitting on the bedside table.

"Hi," he said. "How do you feel?"

"Lousy," Simon said. "Somebody tried to kill me."

"You have no idea," Morgan said, "how glad I am to hear you say that." Morgan scooted his chair closer to Simon's bed and self-consciously patted his arm.

Simon slowly processed what Morgan had said. He tasted bile in his mouth, and he waited until the nausea passed to speak again. He didn't think Morgan had understood him.

"Somebody tried to kill me," he said again. "I need to talk to the police."

"I know," Morgan said. "I understand. I believe you. But the authority figures here think you tried to commit suicide."

Simon turned his head farther, and then he saw the bars on the lower half of his window.

"Oh, hell," Simon said.

"Exactly."

"He used my own pills. Put them in a Coke bottle. Whoever it was knew I'd drink it eventually."

"I know."

"Get me out of here."

"You're in no condition to go anywhere right now. Just rest until we get it straightened out. Besides, it's going to be damn all getting you out. The hospital is really digging its heels in. Apparently, they had some guy in here last week who swore he accidentally OD'ed and wasn't suicidal. They put him in a regular room and he jumped out the window. His family is suing for zillions. It's all very exciting, really. Judy and Marcus are at the office, digging into your personnel file so that they can get your Uncle Morris's phone number before the hospital does, so he won't agree to commit you."

"Oh God."

"Your doctor had a knock-down-drag-out with the psych guy up here. You could hear them all the way down the hall. Your doc told the other doc that he wasn't normal himself, so how could he tell normal? Then the other guy said your guy was an old country doctor who shouldn't prescribe anything other than penicillin. The nurses had to separate them. It was great."

"Gates believes me, doesn't he?"

"He sure acts like he does. For one thing, you've got a twenty-four-hour guard outside your door. And he and that woman you've got the hots for are at your house with a team of forensic guys. They're looking for evidence somebody else was messing in your house besides you."

That was when Simon noticed that the door on the inside of his room had no handle on it. It didn't upset him the way the window bars had. It made him feel safe.

"On second thought, I don't think I want to leave right now," Simon said.

"Don't blame you, under the circumstances. What no one can figure out is why somebody would want to get rid of a stuffy, harmless history professor like yourself."

"I don't have any idea."

"Me neither."

"I feel awful."

"You're still full of drugs. Go back to sleep. When you wake up, I'll get you a milk shake. Maybe we'll know more then."

When Simon woke up again, it was dark outside. Marcus Clegg had taken Morgan's place. He was sitting in the visitor's chair, reading *Rolling Stone.* He owned every issue printed since 1977.

"Am I still officially crazy?" Simon asked.

"Hi there," Clegg said. "No, not at all. You're going to stay up here because it's secure. At least until you're ready to be discharged."

"When is that going to be?"

"Maybe tomorrow, if you feel like it. David left you a milk shake. It's in the freezer. Want it? They won't take those tubes out of your arm until you start eating and drinking."

"Sure," Simon said.

The texture of the chocolate shake was a little strange, since it had been frozen and then thawed in the microwave. It really didn't taste very good, but his nausea was gone and he knew he should drink it. He forced down about half of it.

"Did you manage to fend off my relatives?" he asked.

"Yes, but it wasn't easy. You should have heard Judy on the phone to your uncle. She was brilliant."

"What about my aunt in Boone?"

"They never found out about her. She's not listed in your personnel file. And I sure as hell wasn't going to tell them."

"So what do we do now?"

"Go to sleep."

"You don't have to stay," Simon said. "There's a policeman here."

"Don't be brave. It doesn't ring true. I've got dibs on the sofa in the waiting room. I brought my pillow and everything."

"Thank you."

Simon woke up only once during the night. He counted the drips from his IV bottle until he fell asleep again.

29

ALL OF SIMON'S ENERGIES WERE CONCENTRATED ON KEEPING down his bland breakfast. Sgt. Otis Gates wasn't making it any easier by sipping on a cup of vending machine coffee. It smelled of burnt cardboard. Simon could taste it in his bowels.

Earlier in the morning, Dr. Ferrell had dropped in to tell Simon he could leave the hospital soon.

"If you didn't have such good insurance, I wouldn't mess with you," he said. "You're time-consuming."

"I understand that you and the psych resident had a falling-out over me," Simon said.

"A minor professional disagreement," Ferrell said. "We've had them before. He's one of these guys who believes the whole world is one big dysfunctional family just waiting for him to organize into group therapy and talk into personal revelation and mental health. The next time he tells me that he understands a patient of mine he's seen for five minutes better than I do, I'm going to stuff him down the laundry chute."

Ferrell told Simon he could go home that afternoon, after some test or another came back with the right reading.

"Please take care of yourself," Ferrell said. "One-hundred-percent-covered patients are hard to come by."

Simon hadn't wanted to talk to Sergeant Gates when he walked into the room a few minutes after Dr. Ferrell left. Simon was tired and a little afraid. He had almost died twice recently.

But Gates sat down and began to drink his coffee, oblivious to the sensitivity of Simon's stomach.

"How are you today?" asked Gates.

"Tell me you have some idea what's going on," Simon said.

"Let's dispense with the niceties and get right down to business, shall we?" Gates said.

Gates took out his reading glasses and perched them on his nose. The glasses looked like doll accessories on his large face. He pulled his notebook from his pocket and began to flip through it.

"Let's go over what I've got and you can tell me what you think," Gates said.

This was not what Simon wanted to hear. He wanted Gates to tell him he had made an arrest and had a confession and it was someone Simon didn't know and that the police would lock the guy up permanently and Simon could go home and forget everything.

"I don't have to remind you that this has happened once before, and that we chalked it up to vandalism," Gates said. "I think that we can discard that theory. It's hardly vandalism to walk into somebody's house and dump pills in an open soda bottle."

"The two could be unconnected," Simon said.

"That's possible, of course. But for safety's sake, we should assume the worst."

"I can live with that."

"First possibility: You are trying to commit suicide."

"No."

"Your doctor and your friends say you're fine. And it's pretty hard to fake mental health. Besides, we've found evidence of an intruder at your house."

Simon was taken aback even though he had expected to hear this. Absurdly, he found himself worrying about his cat.

"The doorknob on your back door and your prescription bottles were wiped clean of prints. Why would you do that? Also, we found a tire track in the parking space off your alley that doesn't match your car or anyone else's in the immediate vicinity. There was a partial footprint a few feet from your back porch that belongs to a foot about five sizes larger than yours."

Tessa had wanted Simon to fill in that low spot in the yard for years. It was always damp. Now he was glad he hadn't ever gotten to it.

"Also," Gates said, "you are a brilliant researcher who would need about half an hour in the library to figure out how to kill yourself successfully."

"Fifteen minutes," Simon said.

"Second possibility: You are not trying to kill yourself; you are only trying to get attention. This is a distinct possibility. You've been, or are, depressed. And again, you are smart enough to figure out how to attempt suicide without actually accomplishing it."

"I've had enough attention to last a lifetime."

"Thing is, the docs are undecided as to whether or not the amount of drugs you ingested would have killed you. Your size makes that hard to figure out. If you didn't want to die, seems to me you would have been more careful on the dosage side."

"We're running out of possibilities."

"Be patient. Third possibility: Someone was trying to make it look like you are suicidal. To make you seem psychologically unstable so that you lose your job. This is serious professional jealousy we're talking about here. This is a real possibility, because Alex Andrus, who hates your guts, accused you of being incompetent right before the first incident."

"It can't be Alex. He's a basket case. And he had an alibi for the first time."

"I wouldn't exclude him from being involved. Besides, you have plenty of other enemies to choose from. Seems you're the favorite to become chair of the department of history after Walker Jones retires."

Simon was thunderstruck. "That's nonsense," he said. "If the college doesn't choose someone from outside the department, there are three other people on the history faculty senior to me."

"Two of them are out of town for the summer, and the other one is Vera Thayer," Gates said, consulting his notes.

"This is crazy," Simon said.

"Maybe Professor Thayer figured if she took you out of consideration, she could have the job after all. Where does she live?"

"Around the corner and down two on Benehan Street—about two blocks from me." Simon knew Vera was mean enough to do anything to get the chair, but he had a hard time visualizing her with her beehive and ultrasuede suits under his car, rigging a booby trap.

"Your secretary told me you'd be shocked," Gates said. "She said you hate departmental politics and never know what's going on. I think the expression she used was 'babe in the woods.' "

"I don't believe this."

"According to her, you're a Pulitzer Prize winner, you generate great publicity for the college at regular intervals, you're a popular teacher, and you're fair and easy to get along with. Oh, and you're cute. In short, you're the history faculty's ideal compromise candidate. Nobody wants Professor Thayer, and you get everyone else's vote after themselves."

"So your theory is that these two so-called suicide attempts of mine are somebody's way of taking me out of the running for chairman, or out of the college altogether? By making me look psychologically unstable and unfit for the job?"

"It seems possible."

"I can't deal with this."

"You'd better deal with it. There's always the fourth possibility."

"What's that?"

"The perp doesn't just want you out of the way; he, or she, wants you dead."

30

THE UNDERCOVER POLICEMAN WATCHING SIMON'S HOUSE MADE him nervous. No one in full position of his faculties could mistake this guy for a student on a bicycle. Every time he hit a cobblestone in the alley, he practically fell off. His blue jeans, T-shirt, and athletic shoes were brand-new and looked like he had bought them at Sears. His haircut came from the shop opposite the police station, which offered a special price to anyone in uniform. His sunglasses screamed "cool Clint Eastwood–type law-enforcement person." Plus, he kept stopping and fiddling with an earpiece that obviously wasn't connected to anything. He didn't have a backpack or books in his bicycle basket. Simon hoped he had a gun in it—a really big gun, like the bad guys had on television.

Simon thought he should probably warn the cop's night relief about the neighbors' intruder alerts. They were mounted on garages all up and down the alley. If the guy cruised all night, the alley would look like a lit-up Christmas tree. Someone might call the police.

Simon felt sorry for himself. He was sitting on the sofa in his living room, wrapped in a blanket, for comfort, not for warmth. This had been quite a year. His wife had left him. He had been accused of incompetency. Someone was trying either to get him committed or to kill him. Right now, a detective sergeant from the Homicide Division of the Raleigh Police Department was interrogating his friends and colleagues. If Alex Andrus and Vera Thayer disliked him before, getting hauled off to the police station certainly wouldn't help matters. He was especially embarrassed that his other friends, including Marcus Clegg, were being questioned, too.

The only bright spot in his barren existence was that Julia was coming to fix him dinner and protect him until around midnight. Then David was going to come and spend the night. Simon hadn't argued with either of them about this.

Simon answered Julia's knock on the door about 6:15.

"I'm a mite anxious," Simon said, taking one of the shopping bags from her.

She reached out and squeezed his arm.

"Don't worry," she said. "Otis will get to the bottom of this. When he turns his whole attention to a case, results happen. Besides, no one would dare try again, not after all this commotion has been raised."

"I hope not."

They carried the bags to the kitchen.

"What are we having?" Simon asked.

"Lamb chops, baked potatoes, salad, and—"

"Please say something chocolate."

"Chocolate decadence pie."

"Thank you, God."

"I hope you don't mind the meat and potatoes. The Irish in me just can't quite give it up."

"It sounds wonderful." He pulled a bottle of red wine out of one bag. "I guess I shouldn't drink any of this. I had my stomach pumped yesterday, after all."

"Good. That means I get more."

Simon uncorked the bottle and poured the wine into one of his mother's old Waterford crystal wineglasses and gave it to her.

"This is wonderful," Julia said. "I don't know which is better, the wine or the glass. I wish," she said, "that I had thought to bring a change of clothes."

Julia was wearing a full suit of regulation office wear: suit, blouse, stockings, and pumps. Her hair was pulled back from her face. She looked hot, wrinkled, and uncomfortable.

"You can borrow some of my clothes," Simon said.

"I couldn't fit into a pair of your jeans if my life depended on it."

"Don't be insulted, but I have a pair of old overalls I think would fit you," Simon said. "They're pretty baggy."

"I am not at all insulted. Where are they?"

"In the bottom drawer of my dresser, right side," Simon said.

While Julia was upstairs, Simon washed the potatoes and put them in the oven. He tried not to think about her undressing in his bedroom. The happy domesticity of the evening so far gave him a familiar contented feeling, and he had to remember that they were just friends, so far at least.

Julia came into the kitchen in the blue denim overalls Simon had worn threadbare working on his aunt and uncle's Christmas tree farm near Boone. She had borrowed one of Simon's white T-shirts and was barefoot. Her hair was loose and pushed behind her ears.

"You look great," Simon said.

She knew it, too. She walked up close to him and her body requested a friendly kiss, which she got. But that was all she wanted. She backed away from Simon's move toward a longer embrace, politely detaching his arm from around her waist and leaning back on the counter.

"You put the potatoes on?" she asked.

"Yeah," he said. "Want to go sit outside?"

They went outside and sat on Simon's porch, he cross-legged on an old wicker rocker and she on a chaise lounge. They talked easily for an hour, until the potatoes were done. Julia went inside to fix the salad and Simon turned on the grill.

When everything was ready, they sat at the old table on the porch and ate it. Simon hadn't realized how hungry he was. He hadn't had a square meal in days. He finished the half a lamb chop left on Julia's plate and had two pieces of pie.

There wasn't much to clean up, and with both of them working, the kitchen was straight in just a few minutes.

Then there was a lot of time left to pass until midnight.

So they did what all members of their generation do when faced with an uncertain social situation. They put on some music and fixed complicated coffee. If it had been winter, they would have lit the fire, too.

At this point, Maybelline wandered through the room and gave them a topic of conversation. Her big belly swung under her, and she went into the kitchen for the lamb bones Simon had left in her dish.

"Looks like you're definitely going to hear the pitter-patter of little paws pretty soon," Julia said.

"I know," Simon said. "I hope so."

"No one wants kittens."

"I think it would be fun."

"They'll wet all over the house and cost a fortune in vet bills."

"It'll give me something to do."

"When they get big, what are you going to do with them? You'll wind up taking them to the pound."

"All my friends will have to take one," Simon said, "if they want to stay on my Christmas card list."

Julia didn't think she'd ever figure Simon out.

"I'll take one."

"A kitten? Good, but you'll have to provide two references."

"I can do that."

Simon put his coffee glass on the table in front of the sofa and took Julia's away from her and put it on the table, too. His intentions were clear. Right now would be the best time to stop this, Julia thought. Simon put his arms around her and kissed her. It felt so good to both of them that they didn't stop until they ran out of oxygen. Julia knew she needed to do something, but that something was to ease into Simon's lap when he urged her to, and they kissed again. Simon unhooked her overalls and put his hands under her—or rather, his—T-shirt. He rubbed her backbone under the waistline of her panties while they kissed again.

"Skin," he said.

"I want some, too," she said. She pulled his shirt out from his belt and put her arms around him and caressed his back and nuzzled his neck with her lips. Both of them began to breathe hard and fast. Simon unhooked her bra and held her breast.

"You are so soft," he said. "You feel wonderful." They lay down on the sofa. Simon stretched himself over the length of her, nestling the lower half of his body into the hollow formed by her slightly spread legs. Neither of them said anything while they touched and kissed for a long time.

They were both wondering if there was a graceful way to get up, go upstairs, and undress without breaking the spell they were under when a tiny but insistent beep began to sound somewhere in the room.

"What is that?" Simon asked.

"My beeper," Julia said. She gently pushed him off of her.

"Don't," Simon said.

"I have to," Julia said. "I'm on call."

"Can't it wait?"

"Until you and I are through making love? I don't think so. Sergeant Gates knows I'm here. If I don't call him, he'll send a police cruiser over to see if we're okay."

She disentangled herself from Simon, got off the sofa, and went over to where her purse lay on a table. She took her pager out of her purse and looked at it. "It's Gates's number all right. It's probably about your case."

That thought drove the libido right out of Simon, and he sat up straight on the sofa. "My case?" he said.

"You knew he was working on your case tonight. He's probably still interviewing people and has a legal question."

Julia went into Simon's kitchen to use the phone, hooking her overall straps as she went.

Simon stretched and tucked his shirt back into his pants. Temporarily, he hoped.

Julia was gone for a rather long time. Simon could hear her murmuring in the kitchen. He, and she, had studiously avoided bringing up the attempts on his life during the evening, and for a time he had exited the emotional twilight zone where he had dwelt since waking up in the hospital. Now, though, he felt the cosmic weirdness of the situation overtake him again.

Julia hung up the phone and came back into the living room.

"Guess what?" she said. "Alex Andrus has confessed!"

Simon didn't know what he had expected, but this wasn't it. "I don't believe it," he said.

"So far, he's just admitted to booby-trapping the car," she said. "He seems to think that the second attempt was more serious, and he denies that one. But not for long, I'll bet. Otis says he's so scared, he's hyperventilating."

"But Alex was supposed to be at Bobby Hinton's apartment."

"The kid lied to help him out."

He would, Simon thought. Why hadn't he figured on that?

"The little bastard," Simon said.

"Andrus said he had no intention of killing you. Just wanted to force you to leave Kenan. I wonder what he thought carbon monoxide poisoning and a drug overdose would do to you."

For a moment Simon could picture his small, cold, dead body curled up on the floor of his kitchen. It might have happened if he hadn't made it to the telephone. And his friends and family would have believed that he had killed himself. He became so angry that it seemed every drop of blood in his body would burst out of the top of his head. He clenched his fists.

"Goddamn him," he said.

Julia went over and put her arms around him.

"It's okay," she said. "It's all over."

"What will happen to him?" Simon asked.

"He'll be charged with attempted murder, of course," Julia said.

Attempted murder and perjury will not look good in Alex's personnel file, Simon thought. He'd never see the man again. He had his life back.

"Look," Julia said, "I have to go. Gates wants me there five minutes ago."

Simon did not want her to leave, for more reasons than one.

"Why do you have to?" he asked.

"Andrus has waived his right to call a lawyer," she said. "The idiot. Otis wants to continue to question him, and he wants me there to be sure it's legal."

"Can't someone else do it?"

"I'm on call. Don't worry, I'll be back in a couple of hours."

She went up Simon's stairs two at a time to change her clothes.

Simon sat down wearily on his sofa. Alex Andrus, damn him. Simon's hands hurt, and he turned them over, to see the deep indentations his fingernails had made in his palms when he clenched his fists. He was deeply angry, angrier than he had been before he knew who his persecutor was. He took deep diaphragmatic breaths, trying to relax.

Julia came downstairs, back in her working clothes.

"I forgot to tell you," she said. "Otis got the report on the bullet back from the lab."

Simon had forgotten all about Anne Bloodworth and the bullet that had killed her.

"And?"

"It's a forty-one caliber."

"Do they know what kind of gun it came from?"

"No," she said. "But it's a big bullet. It must have come from a big gun."

AFTER JULIA HAD GONE, SIMON STOOD IN THE DOORWAY BEtween the kitchen and the living room and pushed on the frame as hard as he could. He used his feet to brace himself and pushed with both hands until his body trembled with the tension. When he heard the wood cracking under his hands, he stopped. Dissipating all that anger was a good thing, but he didn't want to have to replace the door frame.

He called Marcus to find out what had happened at the police station.

"It was great," Marcus told him. "I've never had so much fun in my life. I warmed a bench in the waiting room outside Otis Gates's office and observed humanity. I always thought the state fair or the flea market was the best location in town for that, but let me tell you, the police station has them both beat. I wonder if I could get a grant to study something there. How about 'Comparing and Contrasting the Body Language of the Criminal Element and Law-Enforcement Personnel in a Local Police Station' sound as a title?"

"You never got questioned?"

"Not really. I was just there for appearance's sake, I think. That Sergeant Gates is huge. He must have been some effective beat officer. Anyway, when I finally got called into his office, we talked about our kids and soccer and how hard it is to be a Southern Baptist these days and stuff like that. Then he asked if I would be willing to help him. I said of course. So he assigned me to sit in the waiting room with Alex and make him nervous while he questioned Vera. I was great. I should win an Academy Award. I told Alex that if he was concerned about being a suspect, he should offer to take a lie-detector test because they're very accurate in untrained subjects. He was a wreck by the time I was done. No tranquilizer in the world could have calmed him down."

"How did Vera take it?"

"She was livid. What an affront to her dignity. She must have met her match, though. She marched into Gates's office planning to put him in his place, but she came out looking like she'd been ridden hard and put up wet. That made Alex even more nervous."

"I'm sorry you got dragged into this."

"I wouldn't have missed it for the world. I'm glad it's over, though. I was beginning to feel like Crito watching Socrates drink hemlock. Stay out of trouble for a while, all right?"

Now that he no longer felt strapped to a post waiting for the firing squad to assemble, Simon's big problem became passing the time until Julia came back. He decided to do what he always did when he felt bored, restless, or beat-up: go to the library. Simon left Julia a note in case she came back sooner than she had predicted. Then he called David Morgan and told him not to come to his house to stand guard over him. He was safe now.

THE KENAN COLLEGE LIBRARY WAS OPEN UNTIL MIDNIGHT every night. As he passed through the double entrance doors, bound for the reference section, Simon saw Bobby Hinton reading the *Sports Illustrated* swimwear issue in the seating area next to the door. The boy saw him and raised his hand in greeting, with one eye still on Rachel Hunter. Simon lifted his hand and waved back with a friendly smile.

You little jerk, he thought to himself. Enjoy yourself while you can. The police will be looking for you very soon. After they find you, they'll take you downtown, fingerprint you, slap you in a holding cell, and charge you with obstructing justice. That's a felony, son. You'll have to stay right there in that cell with all the other lowlifes until the family lawyer comes to bail you out of jail. How will that look in the Charlotte papers? Think anyone will want to buy a posh house in Myers Park from a felon?

As he looked up the call numbers for gun catalogs, Simon hoped he would get to testify against someone, anyone. He allowed himself to contemplate the sweetness of revenge, then put it aside and set himself the task of finding out what guns were available in 1926 that took .41-caliber ammunition.

Contrary to popular opinion, not every southerner drives around in a pickup truck with a selection of firearms mounted on a gun rack behind the cab and a revolver in the glove compartment. There were a lot of guns in the vicinity of Boone, North Carolina, when Simon was growing up, but his parents didn't have one. A couple of his aunts' husbands were hunters, and he had enjoyed the fruits of the sport many times, but hunting guns were tools, and when they weren't being used for their intended purpose, they were kept locked up in a gun cabinet. So Simon was completely unfamiliar with the gun as toy or macho accessory. On this night, he found out quickly just how fascinating firearms can be.

The gun catalog Simon had in hand was the fourteenth edition of the *Gun Trader's Guide.* It was five hundred pages long and profiled an average of eight guns on each page. There were a lot of guns in the world, a whole lot of guns. However, Simon was able to eliminate most of them immediately. The murder weapon was obviously not a shotgun, which used cartridges filled with shot rather than bullets, so he skipped that section. As he slogged fruitlessly through the rifle section, Simon suddenly realized that a rifle with a barrel 41/100 inches in diameter would be damn heavy. There were just not many of them. Almost all rifles were .22s. Feeling stupid, he turned to the handgun section.

Despite himself, he soon became caught up in the history and, yes, the romance of some of the famous handguns of the world. As he browsed among the Lugers, Police Specials, Walther PPKs, and Colt .45s, he had to interrupt his fantasies of Wyatt Earp and James Bond and remind himself what he was looking for.

There were not a lot of .41-caliber weapons here, either. The most obvious one was the famous Colt six-shooter, which came in many calibers and was ubiquitous throughout the country. The military had packed them, and the civilian models were known by the famous name of Peacemaker. They were made from 1873 to 1942, and there must have been thousands in circulation in 1926. Most were .45s, though, since that was the caliber used by the military. The Peacemaker was the most famous model, mostly because Wild Bill Hickok killed fourteen men with his. After he died, shot in the back in a saloon, his sister gave the gun to Pat Garrett, who killed Billy the Kid with it in 1881. Too bad Hickok couldn't get to his .32 Sharp's double derringer inside his breast pocket. It was buried with him in Deadwood, South Dakota.

Now the derringer was a fascinating weapon. It took a heavy load, making the stubby weapon absolutely deadly at close range and worthless at any distance wider than a card table. Its ease of concealment, power, and secondary advantage as a knuckle-duster made it the favorite weapon of gamblers, dance-hall girls, and gunmen who needed backup. John Wilkes Booth killed Lincoln with one. The most popular derringer was the Remington-model double derringer with the famous bird's-head grip and over/under double barrel. There were thousands of these in the country. They had been manufactured continuously from 1865 to 1935. They were only worth around five hundred dollars today, but the engraved version with the mother-of-pearl grip was worth about a thousand bucks. That's why Charles Bloodworth's was kept securely locked up in the display case at Bloodworth House.

It took a second for Simon to realize the import of what he had seen. For a second, the air around him went cloudy and red spots swam across his eyes. He put his head down until the faint went away. When he sat up, he saw a librarian walking toward him with a concerned look on her face. Simon waved her away. "Just resting my eyes," he said. She didn't look completely convinced, but she went back to her desk.

Simon looked at the page of the gun catalog. He was positive that a derringer identical to the one illustrated had belonged to Charles Bloodworth. Simon wondered if a ballistics test could be performed on Bloodworth's gun and a bullet that had been in a corpse for seventy years.

As his head cleared and his heart rate slowed down, Simon studied the page. He looked up some other derringers. They did look a lot alike. The original Deringer pocket pistol had been wildly popular and was copied by every gun manufacturer who could think of a way to get around the patent. Simon didn't know anything about guns. He could not be sure that Bloodworth's gun was a Remington, or that it was any model that took a .41. And the caliber was all he knew about that bullet. Finding out was the most important thing in his life, more important even than making sure he was home when Julia came back.

Simon had never defaced a library book in his life, but now he had an overwhelming urge to tear the page illustrating the Remington derringer out of the book and take it right over to Bloodworth House to compare with the real thing. The only thing that stopped him from doing it was the vigilance of the librarian, who kept looking at him in case he fainted. Simon wrestled with the closest copy machine until it gave him a decent copy of the page, then dutifully handed the book to the librarian. He folded the copy and put it in his pocket. When he walked out of the library, he didn't pay any attention to Bobby Hinton sitting and reading his magazines. Just then, Simon was preoccupied with the crimes of the past.

Simon walked across the lawn of the college toward Bloodworth House. The grass under his feet had been cut that day, and it gave off that unmistakable odor of new-mown hay. The tiny insects that lived in the grass had been disturbed by the mowing, and they swarmed around Simon's ankles as he walked quickly toward the house. It was very dark on the campus, except for one light that burned on the back porch of Bloodworth House.

Simon reached the back door, which led into the office, and fumbled for his keys. He found the right one, then opened the door and flicked on the light switch. A bank of overhead fluorescent lights came on, lighting the office like a jewelry store. Simon walked through and into the dining room, where the display case holding selected items that had belonged to Charles and Adam Bloodworth stood.

The lighting here was less invasive, and Simon peered into the case. There was the derringer. He compared it with the drawing in his hand. It was definitely a Remington. The case was locked, but Simon had the key. He opened the case and removed the gun. It was very small. The two pudgy .41-caliber over/under barrels were massively out of proportion to the rest of the gun. At close range, the bullets would definitely kill a person. At any other range, God knows where they would end up.

Simon inspected it closely. Under the grip, the initials C.B., for Charles Bloodworth, had been scratched. On the side rib, the firearm was stamped Remington Arms Co., which placed its manufacture from 1910 to 1935.

Simon had used a paper towel from the sink in the office to pick up the gun, and now he stood hesitating. He desperately wanted to take the gun home, to show it to Julia, and then tomorrow to take it downtown to show Otis Gates and find out if a ballistics check should be run on it. It wasn't dangerous. They had removed the firing pin before putting it on display. But Simon knew it would interrupt the chain of evidence if he removed the gun. It was a stupid worry, since the murderer was dead and there would never be a trial, but he didn't want anyone to be able to question where he had found the gun and in what condition he had found it. So he put the derringer back in the case and locked it. He slumped a little bit, leaning on the case as the adrenaline leaked out of him. He almost wished he didn't know who had murdered Anne Bloodworth.

"Get away from there," Bobby Hinton said. "That's not your property." The kid was lounging in the doorway, scowling at Simon. He must have followed Simon from the library. Every trace of syncophancy was gone from his expression. He looked mean.

"I have a perfect right to be here," Simon said. "I'm on the board of directors and I have a set of keys. Which is more than I can say for you. This is not your property, either."

"It's more mine than yours," Hinton said. He raised his right arm, which held a .38 Colt Special, and pointed it right at Simon. Simon suspected that the firing pin had not been removed from this weapon. His adrenaline began to flow again.

"What do you think you're doing?" Simon said. "Give me that thing."

"You are such an asshole. I've been wanting to do this for a month—ever since you started screwing up my life."

Simon was silent for a few seconds. How could anyone want to kill someone because of a grade? There was serious mental illness at work here. And this seriously mentally ill person was holding a gun on him.

"Listen," Simon said, "if it's that *C* you're worried about, we can deal with that. We can look at the whole issue again. It's not worth somebody's life—mine or yours. You'll go to prison if you hurt me."

"You idiot. You think this is all about a damn grade! This is about a couple million bucks!"

"I don't understand."

"That's what my family will lose if you prove Adam Bloodworth killed his cousin. If you think I'm giving up all that money over some stupid chick who died seventy years ago, you're crazy."

Simon ransacked his mental filing cabinet, and the note cards fell into place. Bobby's family had inherited money, and lots of it, because Anne Bloodworth died and the Bloodworth fortune went to Adam.

"You want to kill me because you think your family would lose the Bloodworth money if I prove Adam Bloodworth killed Anne? You booby-trapped my car, and when that didn't work, you tried to poison me?"

"Dr. Andrus booby-trapped your car. It gave me the idea," Bobby said. "I figured if you took an overdose it would solve all my problems. Even back in 1926 a murderer couldn't inherit from his victim. If you prove Adam murdered Anne, we could lose the estate. I'm not going to let that happen."

"I think it's more complicated than that, Bobby," Simon said. "Besides, I know Adam didn't do it. I cleared him the other day. He had an alibi."

"Sure. You figured out where one guy was on a night seventy years ago. Do you expect me to believe that?"

"The police know someone was in my house," Simon said. "They know I didn't try to commit suicide."

"They've got nothing," Bobby said. "Nothing at all. Especially after you succeed this time, they'll change their minds. Get outside."

"What are you going to do?"

"Just move. I don't want to have to shoot you. I'll have a lot more to cover up if I do, but I will if I have to."

Simon walked back through the office and outside. Bobby flicked off the outside porch light.

"Go over toward the excavation," he said.

Simon went, picking his way over stakes and mounds of dirt. Without the porch light, he walked into darkness just a few feet from the house. Bobby followed him so closely that Simon could almost feel the barrel of the revolver between his shoulder blades. Simon's brain was working as fast as it ever had in his life, but he wasn't coming up with any solutions.

"Stop," Bobby said.

"What are you going to do?" Simon asked.

Bobby laughed. "Don't worry. Before too long, you won't be able to tell anyone the solution to your little mystery."

"I know Adam didn't kill Anne," Simon said. "I know it for sure. Her maid is still alive. She said he was at a local whorehouse with a lot of other people. He's in the clear."

"You're very inventive under stress."

"Killing me would be a big mistake," Simon said. "You'll spend the rest of your life in prison. You won't be able to spend your money on anything other than cigarettes and candy bars at the prison store."

"I'm not going to get caught."

"Everybody gets caught. Stop this now, and maybe you'll get off with probation and counseling."

"I won't get caught, because you've tried to kill yourself twice already. This time, you'll succeed." Bobby waved his gun toward a pile of tools to Simon's left. "Get a crowbar out of there," he said, "and don't get any ideas about using it on me. I'm twice as big as you are and I've got a gun."

Simon picked up the crowbar. It could be a powerful weapon, but Simon knew he couldn't get close enough to Bobby to use it before the gun fired.

"Now pry off that grid," Bobby said. He was pointing to the safety cover that covered the cistern David had found.

Suddenly, Simon was really frightened. His bowels threatened to move and his legs turned to the proverbial rubber. How deep had David said the water was in that cistern?

"I don't think I can," Simon said, stalling for time.

"Bullshit," Bobby said. "If you don't, I'll shoot you and stuff you down it myself."

Simon took the crowbar and easily, too easily, pried the grate off the hole. He looked down into it. He saw a narrow opening, lined with stone, wide enough for a man. A distant shimmer indicated that the cistern was full of water. How deep was it? Very deep, if the underground springs and the storm drains of the neighborhood fed it, the way David speculated that they did.

"Get in," Bobby said.

"Look," Simon said.

"Get in," the kid said. He raised the gun to his eye level and pointed it at Simon. "If you don't, I'll kill you and think of another way to cover it up."

Even if you can't, I'll be dead, Simon thought. At least this way, I might have a chance.

Simon sat on the edge of the cistern and slowly lowered his body into the hole. The stones were worn and damp and slick with moss. He looked into the darkness below him and wondered how many other animals had drowned in it during the past hundred years or so. Halfway in, he hesitated, leaning the upper part of his body over the edge and holding on to a tree root nearby.

"Listen to me," he said.

The kid picked up the crowbar and swung it at Simon's head. Simon ducked, then dropped into the well.

The narrow walls fell away quickly and Simon felt, rather than saw, the sides of the cistern widen before he hit the water. It was very cold, and he did not hit very gracefully. He had reached his hands out in an automatic search for something to hold on to and his mouth was open in a scream. He hit the water flailing and his face went under. He had to spit out filthy water when he surfaced.

Simon remembered getting his Red Cross lifesaving certificate when he was sixteen. He'd had to tread water for fifteen minutes. It had seemed like forever to him. By the time the instructor had called time, his lungs were heaving, his legs were exhausted, and he no longer gave a damn whether he got the job at the faculty club that summer. He was a kid then. How long could he last now? Fifteen minutes was no time at all. It was late at night on a deserted campus. There was no way anyone would find him. If he screamed, the sound would be dissipated by the well and the earth and would lose itself in the other noises of the night.

He held his breath and forced his body down into the cistern until he stood on his tiptoes on the bottom. As he had already guessed, the water was several inches over his head.

He padded over to the wall of the cistern. He guessed that the circumference was about four times the width of the opening above. He slowly circled it, feeling carefully with his hands and feet for something to hold on to. Nothing. He dived to the bottom and felt along the edge, where the stone walls met dirt. He was looking for a channel of some kind. He found several gaps in the stone, but none large enough for him to squeeze through. Even if he could, he would probably drown before he got to the first storm drain. The nearest grate on campus he could think of was many yards away.

The bottom of the cistern was full of sludge and objects that Simon couldn't identify when he touched them. He went back up to the surface of the well. He plastered his body up against the stone wall, hoping friction would help keep him afloat. He looked up at the cistern opening above him. He could see a few stars and hear night noises, but no people. He wondered if he should start screaming, but he decided not to unless he heard voices. It would just exhaust him.

Simon figured he was going to die. He tried to think, but his blood supply seemed concentrated in his extremities, where his muscles were fighting to tread water and to cling to a few bumps in the stone wall of the cistern. Fear consumed him for a minute and he lost the contents of his bowels and his bladder. Then his head cleared and he began to think again. He was getting cramps in his legs, so he rested them by floating on the surface of the water, using his arms to stay afloat. The cistern was too wide here for him to brace himself against the opposite wall, and he couldn't climb into the narrower opening above him. There was no way out, no way he could survive. That stupid kid had killed him.

As he floated, Simon wondered if he could write a message before he died. He wanted to tell Otis Gates who had killed him, and tell the world who had killed Anne Bloodworth. But in his rush to leave the library, he had left his notepad and pen behind. It was a stupid idea anyway. Odds were that his body would never be found.

Simon was exhausted. He felt himself sinking into the water, and when water covered his face, he struggled to the surface again. His legs and arms were so heavy that he could no longer move them. He sank again, holding his breath.

Simon had no comforting out-of-body experiences as he began to die. He saw no bright welcoming lights, heard no heavenly chorus, and saw no visions. His parents didn't beckon to him from some celestial shore to show him the way. Instead, cold, filthy water filled his mouth and nose and trickled into his lungs. His brain signaled his arms and legs to propel him upward one last time, but they refused. The most primitive part of his brain screamed out in protest as his body extended itself along the bottom of the well.

The last thing Simon sensed was a disturbance in the water around him, then a sharp pain in his left forearm as someone stepped on him and cracked the bone. Two massive hands grasped Simon under the armpits and dragged him upward.

"Cough, damn it," Otis Gates said.

Simon struggled as Gates pounded him on the back. He began to breathe painfully, then vomited over the policeman's back.

With both feet planted firmly on the bottom of the well, and his head and shoulders well above water, Otis Gates held Simon over his shoulder like a toddler. Like a child, Simon clung to him with his legs and arms while he got used to breathing again.

"God, get me out of this place," Simon said.

"It'll be a few minutes before the fire department gets here with a block and tackle," Gates said. "It's okay, I've got you, and I've got nothing else better to do."

Simon realized that he wasn't going to die and tears came to his eyes.

"What I want to know is, who the hell told you that you could leave your house tonight? Didn't I tell you to stay at home and with someone until I said different? I'm a policeman. You're supposed to do as I say."

"I thought it was all over," Simon said. "I thought Alex Andrus had confessed to everything."

"You can solve all the historical mysteries you want," Gates said, "but you let me deal with the present."

"Her father did it," Simon said.

But Gates wasn't listening.

"Where is that block and tackle?" he was shouting up. "It's cold down here."

"It's coming," a voice called back.

A leather harness on a rope dropped into the well. Gates strapped Simon into it. Then Simon heard the whine of a winch, and he was pulled upward into the warm night.

David Morgan was there to help assorted firemen, paramedics, and police officers disengage him.

"Short people should stay away from deep wells," Morgan said.

"Archaeologists should put tighter covers on very dangerous old cisterns," Simon said. "I should sue. I'll probably need psychotherapy for life."

"What you need is a shower," Morgan said. "You stink."

Gates was a tight fit in the narrow opening. Simon could hear him swearing as he was winched out of the cistern by a fire truck. Soon he was standing in front of Simon, dripping wet.

"I'll have you know," he said, "that this is the best suit money can buy at Derrick's Discount Big and Tall out on Airport Road. The color brought out the brown in my eyes."

"I'm sorry," Simon said.

"You need to be real careful in your life from now on," Gates said. "You've used up all your luck tonight. When we broke Andrus and he confessed to the first incident but we couldn't budge him on the second, I knew there was someone else involved in all this. And I knew it had something to do with this damn house and that girl's murder. It's the only thing in your life that is different from where you were a month ago. Then Julia remembered this conversation we had with the kid at the Bloodworth woman's funeral about inheritance. Then we called you and when you didn't answer, I went to your house and found the note you left for Julia. You are so damn lucky," Gates went on. "The librarian told me you had left just minutes before I got there. I ran into Morgan here outside the library. He saw the office lights on at the house, so we went that way. We ran into the Hinton kid running off with a crowbar in one hand and a gun in the other. We convinced him that it was in his best interests to tell us where you were. Or rather, Morgan here convinced him. I was concerned I'd violate his constitutional rights."

"Thank you," Simon said to both of them. "Thank you very much."

The paramedic, trying to insert an IV needle, handled Simon's left arm, and Simon hollered.

"I think it's busted," Simon said. "My delivering angel here stepped on me."

"I thought I felt something crack," Gates said. "Sorry."

"I am not complaining," Simon said. "Don't put that thing in me," he said to the paramedic, who was trying to insert an IV into his other arm. "I've had more than enough fluids tonight, thank you."

"All right," the medic said, "but you need to go on to the hospital. You want to get that arm set or it'll hurt like hell, and you should get a chest X ray. You might have aspirated something horrible down there."

"I'll do anything you say except stay in the hospital," Simon said. "I've spent enough time there recently."

"I thought you looked familiar," the medic said. "Kind of accident-prone, aren't you?"

"Looking at me, I'm sure this will be hard for you to believe," Simon said, "but I have been the target of multiple murder attempts."

"He's not kidding," Gates said. "This guy has been more trouble to me recently than all the dope pushers, bank robbers, and other assorted criminals I've arrested in the past year." He turned to Simon. "I'm going to radio Julia and tell her you're safe. Then I'm going to get cleaned up and follow you to the emergency room to take your statement. Don't move without letting me know where you are. Hear me? I want to get home before dawn."

"You know," Simon said to Morgan as he helped Simon into his car to go to the hospital, "her father killed her."

"Who?" Morgan asked. "What are you talking about?"

"Anne Bloodworth," Simon said. "Her father killed her."

"How you can be interested in how some girl died in 1926 when you don't even know the whole story about how you practically got murdered amazes me."

"This is more interesting," Simon said.

"Fathers don't kill their children."

"Sure they do, sometimes. Besides, it could have been an accident."

Simon talked Morgan into stopping by his house on the way to the emergency room so that he could shower and put on clean clothes. He knew he wouldn't have a chance to get really clean once his arm was in a cast. Julia was going to the hospital, and he didn't want to smell like a sewer.

At the hospital, Simon refused to be admitted, so he sat in a corner of the emergency room waiting for the plaster to dry on his cast and for someone to read his chest X ray.

Julia was holding his good hand. Simon was a little disappointed that she hadn't thrown herself into his arms and wept over his injuries when she saw him, but she did kiss him on the ear.

"You deserve to be dead," she said.

"The woman's crazy about you," Morgan said.

"Listen," Simon said. "I didn't know I was still in danger. I thought it was okay to go out."

"I assumed you were safe, too," Julia said. "In fact, I sent the bicycle cop home. But Sergeant Gates thought from the beginning that more than one person was involved."

"Why?" Simon said.

"The two attempts were very different. The first is what we call a disorganized crime. It was a mess—ineffective and sloppy. The second was much better planned and executed. In fact, it almost succeeded. If you hadn't made it to the telephone, we might always have thought you killed yourself."

Sergeant Gates arrived with a police stenographer. The sergeant was dressed in a splashy blue uniform, complete with brass buttons and braid.

"I love a man in uniform," Julia said.

"Shut up," Gates said. "I had no choice. I went to the fire station on Oberlin Road to shower and change. This was the only thing they had that would fit me."

"You could pass for John Wayne," said Simon.

"A little respect, please. I'll have you know this is the full dress uniform of a major in the Raleigh Fire Department. Its owner played football with me at State."

He sat down and signaled the stenographer to open his notebook.

"You okay?" he said to Simon.

"We're just waiting for my X ray," Simon said.

"Okay, let's get to work," Gates said.

Simon told Gates everything that had happened since he left his house that night. When he had finished, the stenographer carefully read everything back to him. Simon added a little additional information.

"Okay," Gates said, "I'll get this typed up and take it over to your house in the morning."

"Can you explain this to me a little more completely?" Simon asked. "Why did these two guys try to kill me?"

"Andrus's little trick with the car exhaust was apparently a spur-of-the-moment thing. He was furious because of all the attention you got at the Bloodworth funeral—you know, the press and the president of the college and everything. He just happened to walk by your house after the reception and saw your car and the garden hose sitting there. He got the idea of faking a suicide attempt and running you out of your job. It didn't happen that way, and when I started asking questions, he got scared and asked Bobby Hinton for an alibi. I guess the kid owed him."

"Then," Julia said, "Hinton got this idea to take it further, to kill you and make it look like suicide. He'd been really worried about you finding out that Adam Bloodworth killed his cousin. He had done some careless research on the laws of inheritance and thought he'd lose his money. Apparently when he talked to his mother, as you asked him to after the funeral, she told him that the family always suspected Adam of killing his cousin. That worried him. He decided that you either had to be distracted from the investigation or die for his family to keep their money."

"Plus, he had a lingering dislike of you because of that C," Morgan said. "Because of you he couldn't go to graduate school, either."

"That's why Andrus has been such a wreck the last couple of days," Gates said. "He knew the kid's plans, and he was terrified he'd be implicated if you were murdered. But he was too cowardly to tell the police, because he knew the first incident would get him fired."

"I cleared Adam a couple of days ago," Simon said. "But I hadn't told Bobby."

"Smart move," Morgan said, "but now that we've dispensed with this, tell us about the Bloodworth murder. Since we're all gathered in the drawing room sipping our port, so to speak."

"Charles Bloodworth killed his own daughter," Simon said. "Nothing else fits. She was in love with someone absolutely unacceptable and was going to run off with him. All the servants and Adam were out of the house. She packed a bag, but either he caught them slipping away or they went to tell him before they left. He was furious. And he had been drinking. He pulled out his derringer and shot at them as they walked away. The derringer had two bullets in it. One hit Anne in the back of the head and the other wounded Joseph Weinstein in the shoulder. He might have been shooting just at the boy—over any distance, derringers are completely unreliable."

"Imagine how he must have felt once he realized what he had done," Gates said.

"I can't," Simon said. "Anyway, the boy took off and got to a black doctor, got patched up, and left town, never to return."

"Why didn't he call the police?" Julia asked.

"Who knows? Maybe he didn't care at that point. The girl was dead. Maybe he was afraid. Perhaps he thought the community would be on her father's side."

"Then what?" asked Morgan.

"Charles buried his daughter, almost ritually, under the dirt floor of the old kitchen. He buried the carpetbag, too, maybe because it had blood on it or something. Then he went to bed and put on a great act the next morning. Of course, he made sure that the house and grounds were trampled over, and I guess he prayed real hard that Weinstein would keep his mouth shut."

"What made you suspicious of him?" Julia asked.

"After I cleared Adam, I kept remembering that Charles settled his business with Pinkerton just a few months or so after she disappeared. That didn't make any sense. Most distraught fathers with money would search for a missing child forever. I would. Then when the bullet came back and I went through the gun handbook, I remembered that Charles had a derringer. So I went to the house to look for it."

"Bobby Hinton saw you leave and followed you. The last he knew, Adam was still your chief suspect. You almost bought it this time," Gates said.

"I laugh at danger," Simon said.

Julia drove Simon home. When they stopped in front of his house, she leaned over and kissed him.

"Aren't you coming in?" Simon asked.

"I can't," she said.

"You're kidding," he said.

"Listen, babe, the ADA on duty tonight is a baby lawyer. I'm going to have to walk him through everything. There will be a preliminary hearing on Andrus and Hinton tomorrow. We're going to try to deny them bail. All the documents have to be perfect."

"But they confessed."

"Confessions are worthless in court. They get thrown out like used Kleenex. All Andrus's lawyer would have to say was that the man was taking tranks and wasn't responsible for what he said. The case against the two of them has to be perfect without the confessions."

"Oh."

"Besides, you're not up to it."

"Try me."

"I'll come by tomorrow morning with breakfast. How do you like your cinnamon rolls?"

"With raisins and walnuts. And bring lots of coffee."

"Cinnamon rolls all the way."

"By the way, could Bobby have lost his family's money if I'd proven Adam was guilty?"

"Almost certainly not. Today we have a statute that bans convicted murderers from inheriting the estates of their victims. It was passed in 1961. In 1926, the law of trusts had exactly the same effect. But the salient point here is that Adam Bloodworth is dead. Even if he had killed Anne, a dead person can't be tried and convicted of anything. Hinton missed the point completely."

"Where on earth did he get the idea he could be cut off in the first place?"

"He checked a few books in the library, then talked to a legal services attorney. But he didn't give him all the relevant details, so he didn't get an accurate opinion."

"Primary research was always his weakness," Simon said.